Death at Beggar's Knob

And Other Adventures

(A John and Mary Braemhor Mystery)

by

Owen Magruder

For information, email **Cozy Cat Press**, cozycatpress@aol.com or visit our website at: www.cozycatpress.com

COZY CAT
P R E S S

ISBN: 978-1-939816-61-0

Printed in the United States of America

Cover design by Paula Ellenberger
http://www.paulaellenberger.com/

1 2 3 4 5 6 7 8 9 10

To Nellie

CHAPTER 1

"What is it, John?" Mary Braemhor put aside Durant's *Caesar and Christ*, and turned to her husband.

John and Mary Braemhor were in the sitting room of their B&B, Dunmoor Cottage, in the small village of Daraichburn, nestled in the Scottish lowlands. The cottage served as their retirement activity since John had retired as a member of the Rhodesian constabulary. Though officially retired, John kept an active hand in criminal investigations as he came upon particularly interesting and intriguing cases either through his many contacts in the Scottish constabulary or newsworthy items in the press. Daraichburn was a short train ride from Mary's ancestral home, Dunmoor Castle, north of Glasgow near Blanefield.

"This story in the *Telegraph*. There's been a series of unexplained disappearances near Fort Ewen, close to Loch Ness. Here." John handed her the paper and pointed to an article titled, *Police Baffled by a Series of Strange Occurrences.*

According to the story, several people had vanished over the past few months. All had been working in their gardens when last seen. One woman reported that her husband had been hoeing beneath one of their hawthorn trees when she thought she heard faint sounds of revelry, even the strumming of a stringed instrument. When she went outside to see what the noise was, he was gone. And so was his hoe. The local constabulary ascertained there were no bands of strangers in the vicinity, and the man had no known enemies.

"Maybe it was Nessie," Mary offered with a slight smile.

"I think not." John returned her smile. "She would have left very large footprints and probably puddles of water. But it is interesting that his garden implement was also missing. And all of the victims were in their gardens near hawthorn trees."

"It's the fairies," announced Aunt Rita, as she joined John and Mary in the sitting room. Rita Erskine, Mary's eccentric maiden aunt, had just arrived the day before from Blanefield for one of her many visits with the Braemhors. Her white hair was tied in a bun on the back of her head and she wore that impish smile she was noted for in the family.

John turned to her. "The what?" he queried. He looked at Mary and rolled his eyes. "You're not serious, Rita, are you?"

"Of course I am. Don't you know that the fairies form their circles under hawthorn trees and lure some unsuspecting person into their circle? And then the person disappears."

"Aunt Rita, that's just an old superstition. No one believes the fairy stories." Mary joined the conversation.

"Sir Arthur Conan Doyle did!"

"The author of the Sherlock Holmes tales?" John asked.

"Yes, and he went all over the world researching the supernatural. He even took Holmes with him on several occasions!" Rita was adamant.

"Wait, wait. Sherlock Holmes is not a real person. He's a fictional character."

"Well, fictional or not, he was there helping Sir Arthur prove fairies were real. And did you know you have a fairy circle under one of your apple trees, John?"

Rita took smug pride in that revelation, as she went into the kitchen for a cup of tea.

"Maybe we should entice Rita to go into our fairy circle." John twinkled.

"Shush! She'll hear you!" Mary put her finger to her lips as Rita reentered the room.

"Care for a brief holiday to Fort Ewen?" John quickly changed the subject.

Mary recognized the signs—the renewed alertness in John's voice and the sparkle in his eyes—and knew there was no point resisting. She turned to Rita, "Aunt Rita, would you mind looking after the cottage for a few days?"

"Not at all, dear; it will give me time to read Sir Arthur's *The Coming of the Fairies.*" Rita smiled coyly.

John, looking overly serious, said, "But you must promise us one thing."

"Oh?"

"Yes, please do not go into the fairy circle under the apple tree."

* * * * * *

Next morning, John put his and Mary's small valise in the boot of the Vauxhall, and, waving to Rita standing in the cottage doorway, they headed west on the A72.

"What did you think of Rita's fairy tales?" John asked as they drove toward Fort Ewen.

"Oh, I just think she keeps herself amused with folklore. There are such circular growths called fairy circles, you know? They're usually circles of fungi in forested areas and can grow quite large at times, as much as 10 metres in diameter; some in France reach a diameter of 600 metres. They've been studied for years," Mary responded.

"I don't think Rita is so much interested in the scientific research," John opined.

"No, her interest is in the folklore, which, by the way, dates back to the 13th century, spinning tales of enthrallment by those mortals who come upon the fairies dancing in their circles. The literature says that those who enter the circle disappear and are never seen again, though there are some stories of their rescue. But even those rescued are doomed when they return from their travels in fairy land, according to many of the tales. There is even a rock formation called the Pixies' Church in Dartmoor. The mythology of fairies is quite extensive."

"So I gather, but where did you learn about the fairies and their circles?" John was mildly astounded at Mary's obvious knowledge.

"Aunt Rita. She taught me and my brothers all about the fairy folklore when we were growing up at Dunmoor Castle. Scared us worse than the Brothers Grimm. You can believe that we never stepped inside a fairy circle when we found one on the estate. It was part of growing up in the Highlands," Mary concluded.

* * * * * * *

The trip north took the Braemhors through the village of Glencoe where they stopped for an early midday meal at the Sleat Inn. The clerk looked up from his bookwork and greeted them with a broad smile. "Welcome back, Mr. and Mrs. Braemhor. Are you going to stay with us again?'

"Not this time," John answered.

"We're headed farther north, to Fort Ewen," Mary added.

"Do you hear from the MacIains?"

"No, we seldom hear from our cottage guests, but I suppose they're happy to be back home in America after their experience here," Mary offered. The MacIains were the American couple that last year had been caught up in the Campbell feud in Glencoe.

"I suppose so. Have a seat in the pub and I'll get Annie to serve you." The clerk smiled and directed the Braemhors into the pub next to the reception.

Annie, a short, round young woman in her thirties with dark red hair tied in a bun, took their order and on her way back to the kitchen told another waitress, "That's the famous Braemhors what saved the two Americans last year." She was proud to be in the know on Glencoe's most famous mystery of recent times and wanted to be certain that Pattie knew she knew.

"I guess we're well-known here in Glencoe, John." Mary smiled.

"It's a very small village," John grunted as he studied the menu.

As John and Mary were eating their shepherd pies, John continued, "I want to stop in Fort Lochiel to see DI Ferguson, Ron Ferguson."

"How do you know him?" Mary was always impressed with the range of members of the constabulary John knew.

"I don't, actually, but while you were packing our valise this morning, I called Don Livingstone. You remember, the DCI from Glasgow?"

"Oh, yes, helped you wrap up the Glencoe-MacIain affair."

"Helped *us.*"

"Yes, well what did you learn from Don?"

"Not too much. He turned the case of the disappearing people up around Fort Ewen over to Ferguson. He's a new, young DI, but quite capable,

Livingstone said. This is his first big case and Don thought he'd welcome some seasoned assistance. Don said he'd call Ferguson and let him know we were coming and who we were." John looked at his watch. "We should be able to stop and talk with him before we go on to Fort Ewen. Shall we be off then?"

* * * * * * *

Though the weather was the usual chilly Scottish mist, the scenery along the A82 was breath-taking. The slate grey hills to the east, crowned by Ben Nevis, observed their northward journey, while Loch Linnhe to the west lay contrapuntal to the mountain views eastward.

"This is a geologically interesting area." John swept his hand east and west. "Many mineral deposits in the area, everything from lead to garnet. In fact, lead mining was a major industry over in Strontian until the 1870s." He waved his hand toward the Loch on their left. "And, of course, we know about Ben Nevis because of our MacIain friends." He pointed to the right and the grey behemoth arising from the valley floor.

As Mary and John entered Fort Lochiel, they were awed by the surrounding scenery. Nestled as it is at the northern end of Lock Linnhe, the city's residential areas rise up the stunning mountains to the east like so many wandering sheep herds only to be clothed in the blue mist of Scotland.

John parked off High Street, now a pedestrian way, and he and Mary walked to Cameron Square and the Town Hall.

"It would have been so nice to have supper at McTause's," Mary reflected.

"Too bad it burned in '06. I wonder if they'll ever rebuild it," John remarked as they entered the Town Hall in search of DI Ferguson's office.

"Yes, sir," the bushy-eyebrowed clerk responded to their query. "DI Ferguson is just down that hall," he pointed. "Are you the Braemhors?"

"Yes, we are." John was a little surprised that their identity was so widely known.

"He's expecting you, sir." The clerk smiled and went back to his paper work.

Interesting clerk, Mary thought, *looked like seated death.*

The door was labeled simply: R. Ferguson. John knocked. The sound of footsteps echoed on the other side of the door, and the door opened revealing a tall, slender man in his thirties, with a well-trimmed shock of reddish brown hair surrounding a freckled face and a broad toothy smile.

"You the Braemhors? Come in, please." He grasped John's hand firmly and then took Mary's more gently. "Don has told me a lot about you. Says you might be willing to help out, if I need. And I do need. These fairy circle disappearances are a real puzzle. Here, have a seat." He pointed to two chairs in front of an oversized desk which was covered with papers and a small pipe rack and ashtray. He smelled of aromatic pipe smoke.

"We've had the appearance of many more fairy circles than usual this year. You know what fairy circles are?" Ferguson started right away.

Both John and Mary nodded their assent.

"Well," Ferguson continued, "the area, particularly around Fort Ewen, is just covered with fairy circles, but we've had an unusually damp year so far, so that's not too surprising. And, of course, the locals around Ness seem especially susceptible to all of the mythology surrounding these fungal growths. Some have even

hired witches and warlocks—charlatans, I call them—
to perform anti-fairy rituals and dances." His ever
present smile broadened as he spoke.

"It would all be quite humorous, and instructive, if
the Fort Ewen area had not had several unexplained
disappearances."

"Tell us about them," John interjected.

"The first was up near Cein. Flora Fraser, about two
months ago. She lived with her maiden sister, Lily, on a
hillside just outside the village. They operated a B&B
on land that had come down through the family. They
had noticed a series of fairy circles around their small
grove of apple trees this year, and one day Flora had
gone out to investigate the fungal growths. I don't think
either sister was superstitious. Lily was watching her
sister from the front parlor window, but had to turn
away for a moment when the postman rang. When she
turned back, Flora had disappeared."

"Disappeared?" Mary asked.

"Yes, she said it was as if the ground had swallowed
her up. One moment she was there. The next, she was
gone. Lily went running out, but her sister was nowhere
to be seen, just a slight, wet indentation in the fairy
circle."

"Underground bog?" It was John asking this time.

"First thing I thought of, too, Mr. Braemhor. We do
have some peat bogs in the area, but not on the Fraser
land. I probed the area with a stake—from outside the
circle, of course." A twinkle lit up Ferguson's face
momentarily. "And the ground seemed quite solid,
though soft. I don't think she was sucked into a bog
from the looks of the area, but it's still a remote
possibility. As you can imagine, her sister is quite
distraught. In fact, she's decided to sell the property as
soon as she can find a buyer. Nobody local will touch
it. Superstitious bunch." Ferguson harrumphed.

"The next occurred about a month ago just north of Tuaidh, near Creagan an Fhithich, the Raven's Rock, where the old Glengarry Castle ruins are. Reginald MacDonell, descendent of the famous MacDonell clan of the area and still owner of large tracts of land there, was out walking his dogs—two red and white King Charles Cavaliers. When he and the dogs did not return at their usual time, his wife sent their house steward out to look for them. He found the dogs but not their master. And strangely enough, the dogs were very subdued, almost morose, his wife said."

"Usually Cavaliers are most friendly and affectionate. Constantly wagging their tails, I'm told," Mary added.

"Quite so, but not these two. Showed very little affection. Never wagged their tails and spent the next few weeks lying flat on the hearth following anyone who entered the room with their eyes, but not moving a muscle otherwise. And all we ever found of Sir Reginald was his walking staff right next to a fairy circle. His lands were searched, but to no avail."

"I assume the oldest son inherits his estate?" John queried.

"Yes, John MacDonell, but both he and the second son, Ranald, have vast land holdings of their own, so I don't think there's a motive there. Although John technically will head the estate, he's arranged for Sir Reginald's wife to live there and see to the day-to-day management of things. She'll be financially well set up. However, there's a third son, Morgan."

"Yes?" John asked.

"He's the black sheep. Lives in a cottage on his father's—now his brother's—estate. Never really settled down and seems, as far as we can determine, to live from party to party. However, he appears to husband the allowance his parents allot him well and seems to stay ahead of whatever gambling debts he accrues. There was nothing to implicate him in his father's disappearance. Of course, many of the local people think the fairies got him, but I don't put much stock in fairy tales." Ferguson smiled.

"Quite so. And there was another, more recent disappearance?" John asked.

"Yes, the one you read about in the *Telegraph*. It was on land adjacent to the Frasers; a Mr. Cameron disappeared while he was hoeing beneath one of the hawthorn trees on his property."

"And I understand his garden implement went missing as well."

"Yes, that was the oddity about Mr. Cameron's case. Both he and his hoe, gone. I wouldn't have thought the fairies would have been much interested in a garden tool, much less borne the weight of it." Ferguson smiled again at his own levity.

"So have all of these disappearances occurred on adjacent properties?"

"Certainly with the Fraser and the Cameron cases. Not so with the MacDonell. There are two large tracts, formerly owned by the MacMasters and the MacCleans, separating the MacDonell estate from the Cameron land."

"Formerly?" Braemhor queried.

"Yes, bought about two or three years ago by S&L Limited, an English electronics firm."

"Isn't it a bit odd for an electronics company to be in real estate?"

"Probably not. Now-a-days with globalization a company starts out in one field and expands into all sorts of unrelated businesses. Look at some of your online merchandisers, start out selling books and ten years later sell everything money can buy."

"True. True." John looked at Mary, and then to Ferguson, "Well, we've taken enough of your time. I think Mary and I will be on our way to Fort Ewen. Is it all right with you if we interview Lily Fraser, Mrs. Cameron and Lady MacDonell?"

"Quite. I'll call them and let them know that you will be coming to interview them and who you are. And, Mr. Braemhor, I'll appreciate anything you can add to the cases. As I said before, they have constituted a real puzzle so far."

John and Mary rose to go as John said, "It will be a pleasure to help all we can, and we'll stay in close touch with you as things develop." With that, the Braemhors went back to the Vauxhall and drove on to Fort Ewen.

"What do you think, John?" Mary queried as they drove north on the A82 toward Fort Ewen.

"I don't think it's the fairies." John smiled faintly. "But we'll know more after we talk with the surviving members of the families tomorrow."

* * * * * * *

The Nessie Hotel was on a private road just off the A82 and rested on the shores of Loch Ness. The Braemhors had stopped there several times on holiday and were no strangers to the proprietor, Harold Duncan.

"Aye, and it's good to see you again, Mr. Braemhor, Mrs. Braemhor," Duncan boomed from behind the reception. "Your usual room?"

"That will be fine," Mary responded. "Dinner at the usual time?"

"So it is. The dining room is just about to open, but there's time to get you settled in your room before then. On holiday again?"

"Not exactly. This is more of a business trip," John answered.

"But I thought you'd retired, Mr. Braemhor."

"He has. . .sort of." Mary smiled.

"I see. It's about the fairy circle business, I'll wager." Duncan held the register while John logged in. "Bad business, that. Miss Lily is still beside herself. Can't believe Miss Flora's gone. And Sir Reginald, too. I understand even his dogs are inconsolable. The whole area is in a panic, I'll tell you."

"How do you explain it, Mr. Duncan?" Mary asked.

"Oh, the fairies got 'em, for sure. No other explanation I can see. Flora, Sir Reginald, even Mr. Cameron. Nice people, never bothered anyone. Oh, Sir Reginald was a bit pompous at times, like he owned the countryside—which he did, actually—but a pretty reasonable person."

"I understand he has a son that lives on the estate?" John asked.

"That'd be Morgan MacDonell. Don't see much of him in the village. Stays to himself in the Black Rock Cottage. Gambles a lot, I understand, but I never see much of him."

"Why do you think it's the fairies?" John was fascinated by the persuasiveness of the fairy mythology, even in this otherwise intelligent, thoughtful innkeeper.

"'Cause they're mean creatures, they are. Don't take kindly to anyone disturbing their plots. Make them disappear if they step into the circles."

"But I thought that was all myth and superstition," Mary added.

"No superstition 'round here. The fairies have been around for nigh on ta five, six hundred years. Old Mr. Carpenter saw 'em one evening dancing under one of his apple trees. Went blind he did, right after. Doc Cook said it was the fairies. Just took his sight away. Nothing he could do. Said the blood vessels in ole Carpenter's eyes just started to grow and took away his sight. In both eyes. Terrible tragedy. All because he saw the fairies. Terrible business, that."

"Well, thank you, Mr. Duncan. I think we'll settle into our room and then get some supper." John quickly intervened as he guided Mary away from reception and toward the stairs to the rooms above.

"Mr. Duncan sounds like a true believer," Mary said as they entered the small, cozy room.

"Clearly, but it sounds to me like Mr. Carpenter suffers from macular degeneration, not eyes clouded with fairy dust. Mythology is hard to combat."

* * * * * * *

Breakfast the next morning was large helpings of smoked herring, baked beans, fried tomatoes and the ubiquitous burnt toast.

"Who shall we see first?" Mary asked as she finished the meal.

"I think it should be the MacDonells. They may be central to these events. Hopefully, we can see both Lady MacDonell and her son, Morgan. I'll call them and see if they're available." John went to the phone in reception.

Upon his return John offered, "They'll see us for elevenses. Shall we stroll the village 'til then?"

* * * * * * *

The village of Fort Ewen was small, only about 700 inhabitants, perfect for a morning walk. After crossing the Caledonian Canal, John and Mary walked past one of the many village restaurants and were confronted by a smallish stone building with second floor dormers.

The sign over the door caught John's eye—*The Witch's Cauldron. Spells and Fortunes.*

"John, you don't suppose they deal in fairy circles, do you?" Mary asked with a glint of impishness in her eye.

"I'd say serendipity is working for us. Let's go in." John smiled.

The shop was a treasure of amulets, tarot cards and other magical paraphernalia. The strong smell of incense filled the room. One corner held a library of books on the occult, black magic, spell casting and breaking, and how to hypnotize. There were several books on fairies and fairy circles which Mary was perusing when a breathy, raspy voice from behind the shadow-hidden main counter broke the silence. "Can I help you?" Startled, both John and Mary turned to see an extremely tall—he must have been over six and a half feet—gaunt man with parchment-colored skin and bushy, thick eyebrows overhanging his black eyes which seemed to grip whatever they focused upon with a vice-like tenacity. He was attired in a white collarless shirt beneath a black jacket with gold trim. His black pants were as tight as an onion skin and sported a gold strip down the outside seams. His hands—also parchment-like—were graced with excessively long fingers, each adorned with unusually long and tapered nails. In short, he looked like something out of Dante.

John and Mary turned sharply to confront the voice, which then continued: "Ah, Mr. and Mrs. Braemhor. I wondered when you would come."

"How did he. . . ." Mary started before John signed to her not to complete her thought.

"That's right." John strode forward, extending his hand as he approached the image behind the voice. "Mr. ????" John asked.

"Zauberin, Heinrich Zauberin." A faint grimace-like smile crossed the paper-like facial features of the proprietor as he stepped out from behind the counter with the fluid movement of a classically trained dancer. He stood over the Braemhors, his hands crossed on his chest, denying John his hand.

"You expected us," John stated matter-of-factly, not as a question.

"Exactly."

"Your brother in DI Ferguson's office in Fort Lochiel told you we'd be coming." John met Zauberin's cold stare with icy concentration.

"How. . .ah. . .how did you know?" Zauberin was clearly flustered, having been beaten at his own game of mystical revelation.

"You and your brother look very much alike; it's a sparsely populated area, and how often do you have people disappearing near fairy circles? And, like you in your business, I make calculated guesses in mine. Now that we understand each other, we can have a straightforward conversation. Agreed?" John would not let go of his advantage.

"Yes, yes, of course, Mr. Braemhor. You will have to forgive me, but I make my trade in the occult— surprising revelations to entertain the tourists, you see. I find it gives me a certain . . . advantage with people who are—forgive my phraseology—spellbound by mysticism, the occult, and things unworldly. The recent disappearances have been a real boon to my trade, you understand. Now, how can I help you?"

John, more cordial and less confrontational now, shared with Zauberin a little of what he and Mary knew of the disappearances. "What can you add?"

"Not a lot." Zauberin also relaxed and became more affable. "But I will tell you that the people in this area are very suggestible. When Sir Reginald disappeared, I was delighted. Not that he disappeared, you understand, but that it happened near a fairy circle. It was like manna to someone like me in mysticism, you see. Business quickly doubled. I even had to resupply my library of fairy circle books. And amulet sales went through the ceiling. I also received frantic calls for witch's potions and anti-fairy rituals. One group wanted me to give séances to protect the community. Oh, it was delightful." Zauberin's face lit up as if he were going into ecstasy.

"Yes, yes, I'm sure it was good for your business, but what more can you tell me about the events and the people involved?" John was becoming exasperated with the length of Zauberin's narrative.

"Of course, of course. Sorry. I just get carried away with my good fortune of having a shop here in the midst of other-worldly events."

"You said the locals are a suggestible lot."

"Oh, yes, even Sir Reginald, though not as much as his son, Morgan. One of my best customers."

"Buying what?"

"Fairy circle literature mostly. He's bought almost every book I can find for him."

"I understand he's the black sheep of the family."

"My, you do gather information rapidly, don't you?" A prissy smile crossed Zauberin's face.

John ignored the remark, "Tell me more."

"Well, Morgan and his father don't get along. A year or so back, he took up with Julie Mackenzie from the islands. His father, Sir Reginald, flew into a perfect rage. He would not have anyone in his family associating with a Mackenzie. 'Over his dead body' I think is the expression. You see the Mackenzies and the MacDonells have been at each other's throats for centuries, yes, centuries, at least since Blair-na-park in the late 1400's."

"And the 1602 Battle of Morar, I believe," John added.

"My, my, you certainly are up on your Scottish history."

"It's my hobby. Go on." John requested sternly.

"Sir Reginald and Morgan had an angry shouting match right here in my shop not two weeks before Sir Reginald disappeared. Morgan accused his father of not living in the 21st century and his father accused him of not upholding family tradition. It was electric. But very bad for business. Scared away some tourists that day, I'll tell you."

"I understand Morgan has a penchant for gambling?" John asked.

"Oh, that too. I don't understand how he has enough money to cover his debts and indulge in the quantity of occult paraphernalia he purchases. But I suppose the family is quite rich."

"What about the Fraser sisters? Their family and Sir Reginald's have not had a happy co-existence through the centuries." John was intent on moving the conversation on and gathering as much information as he could before elevenses at the MacDonell's.

"My, my, my, history again, Mr. Braemhor," chided Zauberin. "But you're right, the Fraser and MacDonell clans did have their differences long ago."

"At Blair-na-Leine on Loch Lochy, I believe," Mary added.

"Well, well, well, Mrs. Braemhor, a pair of history buffs in my midst. This is like a return to my schooldays."

"Yes, yes. About the Frasers." John tried to keep his mystical informant on track.

"Well, Sir Reginald would have little to do with them. I don't think it was clan rivalry. You see, a little neck of their land abutted his and a small trout stream ran across both properties, though it traversed much more of the MacDonell estate than the sisters' property. One morning he was out walking his dogs when he caught the sisters fishing in the stream. He claimed they were on his property; they claimed they were on their own. The local constabulary could not establish who was right, but Sir Reginald claimed that since his property was downstream of theirs, their taking fish from the stream amounted to poaching his game. He took them to court and lost, which only infuriated him further. Morgan took the Frasers' side which only made Sir Reginald angrier."

"So there's enough bad blood to go all around."

"Oh, my dear, I'll say there is." Zauberin seemed to thoroughly enjoy himself.

"What about Mr. Cameron? He was the latest disappearance." John glanced at his wristwatch.

"Oh, I wouldn't concern myself with him, Mr. Braemhor."

"Why not?"

"Man's a tippler. Not sober more than an hour or two each day."

"So you don't think the fairies got him?" John asked.

"Oh, come now, Mr. Braemhor, things occult and mystical are my business, not my religion."

At that moment, the door opened and in walked a couple of what appeared to be American tourists— dressed in the latest traveling gear and loud-spoken. "Look at this, honey; they've got that book on hypnosis I was telling you about," the man boomed. "How much?" he interrupted John's ongoing interview.

John quickly ended his talk with Zauberin. "Thank you for your information, Mr. Zauberin. Perhaps we'll come back to see you later." Zauberin smiled and gushed over his new customers. John and Mary exited *The Witch's Cauldron.*

* * * * * * *

The trip to the MacDonell estate from Fort Ewen took the Braemhors through some beautiful, but rugged, terrain. The house, an immense stone structure built in the late 1800's was west of the Tuaidh Castle ruins. Set on a sloping promontory with a sweeping view of Loch Garry, it exemplified the remains of the class-dominated society of the 18th and 19th centuries. It was opulent even by yesteryear's standards. Sir Reginald had managed to keep the estate together through several economic downturns. The Braemhors parked in front of the massive, two-story high front doors.

The doors swung open with a high-pitched and extended screech.

"I feel like I'm in Transylvania," Mary said quietly to John, who frowned and raised a finger of caution as the butler, a Mister Graves, appeared in the opening.

"Mr. and Mrs. Braemhor?" he asked, raising his eyebrows.

"Yes, we're here to see Lady MacDonell," John responded.

"She is expecting you. Follow me to the library, please." Graves strode into the enormous entry and headed toward the library, a large paneled room on the right with floor-to-ceiling bookcases filled with a mix of modern and classic texts.

Lady MacDonell rose to greet them as they entered the room. "Mr. and Mrs. Braemhor, so nice of you to call. Please come in and have a seat by the fireplace." She turned to the butler. "Graves, see that tea is brought in."

"Yes, m'lady." Graves exited into the entry chamber.

"DI Ferguson told me you're assisting him. How can I help?" Lady MacDonell seated herself on the front edge of a small armless, tapestry-covered chair of highly polished cherry. Sir Reginald's wife was diminutive, small-framed, weighing about seven stone. She stood no more than 5 feet, 2 inches. Her white hair was drawn tightly over her head and tied in a neat bun in the back. The skin on her hands appeared transparent with prominent azure veins demarking crests and valleys. She folded them quietly in her lap and fixed the Braemhors with her grey eyes.

"DI Ferguson told us that Sir Reginald disappeared about a month ago. . . ." John started.

"A month tomorrow," Lady MacDonell interjected. "It started as an ordinary day. After breakfast Reginald took his walking stick and the two dogs and went out for his morning constitutional towards the lake. He always took the same path down near the fairy circles and back. Close to a mile and a half."

"So you have some fairy circles in this region?" Mary asked.

"Oh, yes, quite a few. We've always found them fascinating. Of course, the villagers see nothing but evil superstition in them, but we've never considered them anything but what they are—odd fungal growths—until now."

"A shock like this will make anyone wonder about the veracity of old superstitions," John added. "Has anything odd ever happened before?"

"No, not at all. In fact, the dogs used to play in and out of the circles when on the morning walks. They'd yap and scamper in and out of the circles, chasing one another and their own tails. To them the circles were just play areas. Nothing sinister."

"And the only things found so far are the two dogs and Sir Reginald's walking staff?" John continued.

"That's correct and you. . ." Lady MacDonell turned to the door.

A large woman in a black and white uniform entered the room carrying a large silver service. "Your tea, m'lady. Shall I pour?"

"No, Alice, just put it on the table. I'll pour myself today. Thank you."

"Yes, m'lady." Alice nodded and left the room.

"Sugar and cream?" Lady MacDonell asked.

"Yes, please," John and Mary answered simultaneously and then both smiled at their coordinated response.

Once the tea was served, Lady MacDonell spoke again, "Now where was I? Oh, yes, the dogs. You can see the condition they're in." She pointed to the two red and white furry mounds on the hearth.

"Oh," Mary startled. "I didn't even notice them."

"Yes, they've been that way since Reginald's disappearance. Hardly get up to eat now. Before they were so friendly, just bundles of energy. Now this. It seems like everything was taken away that day." Lady MacDonell put her head down and was clearly trying to control her emotions. Tears moved slowly down her cheeks. But she recovered quickly. "All I have now is his walking staff and two very quiet dogs." She managed a whisper of a smile.

"Could I see the walking staff?" John asked.

"Of course, but why?"

"Just curious. The more I know about Sir Reginald, the more I may be able to help." John smiled.

Lady MacDonell rang for Graves and instructed him to bring the staff to the library.

"Here it is, m'lady." Graves handed a white ash, varnished walking staff about four feet in length to Lady MacDonell, who handed it to Braemhor.

At that instant, both of the Cavaliers on the hearth sat up and began to growl and cower against the fireplace wall. *Interesting reaction,* John thought as he examined the staff. Lady MacDonell went to the pair, calming them with pats on the head and the words, "Hush, hush." After some brief whining, the dogs went back to their lying positions and continued to observe John and the staff.

"Did Sir Reginald often let the dogs chew on his walking staff?" John asked.

"On, no, never. He was very strict that the dogs were never to chew on any of his possessions. Why? Oh, I see." John showed the distal end of the staff to Lady MacDonell. There were clear teeth marks on the staff. "That's strange."

"Perhaps you can tell me more about the estate." John redirected the conversation.

"What would you like to know?" Lady MacDonell seemed to welcome the topic change away from Sir Reginald's disappearance.

"Who manages the estate? I understand you've made it through two very bad economic downturns. As you no doubt know, many of the old estates have had to go commercial to keep afloat—renting or selling land, running tours for the public, that sort of thing."

"We do have an estate manager, a Mr. William Harwell, but Reginald coordinates very closely with him on the affairs of the estate. We do rent some of our acreage to local farmers, but not that we need to. We do it more for their sake, since we own so much land. And since we're not in any financial difficulties, we can let the land at very reasonable rates."

"Keeps everyone happy. The locals can make a living farming the land, we take in a modest sum each year and keep the land working." The voice came from the tall red-headed man who'd just entered the library. "Is there anymore tea, Mums?"

"Oh, yes, dear." Lady MacDonell turned to the Braemhors. "This is our son, Morgan. This is the Braemhors, Morgan."

"Pleased to meet you." Morgan extended his hand to John and Mary. "You must be the private investigator, come to solve the mystery of Father's disappearance." A facetious smirk spread across his freckled face.

"I'm here to help, if I can," was John's sober response. "Do you live here on the estate?"

"You know I do. Don't play games with me, Mr. Braemhor. I talked with Zauberin this morning. I'm not one of your local villagers, you know."

Lady MacDonell cringed in her chair as a look of embarrassed horror spread over her face.

"Quite right," John stayed steady. "I understand you and your father did not see eye-to-eye on managing certain aspects of the estate."

"Ah, yes. The argument at Zauberin's. *Touché,* Mr. Braemhor." A faint smile graced Morgan's lips.

"Now that we understand each other better, what was the disagreement about?"

"Father has the opportunity to sell some of the estate—at a rather handsome profit—but he refuses to do so. Even our estate agent, Mr. Harwell, agrees that this is an opportunity that should not be squandered. But Father is living in the 19th century, and I told him so. I do have a stake in the estate, you know."

"As do your brothers, Morgan," Lady MacDonell added.

"Yes, but they have their own estates, Mums. This one is the only one I have, and I hate to see financial opportunity lost for old-fashioned family traditions."

"Who is the potential buyer? Or are parts of the estate open to the highest bidder?" Braemhor pressed.

"That, Mr. Braemhor, is none of your business." And with that, Morgan turned and left the library.

"I'm so sorry, Mr. Braemhor. Morgan can be so impolite when he has these fits of high dudgeon."

"It's all right, Lady MacDonell, sometimes people need to hide behind a façade of anger, but I'd like to hear more about Mr. Harwell."

"Mr. Harwell joined us a couple of years ago and has been with us ever since. He seems very adept at financial matters and has managed the estate very well—with Reginald's oversight, of course."

"What's his history? What did he do before coming here?"

"He was the chief financial officer for a London-based company, an electronics firm, I believe."

"A bit odd. I'd think he could do much better for himself as an executive in a London firm than as an estate manager in the Highlands," John opined.

"We thought so too at the time, but he said he'd had his fill of life in the London business world and wanted something less stressful, even if he had to take a reduction in annual earnings. We make available a cottage for the estate manager as part of his compensation. And Reginald met with him several times before finalizing the arrangement. In fact, Morgan found him for us when our manager of the past twenty years suffered a heart attack and passed on. Morgan keeps a small apartment in London."

"And you say your last manager died of a heart attack?"

"Yes, he was out on the grounds when it happened. It was down near. . . . Oh, dear." Lady MacDonell's voice trailed off.

"Yes?" John asked.

Lady MacDonell had become quite pale.

"They found him lying near the fairy circle, with both feet in the circle! Oh, dear, Mr. Braemhor, you don't think it means anything, do you? Do you suppose there's something to the village stories about fairy circles?" Lady MacDonell asked in a hushed voice.

"I don't think we need to jump to any conclusions along those lines, Lady MacDonell, but I'd like to know a bit more about the previous manager, Mr.??"

"Smyth, Jonathon Smyth."

"I see, and how did he feel about selling parts of the estate?"

"Oh, he was dead against it. Saw eye-to-eye with Reginald on that. He didn't feel it was necessary, didn't see any reason to sell property. The estate was managing very well."

"Where did the idea come from in the first place?" John was putting together his thoughts.

"Why, I believe it was Morgan who first mentioned the idea. Yes, it was one evening at dinner. Said it might be a good idea to raise some funds by selling some of the property and investing it in developing markets."

"Like?"

"Oh, he didn't say, just that he thought it good idea to invest in stocks since the financial markets were in a bit of a downturn."

"And Sir Reginald didn't agree?"

"Most certainly not. But then the matter was dropped, and Morgan didn't mention it again until after we lost Mr. Smyth and Mr. Harwell joined the estate," Lady MacDonell concluded.

"And since then this has been a continuing point of contention between your son and your husband?" John asked.

"Not continuing. Since the first time at dinner, Morgan has only mentioned it occasionally. Like when the MacMaster and MacClean properties were sold about three years ago. Morgan felt we were missing out on an opportunity and could capitalize by selling some acreage on the part of the estate near those properties. But he didn't press the issue. Raised it and let it drop when Reginald quickly rejected it again. I was so pleased they could disagree without being disagreeable."

John caught Mary's eye and turned to Lady MacDonell. "I think we've taken enough of your time, Lady MacDonell, and I thank you for sharing so much information with us. We really must be going." He rose.

"Oh, Mr. Braemhor, it's been my pleasure. I don't have many visitors of late and this has been a delightful—though I admit somewhat painful—respite. I do hope you both will feel free to contact me again and we can have tea together. And please, please, if you have any ideas regarding Reginald's disappearance, do not hesitate to contact me immediately. I would be most grateful." She rose and extended her hand to John and Mary as Graves entered the library to show them out.

* * * * * * *

"Where to now?" Mary queried John as he drove down the MacDonell estate drive toward the highway.

"I want to stop at the local library before we go back to the hotel and look at some past issues of the *Community News*, do a little research."

"On Mr. Harwell?" Mary half stated, half asked.

"Precisely. He may be the key to at least one of the fairy circle disappearances."

At the library, John and Mary approached the reception, and John asked, "Where can we find back issues of the *Community News*?"

"There, in the periodicals," the young woman at the desk replied, as she pointed to a large side room to the left of the main area.

"You take last year's and I'll take this," John said as he took the back issues of the paper from the cabinet. The search did not take long before Mary said, "Here it is, John."

John joined her at her side of the table and read over her shoulder. The brief article on the front page was titled "Mr. William Harwell Joins the MacDonell Estate" and contained a biographical sketch of William Harwell with a detailed account of his work history for the last two decades.

"Just as I suspected," John muttered.

"You're not surprised, are you, John?" Mary asked.

"Not at all. This information may go a long way to explaining his retiring from the London rat race to manage the MacDonell estate. Now the question is 'what was Morgan's role in all of this?'" He smiled at Mary. "We've made a lot of progress already today. How about some lunch?"

"I'd like that. It's been a long morning."

Once back at the Nessie, they went into the dining area and ordered a lunch of cullin skink.

"Who's next?" Mary asked as she started her meal.

"Mrs. Cameron, I think. If Zauberin is right about Mr. Cameron's excessive drinking, we should be able to dispense with that part of the mystery in short order. Why don't you call Mrs. Cameron and find out if she can receive us this afternoon while I arrange our room for a couple more days?"

By the time John returned, Mary had arranged for them to go to the Cameron cottage and meet with Mrs. Cameron within the hour.

* * * * * * *

A quick drive north brought the Braemhors to the Cameron cottage on a hill on the west coast of Loch Ness, with a splendid view of the Urquhart Castle ruins in the distance. The road from the highway to the cottage ascended in three stages, from small plateau to small plateau. The cottage itself resided on the third plateau where its rosebush-covered front façade welcomed the Braemhors into a humble abode. Mrs. James Cameron, a short, round woman in her mid-fifties, whose permanent broad smile seemed to belie her grief at her recent loss, met them at the door. The smell of whiskey was quite noticeable. Mrs. Cameron had obviously been tippling.

"Seems it runs in the family," John whispered to Mary as they entered.

"Come in, Mr. and Mrs. Braemhor, I've just set out the tea cozy." She led them into the front sitting room, complete with a smoldering peat fire and faux leather settees. "DI Ferguson said to expect you, that you're helping him to find me husband."

"If we can, Mrs. Cameron. Perhaps you could tell us exactly what happened the morning your husband disappeared."

"Yes, sir, well. . . " she spoke as she poured the tea, "James took his hoe and went out to dig in the fairy circle. You can see it out the side window." She pointed. Sure enough under a nearby hawthorn tree was a circular fungal growth about 12 meters in diameter. Inside the circle, near the edge were marks of a disturbance as if someone had been digging. At that point there was a break in the fungal circle, as if whoever had been digging had disturbed a small arc of the circumference.

"Why was he digging in the fairy circle?"

"Well, after all of the goings on here about, you know, Miss Frasier and Sir Reginald, he decided to get rid of the circle. That was me James. Niver waited for others to take action. Always the first to attack a problem. His friends in the village told him it was tempting fate to get involved with the fairy circles. But he scoffed at the idea. 'Superstition. Nothing but superstition,' he said. And out he went. I wish. . . I wish he hadn't, now. He can be so bull-headed. Even when he's sober. Worse when he's in his cups."

"So he went out to attack the fairies directly?" Mary summed up Mrs. Cameron's story.

"You might say, but he niver come back. That's what he got for his bull-headedness."

"Had he been drinking that morning?" John asked.

"No more than usual. Maybe a pint or two. That's all."

"And you never heard anything. He didn't call out or anything?"

"Niver a sound. One minute he was diggin', the next he was gone. People shouldn't tempt the fairies, I always say. But there you are. Now he's gone and I'm alone to keep the cottage goin' and tend the few sheep we keep."

"Sheep? I didn't see any fencing"

"Oh, no, they're free range. We have a couple of dogs that help round 'em up at sheerin' time."

"Is that at all a problem?" John pressed.

"Oh, no, except when they get too close to the bog down the hill. Even the dogs won't go get 'em then. Scared of the bog, I think. They'll go to the edge of the bog and no farther. We've lost a couple in the bog through the years."

"When was the last time?"

"'Bout two months ago. Young one wandered into the bog. Started to sink. James tried to pull her out, but he couldn't do it. And the dogs were no help. Just ran frantically around the edge barking and not helping. Thought I was going to lose me James then. He had one leg in the bog and 'tother on solid ground. Our neighbor, Henry Scott, came along and pulled James free. But we lost a young ewe."

"Are they all accounted for, now?" John clearly thought he was on to something.

"I think so. I could count 'em tomorrow morning. The neighbor boy, Mr. Scott's son, is supposed to come and help with some chores. He could count 'em for me. Then I'd know. Do you think that would help, Mr. Braemhor?"

"I certainly do. Perhaps we could call you in the morning and find out if you're missing any of your sheep. In the meantime, Mary and I need to return to our hotel. It's been a long day."

"Of course, Mr. Braemhor. And, Mr. Braemhor, I'm very grateful for any help you can give. It would mean so much to have my James back." She rose and went to the front door with the Braemhors.

"I'll call you in the morning then, after Mr. Scott's son has had a chance to count your sheep. Maybe then we and DI Ferguson will have more news for you."

"I certainly hope so."

As they eased their way back onto the highway, Mary turned to John. "I know what you're thinking, John."

"Seems pretty obvious, don't you think? But we'll wait for the report on the sheep count before drawing any conclusion, and certainly before talking with Mrs. Cameron again. But for now let's get some supper."

CHAPTER 2

Next morning, Braemhor placed a call to Mrs. Cameron's cottage.

"Yes, Mr. Braemhor, we are missing another ewe," Mrs. Cameron reported, sadly. "Henry Scott and the dogs rounded up the whole herd, and one is missing. I don't know where it could have gone."

"Mary and I will come back later this morning and see what we can find," John reassured her.

John went into the dining room where Mary was already eating breakfast. "She's missing another ewe, just as we thought. We'll go back to the Camerons' as soon as I get a bite to eat."

"And look for a bog?"

"Precisely. I think we'll need our hiking boots and a walking staff each. The gift shop had a bin of staffs, if I remember correctly."

"I'll get our boots from the room and buy two staffs at the shop while you finish your breakfast." Mary rose and shortly returned with the boots and staffs in hand. "Shall we go?"

An hour later, Mrs. Cameron met them at the door. "Bog? Oh, yes, there's the one James almost fell into last month. It's down on the next level. Shall I show you?" she asked.

"No, that won't be necessary. We'll go down and take a look around. See what we can find. We'll leave our car here." With that, John and Mary started walking down the hill to the next plateau.

Sure enough, about ten meters off the road was what appeared to be an extensive hedgerow of heather behind which the ground appeared wet and soggy. The two went to the hedgerow where they found several openings in the dense purplish-green growth.

"Now," John instructed, "no more steps without first probing the ground with our walking staffs. Probe. Step. Probe. Step. Right?"

They slowly moved through an opening in the heather, probing carefully as they went. Just on the far side of the hedgerow, John announced, "Here we are." His staff had sunk a full foot and a half into the soft earth. "Now let's walk very carefully around the circumference and see what we can find. But, Mary, be careful," he warned.

The bog had a variable edge, sometimes reaching a meter or so distant from the heather, sometimes right up to the edge of the hedgerow growth. About halfway around the edge, just near a rather large opening in the hedge, John called to Mary, "Come over here. Very carefully. Better still, go outside the hedgerow and come around. There's a large opening in the row over here."

Mary moved through the row so that she was farther from the bog and came around. As she started through the large opening, she stopped. "John, it looks like sheep tracks in the opening."

"I'm not surprised. Look here." He pointed to where the solid ground edged into the bog near where he held his staff, partly buried in the earth.

"The ground is all torn-up," Mary observed.

"Perhaps like a sheep that has gone a step or two too far and is trying desperately not to be drawn farther into the soft ground. Mary, I think we may have solved the mystery of Mr. Cameron's disappearance. Suppose, while he was digging in the fairy circle, one of his ewes began a desperate bleating from the bog; what would he do?"

"Try to rescue it, of course."

"And if he were in his cups?"

"He might fall in himself."

"And there was no Mr. Scott to save him this time. I think we'd best get back and call Ferguson."

"But what will you tell Mrs. Cameron?" Mary worried.

"Only that the case of the missing ewe is solved. Nothing else. If Ferguson can confirm our surmise about Cameron, he can give her the sad news later."

Back at the Cameron cottage, John informed Mrs. Cameron that it looked like her missing ewe may have wandered into the bog and been lost. He assured her again that as soon as there was any news regarding her husband, either DI Ferguson or he would contact her.

"I'm sorry we don't have any more information now," Mary told Mrs. Cameron.

"I know, I know. But thank you for trying to help. It does mean so much to me that nice people like you are trying to find me James." She dabbed her eyes with the hem of her apron and went back inside her cottage.

"The poor, sad woman," Mary said to John as they drove back to Ft. Ewen.

When they got back to the Nessie, John rang up Ferguson. "If you can get a team to probe the bog on the plateau below the Cameron cottage, I think you'll find Mr. Cameron and his hoe." He then told Ferguson about the missing ewe and his surmise of what may have happened on the morning of Mr. Cameron's fairy circle digging. "There's a large opening in the heather halfway around the bog, where you'll find some sheep tracks. It looks like a sheep was trying to extricate itself from the bog about there. My best guess is that Mr.

Cameron went to the rescue and got sucked into the quagmire. He may be under the bog near the opening."

"I'll get a team up there this afternoon, and I thank you for your help. I'll call you as soon as I have anything. You and the wife staying at the Nessie?"

"Yes, we'll be there for a few days. There are still the MacDonell and the Fraser cases to wrap up."

"Wrap up? You mean you've solved those, too?"

"Haven't solved anything yet. Just some hunches, that's all." John smiled and hung up.

* * * * * * *

That afternoon John and Mary drove to the Fraser cottage near Cein. Flora and Lily's B&B was on the side of a knoll, with a sweeping panorama across the valley. At the bottom of the valley was a fast moving stream.

"No doubt where the ladies 'poached' Sir Reginald's trout," John remarked, pointing down the slope. The road coursed behind the brown hillock as he spoke, and the cottage briefly disappeared until the road circled around the hill and ended at a small car park behind the grey, stone cottage which had a yellow on red sign, Fraser B&B, lagged into the stone wall beside the front door.

Lily Fraser was a large-boned woman with reddish blond hair flowing freely about her head and shoulders. She was tall and could have been an Olympic discus thrower in her youth. "You must be the Braemhors?" her deep contralto voice reached across the valley as she opened the door. "Come to help find Flora," she stated rather than asked.

"I'll show you where she was when I last saw her from the window." Lily Fraser pointed and marched quickly to the side of the cottage where there was a small stand of hawthorn trees, each surrounded by a fairy circle. John and Mary quickly followed her, exchanging raised eyebrow expressions as they went.

"Right there." Lily Fraser pointed again, this time at the middle tree in a group of three. "Standing in the fairy circle underneath that tree. I turned for a moment to get the post, and when I turned back, she was gone. Damnedest thing I've ever seen. I went right outside, of course, but she was nowhere in sight."

"You can't see the approaching road from here. It's behind that hill," Mary observed, pointing to where the road disappeared from view. "Could she have gone down the road? Or could someone have picked her up in a vehicle?"

"You're pretty sharp, Mrs. Braemhor. I thought of that myself, but I doubt it. Flora would have had to run pretty fast to disappear before I got out. And I think I would have heard a vehicle, but. . ."

"But?" John asked.

"One of our guest couples was leaving just then."

"Maybe you heard two cars and thought it was only your guest's car?" John asked.

"Clever idea. Ferguson was right."

"What do you mean?"

"He said he'd heard good things about you two—your detective skills. I like a couple," she said as she looked at Mary, "that knows their business. Let's go inside and talk over some tea." With that, Lily Fraser strode off with a long-gated, masculine stride towards the front door.

The common room of the cottage radiated the warmth of a Scottish B&B. Two settees before the fireplace were covered in the Fraser dress tartan. The green Fraser tartan graced the two overstuffed chairs.

"Have a seat. I'll get the tea." Lily pointed to one of the settees and exited into the serving kitchen.

As they waited silently, Mary gave John her best, brief wide-eyed stare. John smiled faintly and shook his head.

"Well, what do you think?" Lily boomed as she poured the tea.

"I doubt that it was the fairies." John smiled.

"Fairies! I've had enough of that nonsense! Do you know that one of the villagers from Ft. Ewen wanted to do an exorcism under my hawthorns. Said he had the perfect ritual. Bought it from that charlatan, Zauberin. I cannot believe the gullibility of people. No wonder we make progress so slowly. No, Mr. Braemhor, it was not the fairies."

"Who do you think might want to harm your sister?" Mary joined in.

"First one I thought of was Sir Reginald. We had quite a row with him recently; I suppose you know."

"DI Ferguson told us."

"But I've known Reggie all my life. He's not that sort. Oh, he'll bludgeon you in the courts, if he can—always has been a bully that way—but not the sort to do anything criminal. Now I wouldn't trust that new estate manager he's got. He's a mean one, I think. But I think Reggie keeps him on a short leash."

"How do you know Mr. Harwell?" John asked.

"Oh, he stopped by a bit ago to see if we were interested in selling the property. Said he knew of a potential buyer and could arrange a meeting, if we liked. At first I thought Flora was going to hit him. Then I thought she was going to throw him out the front door, literally. I've never seen her so incensed."

"Why so?"

"Well, over the last few months we've had several offers to sell the property. You have to admit it's a lovely location. Flora was dead-set against selling, and I guess Harwell was just the last straw. He went away under his own power, but he was intimidated I can tell you."

"And you were not against selling?"

"No, I agreed with Flora, but I wasn't as adamant about it. This is a lovely property and except for occasional disagreements with Reggie we led a very peaceful and enjoyable life. Now though, now that Flora's gone, I'm not so sure. It's become a little more unsafe for a single woman to run a B&B this far out of the village. Not much crime hereabouts, but it does happen. So, yes, I might sell, if the offer is right."

"Did Mr. Harwell say who the potential buyer was?" John asked.

"No, he didn't. Said it was all sort of hush-hush for now. But I do know that both the MacMasters and MacClean properties have recently sold, and I understand from Reggie's wife that overtures have been made to them. Reggie, I know, would have nothing to do with it."

"Well, who do you think did it, Mr. Braemhor?" Lily Fraser's redirection of the conversation was so abrupt that both of the Braemhors were taken aback.

John recovered quickly. "Did what, Miss Fraser?"

"Took Flora, of course." Lily Fraser's voice made clear her impatience. "That's what we're talking about, isn't it?"

"Miss Fraser, all we know at this time is that your sister has disappeared. We cannot necessarily assume foul play. She could have wandered off on her own for all we know at present."

"Not bloody likely," Lily Fraser scoffed.

"Except when she was working here at the B&B, what other things did Miss Flora do? Hobbies? Activities? The more we know about her, the more we may be able to help." John remained calm in response to Lily's onslaught.

"Well, she took care of the grounds, trees, flowers, and the like. I did the inside. At times she did like to take long walks. Out on the hills. Into the village. Sometimes, in the evenings, she'd walk into the Lodge and visit with the regulars at the pub."

"Like who?" John quickly asked.

"Don't know exactly. Some are local, a few from Tuaidh. There's even one comes down from north of Ft. Ewen on Wednesday nights."

"Not a Mr. Cameron?" John threw out a wild guess.

"Yes, yes, I think that was his name. John. . .eh. . . James. . .yes, it was James, James Cameron. Friendly old tippler. I met him one Wednesday. I think he had a sweet eye for Flora, though she just found him interesting to talk to. . .and share a pint. Sometimes he'd even give her a ride home, if it was late."

"So he knew where you and Flora lived?" Mary asked.

"Yes, but he seemed pretty harmless to me. Why? You don't think he had anything to do with Flora's disappearance, do you? Because if so, you can catch him at the village pub tonight. Like I said, he's a regular."

"But, Mr. Cameron. . . ." Mary started and abruptly stopped when she saw John's expression.

"Maybe we'll do that," John continued, "but for now we've taken enough of your time, and we need to get back to our hotel. You've been most helpful, Miss Fraser. I hope that in the near future we can have more information for you about your sister's disappearance. For now, we really need to be going."

"Well, let me know as soon as you have anything." Lily Fraser sounded crestfallen.

"Oh, we will. You can count on that," Mary concluded, as she and John rose and left the cottage.

"She doesn't know Cameron is one of the missing," Mary observed as John drove the Vauxhall around the mound behind the Fraser B&B.

"Curious, isn't it?" John reflected. "Maybe we should visit the Lodge pub tonight and see if Cameron shows up.

"You're not serious, John?" Mary was incredulous.

"About visiting the pub, yes. About Cameron showing up, no. But who knows what we might pick up from the locals."

* * * * * * *

Back at the Nessie, John called Ferguson. "What did the bog yield?"

"Cameron's hoe, that's all." Ferguson's disappointment was evident. "My team probed the area of the bog you suggested, and no Cameron. I thought your hunch was a good one, but. . ."

"So we still have three people missing and no bodies," John mused.

"What do you make of that, John?"

"I don't know yet, but I've got some ideas. I'll call you tomorrow after I see what I can find at a nearby pub." With that, Braemhor rang off and turned to Mary.

"No Cameron. Just his hoe."

"Maybe Mr. Cameron didn't fall in the bog. Maybe he threw his hoe in to make it look like he did," Mary offered.

"What?" John had only been half listening.

"Maybe Cameron hasn't disappeared. Maybe he just wants it to look like he has," Mary repeated.

"Of course! Mary you're brilliant! But why?"

"Maybe he just wants out of his marriage. Wants to start a new life with Flora Fraser," Mary opined.

"There are easier ways to do that. Get a divorce, for example. Throw his wife in the bog."

"John, you don't suppose," Mary's voice trailed off in disbelief.

"No, at least not yet. She was all right when we saw her this morning. But the mystery is deepening. Now we've got two Cameron mysteries. The one we started with, that he met with some disaster, criminal or otherwise or that he staged his own disappearance—for reasons as yet unknown. However, if he did stage his own departure, where is he hiding, and why would he continue his habit of visiting the pub in Cein on Wednesday nights?" John answered.

"To see Flora Fraser, of course."

"Or someone else. I think we need to go to the Lodge pub tonight and see who turns up," John concluded.

* * * * * * *

The pub in Cein was a rustic, small room down the hall from reception. Like the Lodge itself it looked like a 19th century drinking establishment, having small, thick tables, most with wooden benches rather than chairs. There were three booths tucked away on the far wall next to the service window. John and Mary took the one farthest away from the window, in the shadow of the heavy ceiling beams. John ordered two pub meals of Scottish meatloaf, smashed potatoes and marrowfat peas—then returned to Mary in the booth with two pints of Guinness.

"Guinness?" Mary observed.

"I didn't want to draw attention to ourselves by ordering our usual sodas. It'll last us the whole evening."

"And we'll still have most of it left then," Mary observed.

"This is a good location. We can see both the hall to reception and the outside door."

The pub was starting to fill even as the Braemhors waited for their order. A massive table in the center of the room was already accommodating a group that looked like young American tourists. As they downed their first pints, their conversation grew in volume, telling the whole room they had visited the Urquhart Castle ruins today and were to search for the Loch Ness monster tomorrow.

John smiled at Mary. "Interesting, isn't it, how many people are captivated by the mythical? I wonder what they'd do if they actually saw a Loch Ness monster?"

"Probably run with fright. Ah, here's our order," Mary said as the young girl brought their dinner order. "It does look delicious," Mary added as she unwrapped her knife and fork and put her serviette in her lap."

The Braemhors were half-finished with their meal when John looked up and whispered, "Look at the threesome that just came in." He nodded toward the front door. There stood three men, one of whom they recognized immediately as Morgan MacDonell. The other two were unknown. One, a tall, thin, dark-haired chap, whose carriage would indicate a well-heeled business man, was dressed in a grey three-piece suit with a dark blue four-in-hand sporting what appeared to be a studded stickpin. A pencil mustache lined his upper lip and drooped down either side of his mouth. The third man, shorter and stockier than the other two, wore work clothes as if he'd just come in from the fields.

Both John and Mary shrank back deeper into the shadows of their booth, the better to observe and not be observed, as the three walked directly towards them. "I think we've been discovered," John hissed. But just as the three seemed about to join the Braemhors in their booth, they turned and went to the booth two down the back row.

"A close one, that," John observed. "My guess is that the business man is from London, while the one in work coveralls is our Mr. Harwell. Unfortunately, they're too far down the row to hear their conversation, but I suspect we're observing the core nest of vipers of our mysteries. I'll even hazard a guess that Mr. Swengali is from S&L Limited."

"The firm that bought the MacMaster and MacClean properties?" Mary half stated, half asked.

"Precisely. Interesting that they'd meet here, instead of in some pub in Ft. Ewen. Yet, here probably affords them more anonymity than closer to the MacDonell's estate."

At that moment, the front door opened again, and in walked a round, jolly-looking man of about sixty. He wore a thick woolen sweater and dark green corduroys. His face lit up when he saw the three in the nearby booth, and the rosy tip of his bulbous nose seemed to light up with his smile. Though he staggered a bit, he maintained a fairly straight course to the booth where the three men were deeply engrossed in conversation.

John leaned forward toward Mary and whispered, "As they say in the Colonies, bingo!"

"Mr. Cameron, I presume?" Mary whispered back.

"Unless I miss my guess. This is a very informative evening, don't you think?"

"But what does it all mean?" Mary asked.

"I think we'll know better before the evening is over, but for now let's just enjoy our meal and order up some cranachan for dessert." John relaxed back into the corner of his bench as a small smile crept across his lips, the same smile that Mary had recognized so many times before when John was beginning to make sense of the many diverse clues of a case.

About an hour later, the three original conspirators, Morgan, "Swengali" and the one John took for Harwell, got up and left, leaving the last to arrive sitting alone in their booth.

John quickly got up and went down the row. "I see your friends have left you. Would you care to join my wife and me for a pint or two."

The round man looked up, smiled and said, "I'd like that very much. You buying?"

"Of course," John responded and led his prey back to where Mary sat.

"How nice. We can have a threesome." Mary looked up as John and his new friend came back.

"This is my wife, Mary," John introduced Mary to the tippler, "and you are?"

"Name's Jim, Jim Cameron. Please to meet you. You tourists?"

"You might say. We're up from Stirling on holiday. Lovely area you have here. You live around here?" John slid his Guinness across the table to Mr. Cameron.

Cameron imbibed almost half the glass of Guinness in one gulp, smiled and let a low belch escape his lips. "Near Ft. Ewen, but I like it better down here. Quieter, you know."

"You look like a business man." John was probing.

"I am, sorta. Just got into a great deal with my friends. You know, those guys what just left. But I can't tell you 'bout it." Cameron giggled. "All hush-hush, you know."

"What sort of business?" John pressed.

"Oh, I can't tell you." Cameron finished John's Guinness and reached across the table for Mary's.

"Well, let me guess." John played Cameron for the sot that he was. "You look to me like you're from the land. So I guess that you're into real estate."

"Oh, I can't tell you." Cameron giggled again. "But you're close." He smiled facetiously. "I don't buy and sell. I just handle the incidentals. Like persuading the owners to sell."

"How do you do that?" Mary asked, putting on her most attentive countenance.

"Some are easy. All I have to do is talk to 'em. Explain why they should sell to the company I work for. Others are harder. Have to use psychology. Say, could I have another pint?"

"Of course," Mary got up and went to the service window. "But I want to hear about this psychology you use when I come back."

Cameron's third pint greased the tracks even more. "My, that's good." He smacked his lips. "Now, where was I?"

"Using psychology, I think," John replied.

"Well, you see. Some folk 'round here are very superstitious. And if you tell 'em 'bout how the fairies are takin' over their property, and you can show 'em where the fairies are hiding. . ."

"Like in the fairy circles?" Mary asked.

"Yes, ma'am. They get kinda scared like and want to sell before the fairies get 'em." Cameron giggled again.

"How clever! You are a very clever businessman, Mr. Cameron," Mary cajoled him.

"But don't you still have some that won't sell?" John asked.

"Oh, yes. But we just make them go into a fairy circle and disappear 'em."

"Come now, Mr. Cameron, the stories about people disappearing in fairy circles aren't true, are they?" Mary asked.

"Course not, ma'am."

"Then, what do you do? Wait. . .I know. You throw a gunny sack over them and take them away. Am I right?" Mary continued.

Mr. Cameron beamed with pride, threw his chest out and admitted, "That's pretty close, ma'am." He smiled and took another large gulp of his pint. "But I can't rightly say. Hush. Hush. You know." He giggled.

"And so that scares the others you're trying to convince to sell into agreeing to sell. Right?" John joined in.

"Can't rightly say," Cameron repeated as he looked at his watch. "Oh, say, I have to leave. I've still got some duties to perform." He rose to go.

"Can we give you a ride home? You've had a pretty rough night of it," John quickly asked.

"No, I'm all right. Takes more than a few pints to keep ol' Jimmy down." With that, he went to the service window and ordered two shepherd pie meals. He smiled back at the Braemhors as he leaned on the wall next to the window.

"John, you're not going to let him get away and drive in the condition he's in?" Mary was concerned on two counts, first, that they'd lose their key to the fairy circle mysteries, and second, that Mr. Cameron was a hazard on the highway.

"Go to the car and get ready to drive. I'll help our friend carry his order to his car. Then we'll follow him home where, if I'm not mistaken, we may find the other two missing persons." John rose and went to the window to help Cameron carry the two meals which had just appeared at the window.

"Let me help you, old friend," John offered.

"Mighty kindly, mighty kindly." Cameron handed one of the meals to John for transport to the car outside.

"Thank you for the pints, Mr. . . . ?" Cameron said as he started his engine.

"Bruce, John Bruce," Braemhor lied.

"Ah, yes, Mr. Bruce. Well, hope to see you again sometime."

I'm sure you will, John thought as he ran to the Vauxhall.

"As they say in the gangster movies in the Colonies, 'Follow that car,'" he said to Mary as he pointed to the two tail lights exiting the car park. "But keep a good distance back," he cautioned, as if Mary had never pursued another car before. She frowned slightly as she eased their car in behind Cameron's.

Cameron turned onto the highway and headed towards Tuaidh, where he turned north towards Ft. Ewen. His driving was a bit erratic, and he drove some ten or more kilometers faster than allowed.

"He seems in a hurry," Mary observed as she maintained the distance back from Cameron's car.

"Probably the alcohol as much as anything. I don't think we gave him any cause to worry about us," John responded.

About two or three kilometers south of Ft. Ewen, Cameron turned onto a small dirt road toward the Loch.

"Go past where he turned and park in that lay-by you can see up ahead," John instructed.

Mary did as she was told, turned off the head lamps and engine and turned to John. "Now what?"

"You wait here. I'm going to take a walk down the road that Cameron took and see what I can see. It shouldn't be more than a kilometer to the Loch and my guess is that there are not many houses there. I should be back in an hour or so. If I'm not, call Ferguson—his number's in both our mobiles—and get him and his men here as soon as he can. And, Mary, lock the doors while I'm gone."

As if he had to tell me that, Mary thought as John exited the car and walked back to the road down which Cameron had disappeared.

* * * * * * *

John walked briskly alongside the dirt road, hoping that Cameron had not driven too far off the main highway. He passed several small holiday vans on the Loch side of the road which seemed abandoned this time of year. As the road took a sweeping curve toward the left, an old thatched-roofed 18th century crofter's cottage came into view. It had obviously been modernized, for the glow of electric lights peered out from the modern, glazed windows. It was small, *probably divided into no more than three rooms,* John thought as he went around to the Loch side and approached it in a half crouch.

He peered in the window. There, seated at a simple wooden table, were three individuals. One, an older gentleman in his middle-to-late sixties, had the carriage of an individual of means and a full head of white hair which cascaded down his neck to the top of his collar. He was obviously not happy, glowering at Mr. Cameron, who sat across the table having yet another pint. John could not hear the conversation, but the older gentleman was carrying on an extended rant, which did not seem to be affecting Mr. Cameron in the least—a placid, immobile smile being his only response. Also at the table there cowered a middle-aged woman whose eyes looked as if she'd been crying. The clothing of both individuals was dirty and rumpled, as though having been worn for some time without the benefit of washing or pressing. Both legs of Cameron's two companions were attached by short leg irons to the heavy table in the center of the room.

Braemhor circled the cottage and saw through the front window what appeared to be a bedroom with two single beds and a nightstand between. One door led to the room where Braemhor saw the threesome. *The other door out of the bedroom probably goes to the loo,* John thought. He slipped into the small stand of hawthorns across the road from the cottage and called Mary.

"Mary," John muffled his voice lest Cameron in the cottage should hear. "Call Ferguson. Tell him we need him, a van and several constables right away. I think we've found Sir Reginald and Flora. I don't think they're in any danger right now, but I don't want to alert Cameron to our presence until the constabulary can get here. I don't think he's armed, but he's still very drunk, and if we frighten him he could panic and do something we'll all regret. I'll wait here and watch. You can follow Ferguson in when he gets here."

"John, do be careful," Mary warned just before she hung up.

As if I wouldn't, John thought as he sat down under one of the hawthorns to wait and watch.

* * * * * * *

John looked around as he waited and watched the light-filled windows of the cottage, beneath its thatched roof. He had placed himself where he had a full view of the front and only door. *The part I dislike the most, waiting for something to happen,* John thought. The hawthorn tree under which he sat afforded him some shelter from the evening mist that was starting to settle. As he looked around, he realized that not only was he seated under a hawthorn, but within the fairy circle that surrounded the tree. *Well, we'll soon know if there is any substance to the mythology,* he thought as he smiled slightly.

After fifteen or twenty minutes, the fairies had not arrived, but other more sinister beings had. A new BMW pulled up in front of the cottage and disgorged the three men who'd been in the pub with Mr. Cameron. *Ah, ha, now we're getting somewhere.* Cameron answered their knock and the three entered. It was clear to Braemhor, even from his distance across the road, that the three were not pleased with their tipsy friend. Hardly were they inside when he could hear loud voices in argument.

He quickly called Mary. "Stay where you are. The other three have arrived, and they're having some sort of an argument with our drunken friend. Don't come down the road until Ferguson and his crew get here. I'll try to get closer and hear what's going on."

"John, do be careful. Ferguson is on his way, but it will take him about a half hour more to get here," Mary responded, glad that John could not see the worry on her face.

"Not to worry. I'm sitting in a fairy circle, and I'm sure the little fellows will take good care of me." John smiled. "I'll see if I can borrow some fairy dust to bewitch the villains until Ferguson gets here."

"No time for levity, John. What if Aunt Rita is right and the fairies are going to carry you off to never-never land?"

"I've got more real concerns here. Morgan just came out to the car and is taking what looks like a shotgun out of the boot. I'd best ring off."

"John, please. . . ." He was gone. Now Mary had the anxiety of waiting and not knowing.

* * * * * *

John ran quickly across the road and grabbed the shotgun that Morgan had leaned against the BMW while he was closing the boot. Morgan was so taken aback at the unexpected appearance of Braemhor, all he could say was, "Braemhor!"

"One word, one noise and you'll never see the light of day." Braemhor pointed the shotgun at Morgan's face.

Morgan threw up his hands. A look of abject horror covered his face as Braemhor motioned him to move toward the hawthorns.

"Now lay down, face down," John hissed, "not a word." John had placed Morgan at the base of the hawthorn trunk and pressed the muzzle of the shotgun at the back of his head.

Morgan looked around as best he could from his supine position, his face a ghastly white. He whispered in a tremulous voice barely audible from where Braemhor stood over him. "Please, please, Mr. Braemhor, not in a fairy circle. Not that, please."

"I warned you," Braemhor said as he cocked the hammer of the shotgun. At the metallic sound of the hammer Morgan began to shake all over like an aspen in a morning breeze. After a short wait to allow Morgan to appreciate the depth of his fear, Braemhor slowly, silently returned the hammer to its safe position.

At that moment, light flooded the road in front of the cottage. The door had opened, and there outlined by the backlight stood Cameron, unsteadily holding on to the doorframe for support. "Mr. Morgan, what's keeping you?" He stepped over the threshold and came towards the BMW.

"Over here," Braemhor said in a loud whisper and motioned with his arm. Cameron staggered past the BMW towards the sound of Braemhor's voice.

"Mr. Bruce? What are you doing here?" Cameron was very perplexed, but when he saw what Braemhor had in his hand, his eyes bulged and his perplexity turned to fear.

"Come here and not a word." John held his finger to his mouth.

"Now sit on Morgan," John commanded. Cameron said nothing, but did as he was told, placing his overly rotund body squarely in the middle of Morgan's back. Morgan groaned from the weight.

Cameron looked down at Morgan. "I told you this was a bad idea," he whispered. "It'll be the death of me!"

"It'll be the death of you, if you don't shut up," Braemhor warned. "Now the two of you, don't move and don't make a sound." He stood silently over them.

Shortly, the cottage door opened again. The man John took for Harwell came out. "What's going on out here?" he boomed and came towards the BMW.

Now what'll I do? John was quickly reviewing his options. There weren't many. *Good grief, what's taking Ferguson so long?*

At that moment, car lights came around the curve of the road. *Ah, Ferguson at last,* John thought. But no, they were the lights of his Vauxhall with Mary at the wheel! *Oh, no! What is Mary up to?* She stopped the car and rolled down the window as Harwell approached. John could only watch from the stand of hawthorns.

"What do you want, lady?" Harwell asked gruffly.

Mary put on her most vulnerable, lost look. "I wonder if you could help me? I seemed to have made a wrong turn, and I'm lost. How do I get back to Ft. Ewen? I'm supposed to meet with my nephew at the Nessie Hotel and I'm already late, and I'm afraid I lost my way." Mary hoped it was a convincing story.

"You sure have lost your way, lady." Harwell was a little more consolatory and not quite so aggressive. "You need to turn around and go back to the main road. That'll take you to Ft. Ewen. You can't miss it."

"Oh, thank you so much. You've been a big help." With that Mary put the Vauxhall in reverse, turned the wheel and gunned the motor. The car lurched backward and right into the side of the BMW.

"Oh, dear, now look what I've done!" she fretted as she pulled on the emergency brake and started to get out of the car to survey the damage.

"No, no, lady! It's all right! Don't get out! You just drive back to Ft. Ewen."

"But I've damaged your car. I can't just leave. Maybe I should call the police. They could help." She rummaged in her purse, looking for her mobile. "Ah, here's my phone," she said as she retrieved it from the depths of her bag.

"No, no, lady! It's all right! Don't worry about it! Don't call the police! We'll just pretend it didn't happen!" Harwell was getting frantic.

"Oh, I couldn't do that. Here. Let me pay you something for the damage." She again searched her purse for her money. Mr. Harwell was trying to contain himself and get rid of her as quickly as possible.

"Now go, go!"

"Are you sure I can't pay you something. Oh, I feel so badly about your car."

As she spoke, the light of headlamps rounded the curve in the road, revealing two white, green, and yellow police cars and a van in the light escaping the open cottage door. Harwell immediately began running away down the road, but a constable quickly jumped from one of the cars, chased him down and brought him back in handcuffs.

Meanwhile, Braemhor called to Ferguson from his stand in the hawthorns, "There's another one in the cottage. I've got two over here. Flora Fraser and Sir Reginald are inside also."

Ferguson waved acknowledgement and entered the cottage with two other constables. There was a brief scuffle before Cameron's last companion from the pub was subdued. Ferguson sent one constable to Braemhor to take charge of Cameron and Morgan. Mary stayed in the Vauxhall and watched the efficiency with which Ferguson and his men finished the captures.

After the four had been locked securely in the police van, Ferguson talked over the evening's events with John and Mary.

"I think you ought to have this," John said, handing the shotgun to Ferguson. "The three were about to use it on Sir Reginald and Miss Fraser, I believe."

Ferguson took the gun, opened the breech and announced, "You know it's empty, don't you? Harwell had the shells in his coat pocket."

"Well, that would have been embarrassing if I'd had to use it," Braemhor admitted.

"Or worse!" Mary added.

At that moment, one of the constables came out of the cottage with Flora Fraser and Sir Reginald. Both appeared still in shock from their ordeal.

"Sir Reginald, Miss Fraser, I want you to meet Mr. and Mrs. Braemhor. They're private investigators up from Daraichburn to help out on this case," Ferguson said.

"We're so pleased to meet you and to know that both of you are safe now." Mary took the lead.

Neither of the two responded, but stared vacantly at the Braemhors.

John smiled. "Probably the main thing now is for you to be reunited with your families."

"That's our next move, to see to it that both Miss Fraser and Sir Reginald are taken home," Ferguson added as he waved to one of the constables who brought a car over to where the five were standing. "The constable will see to it that you get home safely now. We can meet tomorrow, and I'll get the details of what you've been through. I'll come up from Ft. Lochiel in the afternoon."

Both Sir Reginald and Flora regained enough composure that they agreed to meet the next day, then briefly said their good-byes and got into the constable's car for the ride to their respective homes.

Ferguson spoke to John and Mary, "I have to get back to Ft. Lochiel and start interrogating our four friends."

"If Morgan gives you any trouble, put him into a fairy circle. I'm sure that will loosen his tongue." Braemhor smiled.

Ferguson looked perplexed for a moment. He was not sure whether or not John was serious.

Then John continued, "Maybe you could stop at the Nessie Hotel on your way tomorrow and fill us in on the wrap-up?"

"That will be fine. I'll see you in the morning." With that Ferguson, wearing an ear-to-ear smile, got into the front of the van, waved to the Braemhors and headed back to Ft. Lochiel with the three suspects.

On the way back to the Nessie Hotel, it was Mary who broke the silence. "I'm sorry. I just could not sit at that lay-by wondering what was happening."

"You realize how dangerous it was for you to come to the cottage?"

"Yes, but I had to do something. Besides, you have to admit that my tête-à-tête with Mr. Harwell gave Ferguson a little more time to get there."

"I know. I know. But you know how I feel about you being directly in harm's way." He reached over and patted her hand.

"We work together, don't we, John?" Mary countered with satisfaction.

* * * * * * *

Next morning Ferguson entered the Nessie Hotel pub while John and Mary were having breakfast.

"I want to thank you both for your help. But how did you manage to get all four of the kidnappers together at one time?'

John told Ferguson the tale of last night and how he and Mary found Sir Reginald and Miss Fraser in the cottage.

"So kidnapping will be the charge?" John asked.

"That's the main charge. And possibly attempted murder, in addition to land fraud dating back several months. Seems the London businessman—Williams was his name—was in charge of S&L Limited's land acquisition section. You knew that Harwell was their chief financial officer before becoming manager for Sir Reginald? It was all an elaborate plan to buy up ore-rich land in the Loch Ness region for the company. Seems there's an abundance of strontium up here. Quite valuable in a number of applications: electronics, cathode ray tube manufacture, optics, medical treatments for osteoporosis and even neurotransmitter measurement and facilitation. The company stood to make a fortune. Probably could have accomplished their ends legitimately, but more slowly. Williams and Harwell just got carried away. Profits weren't growing fast enough for them. Some of the people they approached just weren't willing to sell, and when they found that verbal pressure wasn't enough, they got more direct and criminal."

"But wasn't kidnapping and possible murder a bit extreme?" Mary asked.

"Well, ma'am, if you could see the potential fortune to be made, you'd understand. To them, it was worth the risk."

"So how did you get all of this information out of them?"

"That was curious. At first none of them would cooperate with us. Cameron was clearly the weak link. As he got more in need of a drink, he became more cooperative. We gave him just enough to keep him talking and from going into full-blown DTs. But Morgan MacDonell was very strange. Wouldn't help us at all. Even when we offered some immunity to prosecution to 'save the family reputation.' So we took your advice, John, and took him outside and put him in a fairy circle. Worked wonders. I've never seen a man so reduced to childish fright. I was even afraid he was going to have a heart attack before we took him out of the circle. He was absolutely babbling. Couldn't tell us enough. John, he was actually afraid the fairies were going to carry him off. Can you imagine?"

"Yes, I can, "John answered. "I think we who live in the world of logic and hard reality find it difficult to understand what a strong power the human imagination is, particularly when it's supported by cultural myth. It sounds to me that you have your case pretty well wrapped up."

"Again, thanks to you and Mary." Ferguson beamed and looked at his watch. "I think I'd best be going to see Miss Fraser and Sir Reginald and finish my wrap-up."

"Before you go. . ." John stopped Ferguson as he was about to leave.

"Oh?"

"Something you said just now, about Morgan."

"Yes?"

"You said he looked like he was going to have a heart attack when you put him into the fairy circle. You realize that a couple of years ago Jonathon Smyth, the MacDonell's previous manager, had a heart attack and was found with his feet in a fairy circle. His death was what opened the position that Harwell, on Morgan's recommendation, took on the MacDonell estate. Perhaps Smyth was a very superstitious man and Morgan put him into a circle to precipitate his death and clear the way for Harwell to move to the Highlands. . . . Just something to think about." John smiled.

"Anything is possible in the world of fairy circles, John, but I've got enough on my desk right now. I'd best be off." With that, Ferguson left the pub to debrief Miss Fraser and Sir Reginald.

"Care for some sight-seeing?" John looked at Mary. "Then tomorrow we can stop at the Frasers and the MacDonells before going back to Daraichburn."

"That would be nice," Mary agreed.

* * * * * * *

Next morning, the Braemhors went first to the Fraser B&B where they learned that Cameron had, in fact, picked up Flora Fraser in his car near the fairy circle. Seems he parked his car on the other side of the hill behind the Fraser cottage and enticed Flora into his car with "I have something important to tell you." In the brief moment that Lily had turned away from the window to receive the post, he drove off with his captive and took her to the cottage where John and Mary found her being held with Sir Reginald. Both of the sisters were most appreciative of the Braemhors' efforts and offered them free lodging any time they wanted to go on holiday in the Loch Ness region.

Next they visited the MacDonells briefly. Sir Reginald had recovered from his ordeal and was having tea with his wife in the library.

"I see your dogs have recovered from the experience of your disappearance." Mary noted the frolicsomeness of the pair who now played in front of the fire. They now seemed like King Charles Cavaliers of old, alert and playful.

"Oh, yes," Lady MacDonell said, "they've become their old selves now that Reginald has returned."

"I do have one curiosity question," John stated. "Why did your dogs chew on the base of your walking staff?"

"Oh, that. Well, you see, when Harwell and Morgan proceeded to drag me bodily off from beside the fairy circle, I clung on to my staff. I was so surprised by the attack, I couldn't swing it to defend myself. Both dogs seized the stick in their teeth—I suppose thinking they were helping me. It didn't help, as the staff was wrenched from my grasp and I succumbed to my attackers. But it did show me how dedicated this pair is to me." He rubbed both behind their ears which seemed to satisfy the dogs' need for constant attention. "Why do you ask?"

"Just curious. They seem so well-trained that I was surprised they would chew on their master's walking stick."

"They are a very loyal breed, you see, and an attack on their owner is the same as an attack on themselves. At any rate, they were trying to help in any way they could."

With that and a few words of appreciation from the MacDonells, the Braemhors took their leave and went outside to their Vauxhall.

* * * * * * *

Mary looked at John. "Shall we go back to Daraichburn and see if Rita has stayed out of the fairy circle?"

"She's probably taught the fairies a new dance." John smiled. "But first I want to stop at Mr. Zauberin's shop and pick up a book on the fairies for her."

Zauberin was his usual ghoulish self when they arrived, but was only too happy to show the Braemhors his selection of fairy circle books. While browsing, Mary suddenly stopped and motioned to her husband.

"Look, John, here are two books by a professor at Carter University, in the Colonies." She pointed to two books on hypnosis. "We should add them to our library, and maybe the next time we visit the Howards at Carter we can get to meet the author."

John paid Zauberin and the Braemhors headed home to Daraichburn.

CHAPTER 3

Aunt Rita met Mary and John at the door, excitement written across her face. "I'm so glad you're back. I'm just bursting to tell you the happenings." She beamed a broad smile as John brought their valise in from the car.

"Have the fairies been active?" John asked with a smile and a faint hint of sarcasm. Mary frowned at him and shook her head slightly.

"More than that! They've been having a festival." Rita was as pleased as a child with a large piece of candy.

"A festival, you say? Did you see them dancing or whatever they do?" John asked, trying to sound serious.

"Oh, no, no one sees the fairies unless you go into their circle, but I heard them."

"Musical, was it?"

"No, not really musical. More like a low undulating hum. Rhythmic."

"They play a tune, do they?"

"No, not really. More like a contrapuntal bass to a treble melody. Only there's no melody." Early in her life Rita had been a concert pianist. "Reminded me of Ravel's 'Bolero.' You feel it more than you hear it. But you do hear it. Sometimes it even vibrates the floor—rhythmically."

"I don't hear anything, Aunt Rita," Mary said.

"Oh, no; they're not doing it now. It mainly happens in the evening, inside, not out." Rita was proud of her unique gift of hearing the fairies.

"Let me understand," John continued, "you only hear this—ah, hum—inside and at night. Are you sure it's not the fridge? Or the dishwasher?"

"No, I very carefully waited until both had stopped running and then listened. It was still there. You see, I've learned something from my detective nephew-in-law's investigative ways." She beamed again. "I even went outside to see if I could locate it, but it was more inside than out."

"So you think it's the fairies?" Mary asked.

"What else could it be?" Rita pursed her lips to show Mary what she thought of the question.

Seeing that John was getting a bit irritated at the course of the conversation, Mary interjected, "Aunt Rita, we thought you might like this book we brought you from Ft. Ewen." She gave her the book on the fairies that she and John had bought at Zauberin's *The Witch's Cauldron.*

"Oh, wonderful. Maybe this will tell me about how the fairies hum." With that, she marched down the hall to her room with the book nestled under her arm. "I'll be back later for supper," she said as she disappeared into her room, leaving John and Mary staring at one another and wondering.

"Do you suppose she really is hearing something? Maybe I can find more on this hum business before we eat. Probably not, but we'll see," John said as he went into the den and turned on the computer.

* * * * * * *

Mary and Aunt Rita had already started their meal when John came in to join them.

"Well, Rita, you're not the only one who's heard a humming sound. Very interesting. People have heard it all over the world, mainly in the northern hemisphere, although there was one report of it in New Zealand and one in Australia. Been going on since the 1940's here in the U.K. Even been heard on the west coast of Scotland, just 30 miles from Glasgow."

"But what is it?" Mary was intrigued.

"Nobody knows. Very few people are able to hear it. It apparently isn't tinnitus—you know, a ringing in the ear—the first thing most audiologists think of, but some of the people who hear it don't have tinnitus and, besides, if they move to a different location, the hum goes away. It's only heard by about 2% of the population, mostly older individuals, say 55 to 70. Maybe this is the hum you've been hearing and you're one of those people, Rita.

"Some scientists think it might be tiny earth tremors caused by waves colliding underwater and others have speculated that the sound is the mating call of a certain fish—the Midshipmen Fish." Rita giggled as John continued. "But the hum has been reported in desert areas like New Mexico in the Colonies, so waves and fish don't seem to account for it."

"What about industrial noise, machinery, large lorries?" Mary asked.

"Except that it's been heard mainly in rural areas, away from industry or heavy traffic. Gas lines, power line emissions and even low frequency electromagnetic radiation have been considered, but no one thing seems to explain the hum being heard in all these locations," John responded, then turned to Rita.

"Rita, you said it's like a bass note, didn't you?"

"Oh, yes."

"Well, that much is consistent. The hum I've been reading about is a low frequency sound. It peaks at 56 Hz and has a range of 40 to 80 Hz. So, Rita, I apologize for being skeptical when you first mentioned hearing a hum. For now, it seems it could be real; it fits in with what I've read. Its cause remains a mystery, but no one suggests that's it's the sound of fairies dancing," John finished with a smile.

"But why should some people hear it and others not?" Rita was more intrigued than before.

"Some people can hear sounds that others can't. I don't think that's anything new or unusual. Think of a dog. A dog can hear higher frequency sounds than most humans, so there's a market for dog whistles—high frequency whistles that only a dog will respond to. Yet some humans can, in fact, hear the whistles. So 2% of the population hearing something that the rest of us don't hear is not that unusual. If this is the hum you've been hearing, you have a unique talent, Rita." John smiled at her as he buttered his muffin.

"Oh, I like that idea." Rita beamed.

"Wrong analogy, John," Mary interjected.

"What?"

"The dog analogy is wrong."

"How so?" John was not following Mary's thinking.

"Dog whistles are outside the normal range of hearing, so it's not surprising that only a small percentage of people can hear them. But the hum appears to be within the normal hearing range. Most people can hear a piano key that sounds at 56 Hz, near low C, and even lower, so there must be more involved than the physical frequency of the sound."

"Like what?" John was curious.

"What about volume? Maybe the frequency can be heard by most, but it's at such a low, quiet volume that only a few can hear it."

"Or what about timbre? Maybe fairies are making the hum at different resonances than most people can hear." Rita had entered the discussion, speaking from her concert days.

"Of course, Rita. Maybe the 56 Hz hum is of a different timbre than, say, a piano key at that frequency. Whatever is generating it—and sorry, it's not the fairies—has different resonance qualities than, say, a piano." Mary was enjoying the intellectual game of trying to understand the hum.

"So there may be any number of things that could account for the small percentage of the population that hears the hum," John concluded. "Maybe we should go to the shore and see if Rita hears anything there." John smiled at Rita. "After all, we've been thinking of making a trip anyway."

"Like I'm a human divining rod?" Rita displayed her impish smile.

"Something like that. What do you think, Rita?"

"Oh, I think that would be exciting."

John looked at Mary. "Well?"

"Well we did just get back," Mary said hesitantly, "but, why not? We'll see if Rita can find the hum. But first let me check our bookings." Mary went to the B&B registry. "We could do it Monday, day after tomorrow. We have two bookings for tonight."

"That would be fine. It will give me more time for internet research," John agreed.

In their room that night, John confided to Mary that there was something much more interesting to him on the web than the hum. He'd found that over the last six months there had been an increasing number of near accidents between USA and UK submarines in the Firth off of Una. The story said that the authorities were baffled by the incidents.

"Just the sort of situation to rouse your interest," Mary observed.

"Don't you think it would be interesting to see what we can find? And a few days on the coast would be nice," he added sheepishly.

"And so we fool Rita into thinking we're investigating the hum. Really, John."

"Not totally. I think trying to understand the hum better is a worthwhile undertaking, too, and this way we can possibly solve two puzzles at once."

"John Braemhor, at times you are an incorrigible sleuth," Mary said as she turned to go to sleep.

* * * * * *

Monday awoke in the same grey shroud that the Braemhors were accustomed to except that it was not raining. . .yet. John put the valises into the car and then headed west towards Una, where the hum had been reported since the 1980's.

"Oh, this is beautiful," exclaimed Rita as John pulled into the car park at the Ayrshire Hotel, which sat on a slight rise overlooking the Firth of Clyde. Once inside, Rita went directly to the desk and accosted the clerk with, "We're looking for the hum. Can you tell us where we might find it?"

The startled clerk, with a twinkle in her eye, began a low humming sound and said, "It's right here." She went back to her filing.

"Oh, silly, I mean the real hum, you know, the hum, hum."

"Oh, the hum hum. We wish we could find it, too. In fact, there's a whole organization called The Hummers here in Una. They give excellent concerts." The clerk smiled.

"Concerts?" Mary was close on Rita's heels as she approached the desk.

"Oh, yes, they're a choral group, only they don't sing, they hum. They're giving a concert tonight in our extended bar area. Are you staying with us?"

"Yes, we are." John approached the desk. "We have reservations for two rooms. Braemhor."

"Ah, yes, here you are, right here." The clerk consulted the registration book.

John filled out the registration cards and guided Mary and Rita upstairs to their rooms.

"It might be interesting to hear The Hummers' concert tonight, don't you think?" Mary asked as they sat at lunch in the public room that served the hotel both as a bar and an entertainment space. A small raised stage was in one corner, offering sight lines to the entire room. "Where might we find some of the local people who hear the hum that Una is known for?" she asked the waitress, as their desserts of selkirk bannocks were being set on the table.

"You'd want to start with Gilbert Linsay; he's the leader of The Hummers choral group. He has a shop back on Main near the Tourist Bureau. It's called The Hum. You know The Hummers are going to be here tonight?"

"Yes, we look forward to the concert." Mary smiled and then turned to John. "A walk to The Hum, after lunch?"

* * * * * * *

Linsay's shop was indeed close on to the Bureau. The door was painted a deep maroon with gold trim and in the window was an assortment of books on the strange noises—hums—reported by some of the locals and a few of the tourists. The location—right next to the Bureau—was well chosen for attracting tourist trade. Instead of the usual tinkling bell, a low hum announced the Braemhors' and Rita's arrival.

The shop contained, in addition to the books, sheet music and books of traditional Gaelic music. In a side cabinet to the right were collections of mouth organs and small and large kazoos. Behind the main cabinet, facing the front door, was a rack of cellos and two double basses. The display in this cabinet was more books on the strange phenomenon known as the hum, while the cabinet on the left contained traditional violins and violas. The man behind the main cabinet hummed as he dusted, with sensitive care, the double basses. His back was to John, Mary and Rita.

John cleared his throat.

The proprietor was a short, dark-haired man in his early sixties. He wore a bluish-grey smock, the sort often worn by a bookseller or an artist in clay. His eyes were the grey of his smock and wore a twinkle similar to the waitress at the hotel. The corners of his mouth turned upward in a semi-perpetual smile. He appeared welcoming. John took note of the fingers of his left hand. *A double bass player of long standing*, John thought.

"Mr. Linsay?" John spoke first.

"Hummmmm. Yes. Can I be of assistance?" His voice was soft and melodious.

"Your daughter at the Ayrshire," John was making another of his deductive leaps, "told us where to find you."

"Hummmmm. And what might you want with me?" Linsay's twinkle broadened.

"We're interested in the hum."

"As in music or as in a strange, unexplained phenomenon?" Seriousness enveloped Linsay's features.

"The latter."

"Well, you've come to the right place. Una is the center of the hum, at least for the last thirty years or so. I maintain a large library of hum literature. Perhaps, I could interest you in a book or two."

With that, Linsay began shuffling through the books and pamphlets in the display case in front of him and began to launch into a monologue on much of the information John, Mary and Rita had discussed back at the B&B.

John quickly interjected, "No, thank you. What we're interested in is where the hum is most prominent here in Una and what insights you might have about its origins."

"According to all of the scientists, its origins are unknown, but I and my group know more than they." Linsay smiled.

"And?"

"It is the harmonies of the fairies."

"What? You're not serious!"

"Most assuredly I am. Why do you think that we hear it on the coast, here in Una? They came over from Ireland several centuries ago, settled here in Una and have been entertaining the hum hearers ever since."

"See. What did I tell you? It's the fairies!" Rita exclaimed.

"Rita, please." Mary stepped in. Then she turned to Linsay. "If it is the fairies, why do most people hear the hum inside buildings? Shouldn't they hear it outside, near, say, a fairy circle?"

"The fairies in Una have moved inside," Linsay stated quickly with conviction.

John looked at Mary and under his breath hissed, "This is getting us nowhere. Time to go." He turned to Linsay. "You've been most helpful. We look forward to your concert this evening at the Ayrshire." He ushered Mary and Rita out the door, though Rita only went reluctantly.

Outside the shop and on the road back to the hotel, Rita was perplexed and a bit put off by their rapid exit.

"John, that nice man was going to tell us about the hum," she petulantly stated.

"That nice man, as you call him, is a charlatan, Rita, who makes his living by bilking the tourists. We'd better spend our time searching out the hum ourselves," John responded. "Remember you promised to be a human divining rod for us," John cajoled.

"So I did. So I did. Well, when do we start?" Rita calmed with the expectation of the search.

"Let's see the village first. They have some wonderful shops, I understand, and then we can have dinner and go to the concert. Tomorrow will be a good time to start our search. Who knows, maybe the hum will come to us," Mary answered.

The three walked east on Main towards the shops.

* * * * * * *

The concert that evening was most unusual. The Hummers, a choral group of twenty men and women, rendered their musical pieces—ranging from Celtic folk tunes to classical choral work and ending with Verdi's famous chorus from *Nabucco*—not with words, but with hums. It was an inspiring performance, much appreciated by the audience.

After the applause, Linsay approached the table where John, Mary and Rita sat. "Ah, I see you are music lovers as well as hum searchers."

"That was an excellent concert, unusual and musically exceptional. No doubt you conceived the idea of a humming chorus from the fact that Una, as you told us earlier, is the center of the hum," Mary observed.

"It's logical," Linsay agreed, "but sounds generated by humans and those made by fairies are quite different. We have hummer meetings where we discuss this. You should attend one."

"Perhaps so," John said as he herded Mary and Rita towards the stairs to their rooms.

"Oh, I'd like that," Rita gushed.

"Another time maybe, another time, Rita." John took one arm and Mary the other as they hurried Rita out of the performance area and up to the rooms.

Linsay stood crestfallen as he watched his latest pigeons slip out of his grasp.

Upstairs, John and Mary retired to their room and Rita to hers.

"What do you think, John?" Mary queried.

"Maybe we should go back to Daraichburn tomorrow before Rita gets sucked into Linsay's shell game. Why don't you take her shopping in the morning, while I talk with the local constabulary about our Mr. Linsay. We can. . ." John was interrupted by a light tapping on their door.

Mary opened the door and there stood Rita, an impish smile on her face. "I hear it," she announced.

"Hear what?" Mary asked without thinking.

"The hum, of course. It's right here in the hotel. Don't you hear it? It's very loud."

"Well, let's find it." John entered the conversation as he stepped into the hallway and locked their door.

The three of them walked first up to the top floor, and then up and down the hall outside the rooms, while Rita stopped occasionally and listened. Then they repeated the same path on the other floors and finally ended in the common areas, the bar, dining room and reception. Rita's report was always the same. She heard it everywhere in the hotel.

"But it's particularly loud upstairs, and got softer as we came down."

"Interesting," John commented as the three exited the front entrance. The weather had become ominous, dark and foreboding.

"Looks like we're in for a storm," John observed as he ushered all of them back into the lobby. "Maybe we should turn in. It's been a long day, and at least we found one hum location."

As they ascended the stairs, there was an explosive flash of lightening followed by a crash of thunder that rattled all of the windows in the hotel. And then darkness. The power had failed under the storm's initial onslaught. Quickly, John pulled out a small keychain torch and turned it on. "I think this will get us back to our rooms. And none too soon."

As they moved along the passage to their rooms with the small illumination from John's torch, Rita made an interesting observation. "The hum's gone."

* * * * * * *

After a breakfast of soft boileds and toast, Mary and Rita sought out the many specialty shops near the Ayrshire, while John walked to the police station on Council Street and asked to see the DI on duty.

DI Gordon ushered him into an office. "How can I help?"

John gave Gordon a brief summary of his own police history. Then he said, "I have two things, first, what can you tell me about the recent rash of submarine incidents off the coast and, second, what do you know about the hum?" Gordon became noticeably distant, "I don't know anything about the submarines other than what I read in the papers, but we can talk about the hum."

Braemhor's interest was instantly aroused. He decided on the path of least resistance. "What can you tell me about Gilbert Linsay?"

"Ah, yes, Mr. Linsay. He's lived here since shortly after the hum was reported. Runs the musical instrument shop near the Travel Bureau and dabbles in the hum."

"Dabbles?"

"Yes, he sells books on it and other folklore."

"Like fairies?"

"Fairies, spirits, ghosts, zombies, the hum, you name it. He has a whole arsenal of strange interests and has done a good job of selling the tourists on them."

"Legitimate?"

"As far as we know. Oh, we receive an occasional complaint from a tourist who claims she didn't get her money's worth. But nothing criminal, so far. We do keep a close watch on him and a few others to make sure what they sell or do is on the right side of the law. Why do you ask?"

"He struck me as a charlatan."

Gordon smiled. "Charlatan, yes, but criminal, not so far as we know."

"He seems to have a particular interest in the hum."

"Oh, yes, in addition to our local citizens who hear the hum. He heads two distinct groups of hummers. The musical group. Have you had a chance to hear them? Quite an entertainment. . . ."

"Yes, we went to their concert last night."

"Then you know what I mean about their musical talent. He also has a second group, smaller than the chorus. Five individuals. They regale the tourists with tales of the hum. They have regular meetings on Thursday evenings to which he invites the public—for an admission price, of course. DI Smyth went one night just to check things out. Linsay gives a lecture on the hum, then if he has any hum hearers in the audience, lets them share what they are hearing and ends with a group discussion. Smyth thought it quite entertaining, but nothing more. Linsay told the group that night that the hum was space aliens trying to make contact with earth." Gordon chuckled.

"His story now is that it's the fairies, come over from Ireland," John offered.

"The fairies now, is it? He is, if anything, creative in his, if you'll pardon me, fairy tales." Gordon liked his own pun.

"And who are these others who play Linsay's side of the game?"

"Interesting you should ask. Two of them are local, grew up here and always in trouble from their teen years on. Minor brushes with the law. Nothing major, but local troublemakers. The other three came here about ten years ago from somewhere in the Ukraine, near Karkov, I believe."

"And how are they employed?"

"They have a small electronics shop on Gelway. Sell and repair small electronic devices, you know, cell phones, radios, some tellies, the like. The two locals work for them."

"What about the submarines?" John abruptly changed the subject, hoping to catch Gordon off guard and get more information.

But Gordon was quick. "Sorry, but as I said, I don't know anything about them. Sorry, I can't help on that score."

"Well, you've certainly roused my curiosity," John admitted.

Gordon stared at John and said no more.

The stony silence blended into a moment of awkwardness until John rose to leave.

"I've taken enough of your time and I do appreciate your help. Perhaps my wife and I will attend Mr. Linsay's hum meeting tonight. It could be interesting."

"If you're into fairy tales." Gordon relaxed and smiled again, offered John his hand and opened the office door. "They meet in the large room above Linsay's shop. About eight," Gordon said as they exited his office.

* * * * * * *

"How was the shopping?" John greeted Rita and Mary as they entered the Ayrshire.

"Wonderful." Rita beamed. "This is a lovely town with some very interesting gift shops." She pulled two silk scarves she'd purchased during hers and Mary's walkabout.

"Beautiful," John said admiringly. "What did you find, Mary?"

"These, for the grandchildren." She held aloft a handmade highland doll and a Robert Bruce lego set.

"And what have you learned?"

"That we'll stay another night and go to Mr. Linsay's hum meeting tonight. . . ."

Rita immediately brightened. "Oh, I'd like that."

He told Mary and Rita more about his meeting with DI Gordon as they went into the dining area for lunch, after which John suggested that they spend the afternoon searching for other locations of the hum by visiting local landmarks.

Their afternoon hum search took them to a number of historic sites, including a Neolithic tomb and a private observatory where true north can be sighted even on nights when the north star is not visible. But no hum. Even along the beach coast of the Firth, where some had reported hearing it outdoors.

All the while Rita's disappointment at not hearing the hum grew, and she became increasingly quiet and withdrawn. John, too, seemed little interested in the sights, but maintained an almost sullen detachment from the events around him. Deep in thought. Only

Mary seemed to enjoy and thrive on the excursion around Una, its monuments and preserved history.

Finally Mary broke the melancholy silence that had enveloped the three of them.

"Why so thoughtful, John?"

"Just contemplating the mystery of the hum."

Rita brightened slightly at the mention of the phenomena she alone of the three could directly experience.

"And?" Mary continued.

"That there's another possible explanation for the hum." John smiled slightly.

"What?" Mary queried.

"What if the hum is not acoustic? Remember, earlier I ran across an article that suggested that possibility, that it's instead an electromagnetic wave form. Maybe the people reporting it are not hearing a sound, but another wave form that is perceived by them as sound—a hum."

"Like the Aurora Borealis?" Mary suggested. "A small percentage of people report a crackling sound during a Northern Lights display."

"Yes, yes, that's a good analogy. . . ," John said thoughtfully, "but what kinds of things might generate electromagnetic waves that could be perceived as a hum?"

"Cell phones?" Rita asked.

"Probably not," John responded, perhaps a little too abruptly.

Rita appeared crestfallen.

"Sorry, Rita. It's just that most reports have been in rural areas and cell phones are in greater use in urban locations, but it was a logical idea." John tried to temper his response. He continued, "I did find one article that reviewed several electromagnetic wave generators in use by governments, particularly the Americans, for military and navigational purposes."

"And?" Mary asked.

"Two of them, 'long range radio navigation,' LORAN for short, and 'high frequency active auroral research' or HAARP for short. Both use high frequency radio waves, but too high a frequency, I believe, to be interpreted as a low frequency hum."

"This all sounds like science fiction." Mary observed.

"True," John agreed, "but there's one technology that the Americans have developed that just might account for many of the hum reports. It's called 'take charge and move out' or TACAMO—heaven knows where they come up with these names. It generates very low frequencies for radio communication between aircraft and submarines, and—now listen to this—was developed during the time the hum was first being reported in increasing numbers!"

"So you think the hum is not acoustic and is generated by low frequency radio waves being used for military purposes?" Mary summed up.

"It's certainly a possibility."

"I think you're just trying to tie the submarine near disasters to the hum," Mary said.

"It's certainly a possibility," John said again and smiled faintly as they entered the Ayrshire and went to their rooms for a respite before supper.

* * * * * * *

When Mary and Rita came down for supper, John was already seated in reception reading the local newspaper.

"Here's an interesting item about what I was talking about before," he said as he looked at Mary and held out the paper. "It says here that two submarines had a near collision last night off the coast. And, in addition, the background story confirmed what I found on the internet at home. This is not the first time, and such near-misses have been going on with increasing regularity over the last six months."

"Why is that so interesting?" Rita asked.

"Oh, I don't know. It's just that you heard the hum last night and the submarines had trouble the same night. Probably nothing." John tried to sound casual.

"Well, let's have a good supper and then attend Mr. Linsay's séance," John suggested.

"Meeting, John, not séance," Mary corrected. *He's reaching again,* Mary thought, paying more attention to what her husband had not said than what he had, as she and Rita followed John into the dining room.

* * * * * * *

Linsay's meeting was a disappointment. As Gordon had told John, Linsay, dressed in what can only be described as a wizard's costume, gave an extended, farfetched lecture describing and explaining the hum— as caused by fairies doing their ritual dances.

Rita was entranced, berating John and Mary with, "See. See. I told you so!"

Mary held John in check, preventing him from telling Rita what he really thought.

"Poppy-cock and humbug," he muttered under his breath to Mary. She squeezed his hand as a signal to restrain himself.

Then came the moment Rita was waiting for, reports of personal experiences from members of the audience. Some reports were from along the coast north and south of Una, others from London, on the coast in Southhampton and County Kerry, Ireland. One

American told of hearing the hum in Seattle, Washington.

Then Rita spoke, beaming in her glory as the center of attention. "I heard it right here in Una last night in the Ayrshire. It was very loud and sounded like a deep bass note, until the storm started. Then it stopped."

"Why did it stop?" someone called out.

Rita was at a loss, but not "Wizard" Linsay. "Because fairies stop dancing during thunderstorms," he announced decidedly. "And now it's time for us to break up into small group discussions."

He proceeded to divide the audience into small groups of five or six individuals. He put Mary and Rita in his group where a good deal of the discussion centered on fairies and fairy life, when they dance, what instruments they use to make music, until Rita asked, "Why should an electrical storm interfere with the fairies?"

"Because the powers of nature are even more powerful than the fairies's hum." Linsay smiled condescendingly.

"As if the electrical storm jammed the hum signal?" Mary asked.

"That's it precisely."

"Then the hum is like a radio. Do fairies have radios?" Rita was serious.

"Yes, in a sense. You see, their drums beat out a rhythmic tone, just like your radio," Linsay pronounced with certainty.

"Oh, I see," Rita said, but she didn't.

Meanwhile John was discussing what the basis of the hum might be with two of Linsay's assistants in his group. Though he got nowhere with the hum, he did ascertain that the two of them had a particular interest and expertise in electronics. The more he pressed them, the more circumspect they became until both abruptly excused themselves from the group and left the discussion.

Shortly thereafter, Linsay closed the evening's festivities and sent his audience on its way with a few more fairy anecdotes.

* * * * * * *

"Who was that guy?" Limonov approached Linsay.

"What guy?" Linsay asked rather absentmindedly.

"The one in our group. He kept asking questions about electronics. I don't like it."

"Nor do I," Pavlenko added. "He's not MI6, is he? Or CIA?"

"Of course not. I met him yesterday. He stopped in the shop with his wife and a maiden aunt. Three Scots on holiday. They came to my concert last night. The aunt hears it, so they're here in Una. Nothing more. Stop worrying, the both of you. We're as safe as. . .as a fairy in a fairy circle," Linsay spoke with serious, 'I know best' condescension and left the room.

* * * * * * *

Next morning, while Rita visited Mr. Linsay's shop, John and Mary went to the local library to follow up on John's unsaid questions about the night of the storm and to research weather patterns in Una over the last six or nine months.

"Just as I suspected," John noted after scanning the local papers. "Night before last's storm was the only electrical storm in the past nine months."

"Meaning?" Mary asked.

"Meaning that if the hum is attributable to some sort of radio signals and if interference with those signals accounts for the near-miss submarine incident night before last, we may be able to account for both the hum and the near naval catastrophes recently."

Mary was perplexed. "But there has been no natural electrical interference recently, up until the other night."

"Correct, so if the hum was interfered with on the other occasions of near-misses when there was no storm activity, something or someone else is the culprit."

"John, we don't even know what the hum is, much less if the hum and the naval mishaps are related. Even if I allow for your inferential leaps, why?" Mary was very skeptical of his logic. He seemed to be putting pieces together for which he had no information.

"Bear with me. Imagine this. A government, say the Colonies, is developing a new military communication system based on very low frequency radio waves. It would be to the advantage of other countries, particularly their adversaries, to be able to control or disrupt the system. But we need more information."

"Like?"

"When was the hum reported over the last few months in this area? Did it seem to be more intermittent than usual and when? Let's keep looking."

A half hour later, Mary found an article about hum reportings in the Una area during the last six months. "Now we need to talk with some of the hum hearers," John observed.

"And where do we find them?"

"Through our friend, Mr. Linsay. Let's go. We have to pick up Rita there anyway."

Once again, as so many times in the past Mary noticed the new spring in her husband's step and the enthusiasm that spread across his whole bearing. *It's all coming together in his mind,* Mary thought with loving pride. *I just hope he's right again this time.*

* * * * * * *

The low hum of Linsay's unique doorbell announced John and Mary as they entered the shop again. Rita looked up from her coffee and smiled. "Gilbert and I have been having a most interesting discussion."

"Yes," Linsay said, "your aunt," he looked at Mary, "is very interested in the hum, since she's one of those fortunate individuals who hear it."

"That's why we came to Una, so she could practice her skills," Mary explained.

"Of course, I wondered why you were here." Linsay seemed to buy Mary's story.

"It's a fascinating phenomenon, you have to admit," John added. "I wonder if you might help us?"

"Perhaps." Linsay seemed circumspect.

"We thought it would be interesting to talk with a few others who, like Rita, can hear the hum."

"I know a few local hum hearers. I often contact them when I need to know if the hum is humming." He smiled facetiously. "I don't hear it myself. More's the pity. Ask around; I'm sure you'll find some."

It was clear that Linsay was dismissively ignoring their request for information, so John thanked him, and then he and Rita and Mary took their leave.

Why does he need to know when the hum is humming, I wonder, John thought on their way back to the Ayrshire for lunch.

While Mary and Rita were ordering lunch, John called DI Gordon and posed the same question he'd asked Lindsay. Gordon was much more cooperative and gave John the names and contact information for three or four known hum hearers.

* * * * * * *

John parked the Vauxhall and walked up the gravel path to the door of the cottage just outside the village of Una. Hugh Maxwell, a short, red-faced man in his early fifties answered the door.

"Yes?"

"Mr. Maxwell, I'm John Braemhor, here on holiday trying to learn something about the hum."

"Ah, the hum, is it? Strange sound, you know. Not many hear it, but I do. 'Bout to drive me crazy some nights. Why don't you step in? Now, what would you like to know?" Mr. Maxwell showed John to a small sitting room where they could talk.

"How often have you heard the hum recently, say in the last six months or so?"

"Excuse me for a moment while I get me log book. I keep a record of the hum. Have for the last twenty years." He left the room and returned quickly with a large ledger book. He opened the book. "Here, let me see now. Last time was night before last, just before that awful thunderstorm. The hum started loud and clear, but the minute the storm hit, it stopped just like someone turned off a switch. Strange."

"What about over the last six months?" John asked.

"Last six months. Let me see. Ah, yes, going on pretty regularly, but several times it did like the other night. Started, then stopped all of a sudden. Like it was turned off. Usually it slows to a stop, like it was drifting away, but not these times."

"Does your log tell you when that happened?" John was intrigued.

"Oh, sure, like I said, I keep records. Happened on the second and fifteenth of last month, then on the thirteenth and twentieth of the month before that. . . ."

"Wait," John interrupted, "could you write down those dates for me? The ones where it started and abruptly stopped during the last six months."

"Sure can. Do you want the dates when it acted like itself, too?"

"That would be very helpful."

Maxwell wrote down all of the hum dates over the past six months and gave them to John. "You some sort of college professor or scientist or such?"

"No." John smiled. "Just an interested party. It's so strange, my curiosity was aroused. Came here to Una to learn more about it."

"Well, you came to the right place all right. Been going on here for near forty years."

"And you've been hearing it all that time?"

"Oh, yes, since I was a youngster. Would you like some tea?"

John was anxious to take his new list back to the hotel and compare it with the submarine near-misses, but felt he should keep Mr. Maxwell company for a bit. He seemed a rather lonely person whose whole life's excitement involved the hum. John stayed another hour, learning all he could of Mr. Maxwell's experiences with the hum through the years. It was much more intermittent in the beginning and over the years grew to an almost daily occurrence. Louder, too, than at the start. Finally, John was able to extricate himself graciously from the grasp of Maxwell's loneliness and return to the hotel.

First thing he did was to locate the newspaper in which he'd seen the listings of the submarine stories and compared them with the list Maxwell had given him. *I thought so*, he mused. He took out his mobile and put in a call to Glasgow as Rita and Mary came down the stairs from the rooms.

"That would be fine, Rupert. I'll be there in midafternoon." He terminated the call and turned to Rita and Mary.

"I need to run off to Glasgow for a short bit this afternoon. Won't take long. Then after supper we can see if we can find the hum again."

Rita brightened at the idea, but Mary's face showed a definite skepticism. *What now, I wonder.*

CHAPTER 4

Braemhor returned in plenty of time for supper. Mary met him in the reception.

"Well, where have you been?" she asked.

"Visited an old electrical engineering friend, Rupert Mills. He lent me a radio jammer detector."

"Then you're still considering the hum to be electromagnetic rather than acoustic and probably part of some sort of military communication that uses very low frequency radio waves?" Mary asked.

"Yes"

"And that when the hum is jammed, say by a massive electrical storm, communication is disrupted and navigational accidents happen."

"Now you see the point." John smiled. "Remember what I told you earlier, that some governments are using very low frequency radio waves for communication between aircraft and naval vessels, particularly submarines?"

"Yes?"

"Well, suppose such communication is one source of the hum. Last night Rita reported hearing the hum until the electrical storm started. Then it was gone. Now suppose further that there was some communication—important, directional communication—going on between, say, aircraft and submarines at the time she heard the hum. And something—most probably the storm—interfered with it, disrupting the communication and causing the submarines to suddenly lose their navigational information—and hence a near collision."

"You're reaching, John," Mary cautioned.

"Oh, I realize that. Except that Mr. Maxwell confirmed for me that when the near-misses occurred at sea, the hum performed exactly as it did during the storm the other night. The hum started, then stopped abruptly at precisely those times that the submarines were having trouble. We need now to find out what interfered with the hum then and we'll be a long way toward understanding the accidents and the nature of the hum itself. Now with Mills's detector we have the possibility of solving both riddles at once, if we're lucky. Let's get Rita and lay out plans for this evening." Enthusiasm spread across his face.

* * * * * * *

At supper John deliberately chose a table in a far corner of the dining room where they could talk and eat in privacy. The prospect of searching for the hum again delighted Rita who sat in rapt attention as John outlined his plans for the evening. She was so excited at being a real part of a real investigation that she could hardly contain herself, much less eat.

"Here's what we'll do," John began after an alcohol-free cranachan had been served. "Rita, you and Mary will go up to the top floor of the hotel. There's a sitting area by the large window in the main hallway. Take a book, each of you, so you'll look like two ladies on holiday enjoying the night view and occasionally reading. Mary, you take a pad also, and I want you to record what Rita hears, what time the hum begins—if it begins—and its nature."

"Nature?" Mary asked.

"Yes, does it show its usual pattern of a loud hum that trails off as time goes on, or does it abruptly stop in mid-hum so to speak?"

"Like night before last?" Rita enthused.

"Precisely. Mary, you also call me on your mobile when it begins and when it stops."

"Where will you be?" Mary asked.

"I'm not sure right now, but I think somewhere in the vicinity of the local electronics shop."

"Ah, now I see," Mary said as she began to understand her husband's overall plan. "Leaping again, are we?" A twinkle crossed her eyes.

"Maybe. Maybe. And maybe not. We shall see." John beamed at recognizing that Mary had deciphered his plan. *We're a team*, he thought.

By now Rita was lost, not at all understanding the perplexities of Braemhor's plan, but loving every minute of it. "And I'm to be the hum finder!" she bubbled.

"Now off to our stations and let's hope we're successful." John sounded like a general on a battlefield.

* * * * * * *

Braemhor sat in his black Vauxhall on Main, near the electronics shop. At eight the lights in the shop went out, and the three men inside came out, got into a small white van and drove off. His mobile rang.

"Yes?"

"It's started," Mary reported.

After about twenty minutes, the phone rang again, "It's fading," Mary reported. Five minutes more and she said, "It's gone."

And so this pattern, on-fade-out; on-fade-out went on for the rest of the evening. Finally, a little after midnight, the hum was gone for an extended period, and Braemhor returned to the Ayrshire.

"That's it for the night," he greeted Rita and Mary in the top-floor sitting area.

Rita was crestfallen.

Mary tried to comfort her. "That's the way investigations go. Lots of fruitless waiting until, when you least expect it, something happens. Just not tonight." Mary put her arm around Rita's shoulders and guided her back to her room.

Once in their room, Mary looked at John. "Well?"

John shrugged. "Maybe tomorrow night."

The next night went the same, and the next, and the next.

"Maybe we're getting nowhere?" Mary asked after four nights.

"Maybe. But remember, if I'm right, the baddies, as MacLaine calls them, will be very cautious. They won't try their act every time the hum hums." John was clearly worried himself.

"This could go on for weeks or months," Mary summed up her frustration.

"Let's hope not, but I'm willing to give it a few more nights, at least. What do you think?"

"That's fine, but Rita is becoming increasingly disappointed."

"Maybe we should send her back home."

"Oh, she'd never hear of it. No, let's see what the next few nights bring." Mary clearly wanted to solve the puzzles as much as John. "Is there some flaw in your—our—thinking?"

"I don't think so. We've got to remember that if baddies are involved, they have a lot more to lose than we do. If I were in their shoes, I'd certainly be extra cautious, entering the lists only randomly so that no pattern gives them away. Patience is our only virtue now." And so John turned off the light to sleep, but sleep was becoming even more elusive with each passing night of no results.

* * * * * * *

Six nights on as Braemhor sat in his Vauxhall, his mobile rang with Mary's consistent message, "It's started."

The lights in the shop again went out, but instead of the men exiting the front door as before, nothing happened except that his detector came alive and indicated electromagnetic activity. A strong signal was coming from the shop across the street. *Ah, ha!* he thought.

Mary's voice crackled through the phone, "It's stopped!"

Braemhor had his all too familiar adrenaline rush when a case began to coalesce. *Now we're getting somewhere.* But just as that thought crossed his mind the signal from the detector began to fade.

"What's going on?" he shouted at Mary.

"Nothing. It's just gone."

Damn! he thought, as his signal became fainter and fainter. *They're on the move.* Then the thought struck him. *It's in the van!!* He started the Vauxhall and quickly circled the block just in time to see the white van disappear into a crossroad, perpendicular to the street where he'd been parked.

At a safe distance, he followed the van through the streets of Una, crossing and crisscrossing the town for the next half hour. At one point he had to park and let the van go on without him in the hopes that he could catch it at the next cross street. He was lucky. As he sat waiting for a traffic light, the van turned down the street he was on, but in the opposite direction. A quick U-turn after the van had disappeared around a bend in the road got him back in tandem with the vehicle and its continuous signal.

Finally, his detector stopped its signal, and as the van returned to the shop and pulled into an alley way in back, Braemhor decided it was time to drive on past the shop and back to the Ayrshire.

He walked calmly to the top floor sitting area.

Rita was beside herself with excitement. "We've done it! We've done it!" she gushed.

Mary, in a calmer state, smiled at John and said, "Looks like you were right."

"It looks good right now, but we'll know more with the morning news. For now, we all need a good night's sleep, don't you think?" Mary smiled and took his hand as they walked back to their room with Rita bouncing along behind them.

* * * * * * *

Next morning, the telly news out of Glasgow told Braemhor what he wanted to know: two submarines had collided off the coast near Una between eight and midnight the night before.

"Oh, John, that's terrible. Were there any injuries?" Mary asked.

"Don't know yet. The report was very brief and didn't give much information."

"So you were right," Mary added and then asked, "Now, what will you do with what you learned?"

"It would seem so, but your second question is more of a puzzle. I could go to DI Gordon, but this is a national, if not international, issue. Not something the local constabulary could or should handle. I think I'll call Nigil Street in the Manchester MI6 office first."

He went to a land line in reception.

"I'm sorry, sir, but Mr. Street does not take telephone calls."

"I'm sure he'll take this one. Tell him that John Braemhor wishes to speak with him; I have some information that I think he can use."

The receptionist put Braemhor on hold, and after a long pause the line opened again.

"Nigil Street here. Still dabbling in governmental affairs, Braemhor? I could have had you held under the National Secrecy Acts last time, if you recall." The tone was anything but welcoming.

"As I told you then, had I known that the Gorman suicide was of national concern, I'd have come to you first. This time I *am* coming to you first, because what I have been looking into *is* of national concern."

"Learned our lesson, have we?" Street's voice dripped with condescension.

"Not really, I just wanted you to know that we both work on the same side, though in different ways. I need to talk with an agent in a secure location as soon as possible. Can you arrange that?"

"Of course, but what about?" Street was clearly intrigued. His voice took on an even more serious tone.

"Since we're not on a secure line, I don't want to say much, but it's about the recent underwater fleet incidents near Una," Braemhor answered.

"You're in Una?"

"Yes, at the Ayrshire."

"Very well; I'll take a chance. I can have an agent with you by one o'clock, but believe me, Braemhor, this had better be worth the government's time and expense." Click, and Street was gone.

"Well, that was easier than I expected," John reflected and went to find Mary to tell her the latest.

Street, in the meantime, pushed a few buttons on his desk and called Glasgow to arrange for an agent to meet

Braemhor at the Ayrshire. *This guy may be better than I give him credit for. Well, we'll see,* Street thought. Then a smile crossed his face. *Maybe I should hire him.*

* * * * * * *

Shortly before one o'clock, an attractive red-headed woman in her early thirties approached the table where John, Mary and Rita were finishing their lunches.

"Mr. Braemhor?"

"Yes." John rose.

"I'm agent Logan." She held out her official identification. "Mr. Street said you had some information for the agency."

"Yes, why don't we sit there." He pointed to a small table in a partially hidden alcove. "We can talk there. Excuse me, Mary, Rita." He moved to the table with agent Logan walking behind him.

"What is it you have for us?" she asked as they sat opposite one another.

"We came here to Una a little over a week ago to look into the hum—you know, that strange humming noise a small portion of the population reports hearing here and other places. My wife's aunt—you saw her at the table—is one of the few who can hear it. I also became aware of the problems our submarine fleet has been having in the waters off the Firth. Since one explanation for the hum is that it's generated by electromagnetic radiation, and low frequency radio transmissions are used to carry navigational information between aircraft and submarines, I wondered if the two—the hum and the submarine problems—were related. I discovered that the pattern of the hum was to begin and then slowly fade over time, until it was no longer heard. However, over the last six months the pattern of the hum has changed. On certain occasions it begins and then abruptly stops. I ascertained that it's precisely on those occasions that a number of near mishaps occurred with our submarine fleet.

"Since my wife's aunt can hear the hum, I used her to tell me when the hum was occurring. A little over a week ago, the hum started but was then abruptly interrupted by a large electrical storm. On that night another near-miss occurred at sea. Every one of the previous near-misses over the last six months happened when the hum started and then was abruptly terminated. But there were no electrical storms at those times. I know this because a local hum hearer has kept extensive records of the hum. I assumed then that something, or someone, was interfering with the hum, possibly with some sort of radio communications.

"I then procured a radio jammer detector and, using Rita, my wife's aunt, as a human hum detector, awaited the next interruption in the hum. Last night it happened again. The hum started and then abruptly stopped. But this time, I was able to locate the source of interference. A radio jammer—I assume at the appropriate low frequency—was located in or near the local electronics shop on Main. However, when the jamming signal began to fade, I realized that the jammer was mobile. I discovered it was located in a small white van which I tracked around the village for more than half an hour. Here is the van's plate number." John handed Logan a card with the license number on it.

"So to sum up, you think the hum is some sort of government or military communications system that's being jammed and thereby causing the rash of naval problems over the last six months? And that the interference with the hum comes from a local shop or van."

"Right."

"What do you know about the shop?" she asked.

"Only that it's run by three men who came here from Karkov. Two local troublemakers work for them. They're affiliated with Gilbert Linsay who has the shop next to the Travel Bureau and trades in regaling the tourist trade with fanciful tales of the origins of the hum."

"What do you expect MI6 to do?"

"Whatever seems appropriate. All I wanted to do was to make sure that MI6 had the information I'd come up with. You're the international experts, not me." John smiled.

As agent Logan rose to leave, she left Braemhor one piece of advice. "I'll convey your information to Mr. Street and one thing. . ."

"Yes?" John asked.

"I'd get rid of the radio jammer detector. They're not legal, you know." She smiled, shook John's hand and left the Aryshire as Braemhor went back to Mary and Rita's table.

"Shall we go back to Daraichburn?" he asked.

* * * * * * *

Two weeks later, after taking Rita to the train to return to Blanefield, John received a phone call.

"Braemhor?"

"Yes?"

"This is Street, Nigil Street, in Manchester. I want to let you know your assumptions were correct. The problems we were having were coming from intentional interference. We took into custody the six responsible." His delivery was deliberately clipped and circumspect.

"Six?"

"Yes, the one was not just a musician."

"I see."

"I also want to thank you for your part. I do appreciate your coming to us first." This seemed particularly difficult for Street to say.

"I was glad to help. Perhaps again sometime."

"Perhaps."

CHAPTER 5

Two months later, the Braemhors met Rita's train from Blanefield in Melrose as she, once again, returned for a visit with them at Dunmoor Cottage. They whisked her off for a quick pub meal before returning to Daraichburn.

"What did you say, dear?" A prissy smile graced Rita's face as she stared across the table at John.

"I just asked how your trip was. Did you meet anymore vacuum salesmen?" John raised his voice. He was referring to an earlier visit when Rita spent the entire trip in the club car with a vacuum salesman, drinking her way to Dariachburn.

"Oh, the vacuum salesman. That was sometime ago, don't you remember?" She turned to Mary. "Really, Mary, I think John is going potty. My vacuum salesman friend was several trips ago."

"Sorry, Rita," said John. "It's just that you visit so often, I have trouble remembering one trip to the next."

Mary tried to frown John into a less pointed remark.

"You're having trouble with your memory, did you say?" Rita smiled again.

"No, Rita, it's just that. . . . Oh well, it's not important." John let his voice trail off as he attacked his fish and chips. He turned to Mary and raised his eyebrows in increasing exasperation.

"John just asked how your trip was, Aunt Rita," Mary interrupted.

"Of course, dear. He always has been very inquisitive. He should take the train more often."

"But I didn't. You did."

"Did what, dear?"

"Take the train!" John's patience was wearing thin, despite Mary's facial signals.

Rita's eyes opened widely. "You've got a pain? Where? Mary, should we get him a doctor?"

Mary, stifling a laugh said, "John's all right." She raised her voice, "He just wanted to know if you're enjoying your fish. That's all."

Rita repeated her perky smile. "It's delicious."

* * * * * * *

An hour later back at Dunmoor Cottage, Rita settled into her room with the latest editions of the papers. John and Mary took their tea in the sitting room in front of the peat fire.

"Well, what do you think, John?"

"I think we should urge her to have her hearing evaluated. This is not the first time that she seems to be mishearing the conversation. We noticed it at Dunmoor Castle in the fall and the last time she visited. Will she take our advice?"

"Doubtful. You know she adamantly opposes seeing any physician," Mary responded. "You remember the last time?"

"Oh, I certainly do. She was told she had a rather large tumor in her abdomen that needed at least a biopsy. She refused," John recollected.

"And some charlatan got ahold of her and told her all she needed was a regime of carrot juice." Mary smiled and shook her head in renewed disbelief.

"And then she drank so much of it the physician wanted to biopsy her liver because her skin had turned an orange shade of yellow."

"Even after we got the carrot juice out of her system, she henceforth refused to consult another physician. 'You see,' she said pointedly, 'All I needed to do to get rid of the tumor was to wash it out with carrot juice therapy.'"

"Ah, the wonders of non-medical 'science.'"

"But you have to admit, John, the tumor never bothered her again."

"Mind over matter?" John smiled.

"Well, whatever it was, she's never seen a physician since, but all of this lighthearted reminiscing doesn't solve our problem of getting her to an audiologist."

"Well, I'm sure that if anyone can convince her, you can." John stared down at his tea cup.

"Me? Why me?"

"She's your blood relative, after all. And besides, you're the diplomatic member of the family." John raised the twinkle in his eyes to meet Mary's. "In addition, she probably wouldn't hear me."

"More the other way around, I think. She'd hear your bass voice before she'd hear my treble, which is why you have to be more patient with her and less caustic in your comments."

"You're right, of course, Mary. Sorry. I'll try to restrain myself better in the future, but what about talking to her about a hearing evaluation?"

"I'll give it a try, though I think we'll have to approach it very delicately. Tomorrow, after breakfast, shall we say?"

"Done."

* * * * * * *

Next morning, Mary was preparing soft boileds while John tended his apple trees in the garden behind the house.

"Good morning, Aunt Rita," Mary smiled as Rita came into the kitchen. "Doesn't the sun look nice for a change? Not our usual misty morning."

"I always like the rain." Rita returned the smile.

"But it's not raining." Mary was a little perplexed.

"Of course, it isn't, dear. Just look out at the bright sunshine."

"Aunt Rita, what did you think I said?" Mary asked.

"You said it's a misty morning, didn't you?" Now Rita appeared perplexed.

"No, I said it's a bright, sunny day."

"Oh, well, I guess I misheard you." Rita's smile seemed a little defensive. "I do that sometimes, dear."

"You may be doing that more than you realize." John had just come in through the back door.

"Oh, do you really think so?" Rita asked.

"We both think so, Aunt Rita. And maybe we should have a serious talk about it." Mary pounced on the opportunity.

And so began the long and drawn out conversation about the present state of Rita's hearing, its recent deterioration, and what might be done about it. Mary and John pointed out, with delicate diplomacy, the various recent incidents of her mishearing conversations, and how these incidents appeared to be becoming more and more frequent. John marveled at Mary's tact as she probed, then backed off, then probed again. He did not even think Rita was aware that she was being led to a predetermined conclusion that she should have her hearing tested by a professional to see "if there really is a problem."

Rita liked that approach, not having to admit there was a problem, but recognizing the value of an evaluation to ascertain *if* there is a problem.

"We can probably arrange an appointment for you, if you'd like," John suggested.

Rita stiffened. "Not with a doctor. I will not see a doctor!"

"Of course not, Aunt Rita." Mary took over. "This would be with someone who specializes in evaluating hearing—an audiologist, not a doctor." Mary cut the distinction very finely.

"Oh, well, that would be all right." Rita acquiesced.

"Fine. We'll see if we can find someone nearby who can see you," John concluded as he smiled at Mary.

After Rita went back to her room, John looked at Mary. "My, that was easier than I expected."

"The trick was making a distinction between a 'doctor' and an 'audiologist.'"

"Sometimes they're the same," John reminded her.

"But so long as they are not the same in Rita's mind we'll be able to have her hearing evaluated without a fuss. See if you can find someone close, to see her while we're ahead of the game." Mary began clearing the breakfast dishes as John went into the study to consult the computer for nearby audiologists.

Fortunately, one of the audiologists in Melrose had a cancellation for the next day, and so the three of them headed to Melrose at ten the next morning.

* * * * * * *

The office consisted of two small rooms, one a soundproof room, the other a consulting area. Both adjoined a physician's office.

When they first arrived, Rita became resistant to entering the physician's space until she was reassured that the person she was to see was not a "doctor," but an audiologist who merely had her offices in a physician's building.

"And you must be Mrs. Erskine?" The willowy black-haired woman entered the waiting area, smiled and offered Rita her hand.

"Miss Erskine," Rita corrected.

"Oh, so sorry, Miss Erskine. I'm Ann Murdock. I understand you'd like your hearing evaluated."

"You're not a doctor, are you?" Rita queried quickly.

"I'm not a physician, if that's what you mean." Ann Murdock smiled. "How can I help you?"

"Well, my niece and nephew," Rita nodded toward Mary and John, "seem to think that I'm not hearing as well as I might."

"What do you think?"

"Well, I have to admit that sometimes I don't always follow the conversation exactly."

"Let's go back to my office and see what we can find out, shall we?" She looked at John and Mary and said, "It shouldn't take more than an hour. You can wait here or there's a small tearoom just down the street." With that, she led Rita down a small corridor to her office and soundproof room.

"Like some scones and tea?" Mary asked John as they exited the waiting area.

"That would be nice, but let me get a newspaper on the way." He'd spotted a tiny newsstand across the street.

"I do hope Rita does not give Ms. Murdock any trouble," Mary said after they'd taken a table and ordered at the Beehive.

"I wouldn't worry too much. Ms. Murdock seemed quite capable of gaining Rita's confidence."

He buried his nose in the paper, until a familiar voice said, "John and Mary Braemhor. What brings you to Melrose?"

The query had been made by a tall, slender man with a fringe of white hair framing his bald head

John looked up from his paper. "I might ask you the same question, Jim."

"But I asked first," was DCI James Sinclair's quick rejoinder, behind his usual, broad smile.

"Why don't you two stop playing cat and mouse?" Mary looked up. "We're here with my aunt while she has her hearing evaluated."

"Interesting. I'm here interviewing some audiologists who attended the recent CSCA conference in Edinburgh.

"CSCA?" Mary queried.

"Oh, sorry. The Celtic Society of Clinical Audiologists. One of several smaller professional organizations of audiologists in the UK. They had some trouble at their last meeting. One of their members in the upper administrative echelon of the group—a Dr. Jason Logan—was supposed to speak at a breakfast meeting one morning, but never showed up. When some of his colleagues went searching for him, they found his room open and him dead in his bath."

"Drowned? Heart attack?" John quickly asked.

"We're not sure yet. He practiced here in Melrose. Both he and his wife attended the meeting, but she disappeared the night before. She apparently came back to Melrose on the quiet. So I thought I'd start by interviewing her, his staff, and his family here in their hometown while I wait for the coroner's report."

"Sounds interesting," John observed as Mary noted her husband's new alertness and watched him zero all of his attention in on Sinclair. "What have you found so far?"

"Very little. Parts of his family are in shambles, of course, though others seem strangely unbothered by his disappearance."

"Large inheritance?" John quickly queried.

"Very possible, it's the wife who's very blasé about the whole affair. Acts like she could care less that her husband's gone. Didn't even seem interested in collecting her husband's body."

"And she'd be the first in line for any inheritance, right?"

"According to the will, she inherits everything—money, house, his practice."

"His practice?" Mary asked.

"Oh, yes, she's an audiologist too. They have a very large, very lucrative practice."

"Suspect number one?" John probed.

"Maybe yes, maybe no. I'm just not sure yet. It's just too obvious. I'm not convinced it's going to be that simple and easy. These intra-family cases never are that straightforward, you know."

"Right you are," John said almost absent mindedly as he noticed Mary's facial indications that they needed to get back to the audiologist's office to pick up Rita.

"Well, I need to get back to Edinburgh and see what the coroner and my boys have found. It's been good seeing you both again." Sinclair offered Mary and John his hand.

"Good seeing you again, Jim. Let me know if I can be of help." John rose and shook Sinclair's hand as he and Mary left the tea shop to pick up Rita.

"Interesting puzzle, but it sounds like the DCI has a prime suspect already," Mary observed as they walked back to Ms. Murdock's office.

"Just sounds a little too open-and-shut to me," John added. "Maybe Ms. Murdock can tell us a little more of what went on in Edinburgh."

"But, John, it's not your case."

"True. True. But as you noted it's an interesting puzzle." John took her hand and gave it a slight squeeze as they entered the audiologist's building.

* * * * * * *

Rita was in the waiting room with Ms. Murdock.

"Ah, Mr. and Mrs. Braemhor." Ms. Murdock looked up. "Good thing you brought Ms. Erskine in for an evaluation. I've just been going over her audiogram with her and explaining to her that she has a moderate loss in the higher frequencies. So it's not surprising that she has some trouble with conversations, particularly in noisy environments. She's missing a lot of the consonants.

"As we've just been discussing," she turned to Rita, "I think she could benefit from some hearing aids specifically constructed to address the higher frequencies. I can have them for her in about a week, if that's what she decides. Does that sound all right, Ms. Erskine?"

"That would be fine, but I'd like to think it over for a bit before I make a decision. I'll just stay in Daraichburn and call you when I'm ready to order. Will that be all right, Mary?" Rita turned to Mary and John.

"Of course, Aunt Rita. You know you're always welcome at Dunmoor Cottage." Mary smiled and patted Rita's hand. John silently raised his eyebrows to Mary.

"That's it then. Phone me if you decide to take my advice. As I said, I can have them for you in about a week." Ms. Murdock rose to go back to her office and laboratory.

"Could I have a brief moment?" John had followed Ann Murdock a short way down the hall toward her office.

"Of course, come back to my office." John quickly told Mary and Rita that he'd be a few minutes.

"How can I help you, Mr. Braemhor?" Ms. Murdock settled into her desk chair and motioned him to an overstuffed at the side of the desk, which was covered with an assortment of audiometric devices and piles of paper. It faced a one-way mirror looking into a sound chamber in the next room.

"What can you tell me about the recent difficulty at the CSCA meeting in Edinburgh?" John drove right to the point.

"I. . .I. . .How did you hear about that?" Murdock was clearly flustered.

"I have friends and I read the papers. It's not every day that a noted Melrose audiologist dies at a national meeting. Were you at the meeting?"

"Yes, I was, but. . .what concern is it of yours?" Ms. Murdock responded testily. "Are you some sort of investigator?"

"Retired, but I found the death of Dr. Logan a particularly interesting puzzle—as a former professional investigator."

"Jason Logan is. . .was my colleague here in Melrose. At first, no one thought much of it. Jason has always had a bit of a roving eye. Most of the attendees thought he probably had had some sort of a tryst the night before and slept through the breakfast meeting. He *was* seen with Bertha Warkson at dinner the night before." She laughed nervously. "But later, when we realized that he was nowhere about, several colleagues went to his room to find him. But. . . but. . .why am I telling you this?" The question was as much to herself as to Braemhor.

"Such events can be pretty traumatic, particularly when you know the people involved. Maybe it's just good to talk about it." John momentarily played therapist for he suspected that Ann Murdock and Jason Logan were more than professional colleagues. "Have you known Mr. Logan long?"

"Forever. We trained together. Graduated in the same class. There was a time when we were considered 'an item,' but that didn't last once he met his present wife."

"I understand she's an audiologist also."

"Oh yes, a very ambitious one. They developed an extensive practice, just a few blocks away, not far from here."

"You say she's ambitious."

"Very much so. So unlike Jason. He was always so laid back. He had built a comfortable practice before they met, but he never wanted to make a lot of money. Just to be comfortable. But when Shelley—that's his wife—entered the practice, all of that changed. It was work, work, work, build the practice. They—she— drove all the other audiologists out. Except me. Somehow I managed to keep my practice. I thank Jason for that. Because of our past together. I don't think he would let her drive me out, too. I don't know what will happen now. . . that he's gone."

"It's hard to believe, isn't it?"

"I just haven't been able to wrap my mind around the idea." She smiled nervously as a tear worked its way down her cheek.

"Do you think Shelley Logan is involved?"

"Oh, Mr. Braemhor, I don't like to think bad things of people, but, to be honest, it has crossed my mind."

You're not the only one, Braemhor thought, but he said, "I think that's a job for the police, don't you?"

After a brief pause, John continued. "Were there others who might benefit from Logan's death? Professional rivals? Outraged husbands?"

"Not the later, certainly."

"How can you be so sure?"

"Jason was always very discrete. That's why those who knew him were in agreement that his missing the morning session was not a case of oversleeping from a tryst the night before."

"What about professional rivalry?"

"Oh, there certainly was that. You see, the CSCA is laced with intraprofessional rivalries, animosities, competition, and, I might even say, hatreds. You see, the jewel in the crown for CSCA members is the editorship of the organization's professional journal. The previous editor, in fact, the founding editor, of the journal, liked Jason and thought highly of him professionally. He'd maneuvered Jason into the editorship."

"Maneuvered? How?"

"Well, Dr. Dorne—he was the founder of the journal—wanted Jason to be the next editor, but he had to get the nomination past the Board of Governors. There was a small, politically motivated clique on the board who wanted someone else, someone they could control and through whom they could dictate the workings of the journal. Dorne knew this, but he also knew that there was another possible nominee for the editorship that this group would utterly hate to see put into such a powerful position. You realize that the editor of a professional journal is quite a powerful position. You get to pick and choose who's on your editorial board, you get to control whose articles get published—or rejected. You control a large measure of the communications of an entire profession. You can set the whole tone for the profession during your tenure as editor. Very powerful, if you're inclined to manipulate the journal process. This group wanted that power, or, at least, to control the person who would have that power.

"So what did Dorne do? He nominated both men, a co-editorship—the man they utterly hated and Jason, who they disliked, but still thought they could control! He sent his recommendation to the board and they did exactly as he thought they would. They rejected the co-editorship idea and accepted Jason as the sole editor and have spent the last two years trying to control the journal through Jason. But they badly underestimated him. Though, as I said, Jason is very laid back, he has strong professional principles and thwarted their every effort at controlling who got published and who did not. Jason accepted articles on professional merit; they wanted them accepted on personal connections. The battle has raged ever since Jason took over. They tried packing the journal's editorial board; Jason wouldn't hear of it. They tried to dictate the balance between research and clinical articles—they wanted all clinical articles. I don't think they really understood the research in the field of audiology. At one point they tried to curtail the funds the society accorded the journal, but Jason, at the insistence of his wife I must add, put in his own money to keep it afloat. It's been a constant struggle, Mr. Braemhor."

"But why? How many members are in the society? Are there large funds at stake?" John was astounded at the tale Ms. Murdock was telling.

"Two, maybe three thousand members. That's all. It is just that some people want power and control no matter how small the domain. That's why, I think, Shelley supported him putting in his own funds when things got difficult. She's a power broker, too, and sees the value of controlling a professional journal."

"But with him gone, she'll lose what control she wielded over the journal through her husband, won't she?" John saw this as one piece of inheritance Shelley Logan would not gain by her husband's loss.

"I wouldn't count on it. Shelley is a hard edged political infighter, if she thinks it will benefit her professionally and personally. I would not be at all surprised if she's already laid the ground work in the society for replacing Jason as editor."

"Well, I appreciate your talking with me, Ms. Murdock. You've certainly enlightened me on power politics in a small professional organization." John started to rise to go.

"You've only heard half of it."

"There's more?" John sat down again.

"Oh, yes. You see, last year, before the clique—it's headed by a woman named Medea Hathaway—realized that they could not control Jason, maneuvered to have him elected to a two-year term as president of the society. You can see how badly they misread him. Anyway, once he took office the sparks really began to fly."

"In addition to the political infighting over the journal?"

"In addition. It was like these people wanted nothing better than to keep the society in constant turmoil, hoping, I think, to break Jason and force him to resign. But not Jason. He was determined to fight them every inch of the way."

"For example?"

"Well the first thing Jason wanted to accomplish was to open the membership to more people interested in the field of audiology—the paraprofessionals. Membership requirements are very restrictive, particularly with respect to academic training. But less academically trained paraprofessionals do the public a lot of good, if only by guiding the public towards the more highly trained members of our society. Jason felt that it only made sense to bring these practitioners into the society, so he arranged a vote of the membership to accord the paraprofessionals a place in the society, as associate members.

"A mail ballot was sent to the membership for their vote, but on the day before the members were to mail in their ballots, they received a letter from the clique opposing the proposition with a bevy of half-truths and, I must say, out-and-out lies about what having associate members in the society would do to the 'professional standing' of the organization. Obviously there was no time to get a response to this letter out to the membership before they voted, and so Jason's proposition was defeated.

"Jason just shook his head and said: 'I have to give them credit. It was a very astute political tactic.' But what really galled Jason was that at the next meeting of the board of governors, the clique voted themselves money from the society's treasury to reimburse themselves for the cost of their mailing, though it was not, by any stretch of the imagination, a real piece of society business. They even made him a present of Machiavelli's *The Prince* and a set of Napoleon-styled epaulettes to imply that he was a dictator. You see, Mr. Braemhor, they really are a ruthless, vindictive group of people.

"There's a great deal more I could share with you, but I've taken enough of your time and I do have other patients to see this morning."

John rose to leave. "Could I call on you again if I need more information? I can't say that I'll be able to find out what really happened to your friend, but I'd like to look into the puzzle more. Here's my card, in case you think of anything else that might be helpful."

"Thank you, Mr. Braemhor. You were right. It was good to talk about the situation. Up until now, I've just kept my feelings bottled up inside. Thank you, again. And have Ms. Erskine call me as soon as she decides on the hearing aids."

* * * * * * *

"Sorry," John said as he joined Mary and Rita on the bench in the small park outside.

"Interesting?" Mary asked.

"Very. I'll tell you all about it when we get back to the cottage. Meantime, Rita. . ." He turned to Rita. "What do you think about hearing aids?"

"I'm still thinking about it"

"Well, take your time. It's best not to jump into things."

Mary gave him a quizzical look, but assumed her husband had good reason for having Rita delay her decision.

Back at Dunmoore Cottage after lunch, John told Mary what he'd learned from Ms. Murdock.

"So Shelley Logan is still the main suspect," Mary summed up.

"Yes and no. Certainly she has the most to gain from Jason Logan's demise, but it's just too cut-and-dry. She would have gained all of their collective estate— money, practice, the like—but she has that now. In fact, with him gone she loses the power of the journal, unless she can, as Ann Murdock suggested, finagle to become the editor herself. Then there's this power-hungry clique headed by Medea Hathaway. They certainly wanted him out of the way so they could control the journal and, apparently, the whole society. But why commit a crime for that end? Logan was only going to be president for another year. They could wait out his term and then take over the society. Why risk getting tied up in a felony? We need a lot more information before we can jump to any conclusions."

"Maybe they're just impatient," Mary opined.

"Impatient, yes, but foolhardy, I doubt it. And another thing: why so much political infighting for such a small reward? The society has only two or three thousand members, and all of the membership dues can't amount to much. There's no apparent financial gain."

"Maybe it's like Henry Kissinger once said, 'The reason the infighting in academia and professional associations is so fierce is because so little is at stake.'" Mary smiled. "But what's our next step?" John was pleased to hear Mary join the hunt. "And by the way, why were you so relaxed about Rita extending her stay to make up her mind about hearing aids?"

"Her decision is a sheer stroke of serendipity. We need more information about Logan's wife, and what better way than to have Rita get a second opinion. Do you think we can enlist Rita's cooperation—and silence—as part of our investigation?"

"John, sometimes you're as devious as the criminals you pursue. But, yes, I think she'll be absolutely delighted to be a part of the investigation. However, we're going to have to instruct her very carefully."

"Maybe it will be better just to convince her to get a second opinion as a routine approach to medical treatment rather than initially mention anything about an investigation. Are you willing to be our diplomatic leader again?"

"This evening at supper, say?" Mary agreed.

"Excellent."

After a hardy supper of Mary's shepherd's pie, John opened the conversation, "Well, Rita, what was your hearing evaluation like?"

"Very interesting. First she put some earphones on me while I was in this small room—she said it was a soundproof chamber. It sounded as if there was a great deal of pressure on my ears, almost like sitting under water. I couldn't hear myself think." She gave her characteristic little giggle.

"Then she played some tones into one ear at a time and asked me when I first started to hear them. After that, she said some words to me through the earphones and had me repeat them to her. That was the hardest part."

"And what do you think about getting hearing aids?" Mary joined in.

"I just don't know. I did get most of the words she said to me."

"But not all," John reminded her.

"Yes, that's true, but I'm just not sure I need hearing aids. . .yet."

"Maybe you ought to get a second opinion. That's what a lot of medical people recommend if you're not sure of the first diagnosis and suggested treatment." Mary directed the conversation towards her and John's intended end.

"No harm in seeing what a second professional recommends," John added.

Rita frowned thoughtfully. "I suppose you're right. I should see what another audiologist thinks. Are there any others nearby?"

"As a matter of fact, there's another one in Melrose. A Dr. Logan."

"Not a 'doctor' doctor?" Rita started to stiffen.

"No, no," Mary soothed. "She has a doctorate in audiology, just like Ms. Murdock. She teaches audiology and does clinical practice. I'll call her office and see when she can see you?"

"If you think it best, Mary."

"I do. And, as John said, no harm can come of it."

"All right then." Rita acquiesced and John and Mary sighed a collective sigh of relief. *First phase accomplished. Now we just have to keep her from telling Shelley Logan that this is not her first hearing evaluation and that it's really part of a broader investigation into Jason Logan's death,* John thought. He went to the telephone to call Shelley Logan's office while Mary continued to bring Rita full into the investigative plan.

"Rita, you've always been interested in John's investigative cases."

"Oh, yes, I find them fascinating." Rita's countenance lit up.

"Well, how would you like to be a part of one of his cases?" Mary asked casually.

"Oh, I'd love that!" Rita gushed.

"All right then, here's the plan. . . ." Mary then instructed Rita, first giving her the background she and John had learned so far and explaining how her second evaluation was a cover for learning more about Shelley Logan and her relationship with her husband, Jason. Rita was like a small child with a new lollypop.

"But it's very important that Dr. Logan not suspect that you're more interested in learning things about her than you are in her learning about your hearing. You have to be naïve about the hearing evaluation. You cannot under any circumstances let on that you know anything about the testing. It's all absolutely new to you. Understand?"

"Yes." Rita became deadly serious. "I'm to pretend that this is all new to me."

"Precisely. Just be your natural self. A new patient coming to have her hearing evaluated." John had returned from his telephone call.

"John, this is so exciting! I'll be the best little sleuth ever, I promise."

"No sleuthing necessary, Aunt Rita. Just get your hearing evaluated and pay close attention to what sort of person Dr. Logan is. And don't mention her husband. Particularly his recent death. If she brings it up, fine— listen, but don't indicate that you know anything about it," Mary continued her instruction.

"But I do!"

"What?" John could not quite believe what he was hearing.

"It was in yesterday's Melrose newspaper. I read all about it while I was waiting for Ms. Murdock to go over my audiogram with me. Very strange, the way he just died and missed that morning meeting. And his wife was there at the convention, too!"

John rolled his eyes to Mary before turning to Rita and saying, "We're very lucky. Dr. Logan can see you tomorrow."

Later, in the quiet of their bedroom, Mary gave John a worried look.

"Are we making a mistake, John? We're not putting Rita in any danger, are we?"

"I think not. We have no indication that Shelley Logan is anything but a practicing audiologist who's recently lost her husband, but I'll call Sinclair and double-check on what he has on Logan so far." He raised the receiver and punched in Sinclair's private home number in Edinburgh. The call was short and as

John re-cradled the hand piece, he turned to Mary and said, "I explained to Jim what we have in mind and he sees no reason such information gathering should be dangerous. . .or fruitful, he added." John gave a wry expression. "I did tell him about Medea Hathaway and her political gang and he's going to follow up on that lead. But I still think Shelley Logan is our best bet for now."

"Well, it will be interesting to see what kind of a detective Aunt Rita makes, don't you think?" Mary mused.

"Interesting. Yes, interesting," John muttered as he turned out the light.

* * * * * * *

The waiting area was palatial, unlike Ann Murdock's small, cramped space. Wood paneled throughout with enough sitting space to house several dozen people. In the center of the room was an exceptionally large fish tank with at least a dozen colorful tropical fish, guppies, mollies, goldfish, loaches, African cichlids and the like.

"How pretty," Rita gushed. She was still admiring the tank and its contents when the secretary from behind a glass enclosure called her, "Miss Erskine? I need you to fill out this information sheet." She handed Rita a clipboard with the required information form and a pen on it.

Shortly after Rita completed the form, an assistant emerged from a door next to the secretary's window and led her into a massive complex of interview rooms. Rita gave Mary and John a quick smile as she followed the assistant into the treatment/evaluation area.

John and Mary sat down to await the results of Rita's venture into the world of investigative data gathering. Mary was clearly not fully comfortable with sending Rita on this adventure. She tried to read a magazine, but could not bring herself to concentrate on the words on the page. John, however, was quite comfortable with Rita in the role of detective, although he was concerned that she might give away the scheme.

A little over a half hour later, Rita, smiling broadly, returned with Dr. Logan in tow. "Doctor says I need hearing aids," she proudly announced, "says I'm not hearing all of the consonants I should."

"Your aunt's hearing is borderline." Shelley Logan turned to Mary. "She's missing some in the speech range and definitely could benefit from some hearing aid assistance. Not at all unusual for her age. I'd certainly recommend that she get the help she needs now, before the problem becomes worse. Sometimes people with the sort of loss your aunt has live in a world of denial until the problem gets so bad that it becomes socially debilitating. However, she's determined to not do anything about the issue for now."

"Oh, I'm not surprised." Mary walked with Dr. Logan across the waiting area while Rita joined John near the fish tank. "Aunt Rita's a very independent soul. Likes to consider all options. It will probably be best to let her come to a decision in her own time. We can call you, can we not, if she decides to get hearing aids?"

"Of course. I'll have all of her records here and can have aids made at any time. By the way, I must say your aunt is quite an inquisitive person." Mary shuddered at what might be coming next. "She asked me all sorts of questions. And she's very much up-to-date. Wanted to know all about my husband's death in Edinburgh."

"Oh, I'm very sorry. She gets on an issue and will not let go. I believe she read about your husband in yesterday's paper—we all did. We're so sorry. Have the police been any help?" Mary did not want to miss this opening.

"No, and I doubt that they will be, but I must get back to other patients. Right now I'm carrying my own case load and Jason's as well." With that, Shelley Logan turned abruptly and went back into her office area and Mary gathered John and Rita for the trip back to Daraichburn.

John opened the conversation once the car was on the road. "Well, Rita, what did you learn?"

"Some of the fish in Dr. Logan's tank are quite rare and expensive. Why, do you know that the little orange and black ones can run as much as £50! She must be very rich!"

"Not the fish, Rita, her husband." John's irritation was very obvious.

"You don't understand, John, the fish are very important. You see, Jason Logan's hobby was tropical fish. When I admired the tank in her waiting area, she told me that fish were not a hobby she shared with her husband. He had all kinds of species. The tank in the office is only one of many tanks he owned. He had even larger tanks and fish at home. She said he was always buying new ones to add to his collection. Especially when they went on trips, like to professional meetings. She thinks fish are something you buy at the market, bring home, cook and eat, not something you put in a tank and feed and talk to like pets or children.

"During the meeting in Edinburgh, she said, he found a new tropical fish store. Just opened and had a great variety of species, some he'd never seen before. He even had one in his hotel room. Said a friend bought it for him. Planned to bring it home after the meeting and add it to the collection. A disaster had happened to the fish in the office tank about two months ago. Someone had put several piranha into the tank and they ate all of the other fish. She did not seem too distressed at the loss, but her husband was slowly rebuilding the office collection, so he was very happy to have another to add to the tank."

"Where's the fish now?" John interjected.

"I don't know. She didn't say, and I didn't ask. Oh dear, I should have asked, shouldn't I? Here's my first assignment and I bungled it." Rita went quiet.

"No, no, Rita, not at all. You did very well. Now what else did you learn?" Mary asked.

"Well, it seemed to me that it was most unusual that she was back at work so soon after her husband died, and do you know what she said?"

"Yes?" John asked as he turned into the small road to Dunmoor Cottage.

"She said, 'life has to go on.' Just like that! Can you imagine?"

"You did very well, Rita. Was there anything else you learned?" John pressed on after they entered the cottage.

"I did ask her if she had any idea why anyone would want to kill all of the fish in their tank, and she said that she thought she was not the only one who didn't share her husband's hobby. In fact, she even said she wished she'd thought of killing all of the fish herself first. 'He spent too much money on those little, scaly things.'"

"Well," Mary intervened, "would you two like some lunch? Maybe a meal and some afternoon rest would be nice."

"Yes," John and Rita spoke simultaneously, then looked at each other and laughed.

"Detective work has made me very hungry." Rita smiled as she went into the kitchen to help Mary set out the food.

* * * * * *

After lunch, Rita went to her room to take her afternoon nap, and John and Mary settled into the sitting room to review where 'the case of the dead audiologist' stood.

"So what do we know so far, John?" Mary opened the discussion.

A wry smile crossed John's face. "We know that Rita needs hearing aids."

"Not humorous, John."

"Rita has discovered a fish story?"

"Oh, John, please!"

"I'm not actually kidding. I think Rita is on to something."

"Really?"

"Really. I think I'll call Sinclair again. I want to know what happened to the new fish Logan had gotten for his tank." He rang up Sinclair in Edinburgh.

"Sinclair here." The voice boomed through the phone.

"Braemhor here, John Braemhor. Jim, I have a few questions about the Logan investigation."

"Not much new on that front. I did interview the Hathaway woman. Interesting. Did you know she'd been in Melrose a couple of months back?"

"No, I didn't. Why was she there?"

"Visiting Shelley Logan. Said it was society business, but she timed her visit to coincide with Jason's being away on other society business."

"Doesn't feel right," John stated.

"To me either, but I can't hold a person because they make a business trip."

"Right. By the way, did you find a tropical fish in his room?"

"Yes, we did. How did you know?"

"Just a guess. Where is it now?"

"It's here in my office. We're holding it until this case is resolved. I asked his wife about it but she said she didn't want it. She doesn't like tropical fish. It was her husband's hobby."

"I think I'll come to Edinburgh," John added abruptly.

"Why?" Sinclair was puzzled.

"Let's say I'll be on a fishing trip. If I can find what I need here, I'll be there tomorrow, otherwise I'll call you tomorrow. And don't put your fingers near that fish. Some of those tropical fish can be quite dangerous." Braemhor hung up and immediately punched in Ann Murdock's number in Melrose.

"Ann Murdock's office," was the crisp response on the other end of the line.

"Ms. Murdock. John Braemhor here. Was a picture of all of the attendees at the CSCA taken at the meeting?"

"Oh yes; they do that towards the end of every national meeting. A memento for each of the attendees."

"Do you have your copy?"

"Yes, I believe I do. Why?"

"I wonder if I might borrow it for a day or two. It might help me to understand better the tragedy of your friend."

Ann Murdock was a bit perplexed, but told Braemhor that he could pick it up from her secretary any time he wanted. "But I don't understand how a picture will help you."

"Well, for one thing I want to see what Medea Hathaway looks like."

"Oh, I see. Come by anytime. It will be at my front desk, and I'll mark which one is Hathaway and which one is Jason."

Braemhor quickly told Mary what he was about and headed East on the A72.

About an hour later he returned, parked the Vauxhall in front and briskly entered Dunmoor Cottage. He handed the photograph to Mary and smiled broadly. "Now we're getting somewhere!"

Mary looked at the photograph then at John, "So what do we know now?"

"Look at the picture. Who's not in it?"

"I don't know, John, I don't know any of these people. How am I supposed to know who's not there? Stop playing games, John." Mary was becoming a little irritated.

"Let me put it another way. Who do you recognize in the picture.?"

Mary studied the photo. "Well, I see Ms. Murdock. And I suppose the two on either side of her whose faces have been circled are of significance, but I don't know who they are. I suppose the male is probably Jason Logan." There was a brief pause. "Oh, I see. Shelley Logan isn't there."

"Right! And this photo was taken the evening Jason Logan disappeared! Wouldn't you think his wife might have been there? Instead, Jason is standing with his old paramour and his society nemesis."

"Maybe she was off having a tryst of her own." Mary smiled.

"Possible, but I doubt it. Care for a trip to Edinburgh tomorrow?" John asked abruptly.

"Fine. Should we take Rita?"

* * * * * *

Next morning, Mary and John headed North on the A702 to Edinburgh. Rita had agreed, though grudgingly, to stay and look after the cottage. "But I want a full report when you get back," she admonished them as they drove out onto the cottage lane.

As they entered the city, Mary asked, "Where to first?"

"I want to stop at The Fish Tank, a tropical fish store just two blocks from the hotel where the CSCA held its meeting. According to their webpage, they deal in rare species." John parked across the street from a low building with a totally glass front.

"It almost looks like a gigantic fish tank," Mary observed.

"Clever, don't you think?" John rejoined as they entered the shop.

Inside there was a myriad of fish tanks, large, small, medium, all filled with a variety of tropical fish and all bubbling rhythmically. Several tanks were marked "Danger. Do Not Touch."

"Can I help you?" the dark-skinned man behind the main counter asked. His eyes were exophthalmic and set too wide apart in his face.

Reminds me of a Black Moor goldfish, Mary thought, then she saw his forearms. They were covered with scales.

The proprietor, a Mr. Trawler, noticed Mary's gaze, smiled and said, "It's a mild form of ichthyosis. It's not contagious. Actually, it's hereditary."

"Oh, I'm so sorry; I didn't mean to stare." Mary was embarrassed.

"No, no, it's all right. Most people stare when they first come into the shop. I'm used to it, and I suppose for many it's a bit jarring to see the proprietor of a fish store who looks like his products. Now, can I help you?"

John stepped forward. "Well, I wonder if you recognize anyone in this picture?"

"Why? You a copper?" Mr. Trawler became noticeably defensive.

"No, no I. . .we're just trying to find a friend and since their hobby is tropical fish, I thought they might have stopped in your shop."

Trawler relaxed somewhat, took the photograph from John, and scrutinized it. He looked at John.

"Yes, I recognize a couple. First, this one whose face is circled. I remember her very well. Came in about two months ago. Asked if I had some nice vicious fish, the kind that would eat all the other fish in a tank. Imagine, someone asked specifically for a dangerous fish. In fact, she reminded me of a large black dragon Betta. Gave me the shivers, but I sold her two of my largest piranha. Told her I thought they'd do the job. She wasn't someone you'd forget."

"Any others?"

"Ah, no. . .wait. This one. Reminded me of a jumpy guppy. She came in recently and bought a puffer. Said she had a friend whose hobby was tropical fish. Sold her a small plastic bowl, but I told her the fish wouldn't last long in that small a tank. Also told her to keep her fingers away from it. Their bite's very toxic and she looked a little naïve to me. Seems I've had a run of people interested in the worst of tropical fish," he concluded, then added, "No. I don't see anyone else who looks familiar."

"Thank you. You've been a big help. And we'll recommend your shop to others." John joined Mary, who by now was exploring the other tanks in the store.

"Did you notice how many tanks he had marked 'dangerous'?" Mary asked as they went back to the car.

"Probably why he was so wary of us as possible 'coppers.' I suspect there are some restrictions on the possession and sale of poisonous tropical fish," John suggested.

"And did you notice, John, how he saw his customers as resembling different tropical fish? I wonder how he'll describe us."

"How about sharks or barracudas?" John smiled.

"I think I'd rather be seen as a goldfish." Mary returned the smile. "Where to now?"

" I think we need to see Jim Sinclair."

Sinclair's office was the usual dingy, glass-enclosed postage stamp.

"How are my favorite citizen sleuths today?" Sinclair greeted them at the door of his office. Behind his desk was a large, 30-gallon fish tank in which was swimming a yellow fish, with leopard-like spots, about 12 cm long.

"Trying to understand the case of the dead audiologist." John smiled. "And we could use some help."

"You and me both." Sinclair returned the smile. "What can I do for you?"

"We'd like to interview some of the Baird Hotel staff and wondered if you could smooth the way. We're going to interview Bertha Warkson later on."

Mary was a little taken back. This was the first time John had mentioned any interest in Jason's night-before dinner companion.

"I'd be happy to, but be aware that my guys have already interviewed her and most of the hotel staff. She was the last person, so far as we know, to see Dr. Logan alive, you remember. What's your intent?"

"I've been able to locate some pictures of most of the participants at the CSCA meeting. We just want to find out if seeing them will shake anything loose from the room staff. For now, we only need to talk with the chambermaids who were on duty the day he died. See if they noticed anything unusual. The Warkson interview is just to get a better feel for Jason Logan, and since she practices here in Edinburgh, we thought we'd see her as well."

"Glad to help, John. I'll put in a call to the management right now and clear the way. That way, by the time you get there, they should be expecting you and Mary." He pushed a button on his telephone. "Can I interest you in a pretty tropical fish? As soon as the case is solved, you can take it back to Daraichburn."

Mary smiled. "We're not much for pets, but if I were you, I'd put a warning sign on the tank and keep my hands away from it. Do you know that puffer fish are considered one of the most poisonous animals on earth? Second only to the golden frog."

"I knew they were dangerous, but not how dangerous," he said as his assistant, Officer Wallace, entered the office. Sinclair looked up. "Ah, Wallace, call the Baird Hotel and inform them that Mr. and Mrs. Braemhor, two of our staff, . ." he winked at John and Mary, ". . .will be over shortly to interview some of their house staff." He turned to the Braemhors. "There! That should do it. I'll need to know as soon as you have something for me "

With that, John and Mary left Sinclair's office and drove to the Baird.

"What are we looking for now, John?" Mary queried.

"I want to see if any of the house staff recognize anybody in the photograph I got from Ann Murdock, and, if so, what they remember of them. It's a long shot,

I know, but we're short on leads at this point. Warkson may also be of value. But, maybe we should get some lunch in the Baird tearoom before starting our interviews. It could be a long afternoon."

After a quick meal of cullen skink and butteries, the Braemhors introduced themselves to the hotel management and set up interviews with all of the chambermaids staff who were on duty the day before Logan missed the morning meeting.

The management gave them a small guest room for interviewing. Five of the house staff had been working that afternoon. The first three were easily eliminated since they did not recognize any of the individuals in the photograph. The fourth allowed that she'd seen Medea Hathaway, Jason Logan and Ann Murdock, but individually and at different times and places within the hotel that afternoon. Mary was interviewing chambermaid number five.

"I want you to look over this photograph and tell me if you remember seeing any of these individuals on the guest room floors the afternoon of the twelfth. Take your time and look carefully." Mary sat back and waited for Ida Brown to inspect the photograph. Ms. Brown was a very small woman in her mid-twenties with auburn hair and green eyes whose face wore a constant puckish smile. She slowly and carefully looked over the photograph.

"I seen this 'un down in the front lobby." She pointed to Medea Hathaway. "She was running through the lobby like she had a terrible important meeting."

"When was that?"

"'Bout half past two, I think."

Then she looked again at the photo.

"And he," she pointed at Jason's image, "was in reception with this 'un." She pointed again at the photograph, "'bout half past four, I think."

She looked at the photo again, enjoying the attention she was getting from Mary and John, who'd now joined the interview.

"Oh, and this 'un was in reception with 'im," she pointed at Jason again, "'bout an hour later, jest before I went home. Whatcha wanna know all this for? "

"We're just trying to understand Dr. Logan's—that's the man—whereabouts that afternoon. You've been a big help. And we'll tell management how much you've helped us." John praised Ms. Brown.

"I'd like that ever so much. Thank you, sir, you've been most kind." And she left the room with, "I'm a good worker, I am."

"I'm sure you are." Mary smiled.

"Well, John, who was the third person she recognized?"

"I'd bet on Bertha Warkson, his dinner companion, but let's go to her clinic and find out."

Bertha Warkson's offices were a cut between Murdock's cramped space and the palatial offices of the Logans.

Bertha Warkson was a short, overweight, matronly individual about fifty. Although her dress was severe, her manner was that of a protective grandparent. Her clinic coat only accentuated her size. The interview was brief. Yes, she'd had dinner with Jason Logan the evening before he missed the morning session. They had eaten at a small oriental fish restaurant near the hotel where they'd had the specialty of the house. But they'd called it an early evening because they both had morning meetings the next day. She'd returned to her room about ten and assumed he went to his. And, no, she was quick to add, it was nothing more than dinner and a chance to discuss a paper she'd submitted to the CSCA journal. She laughed as she acknowledged Jason's reputation as a lady's man.

"He's the editor," she reminded the Braemhors.

"I understand that there's lots of political infighting in your organization," John ventured.

"Always has been, always will be. It's the nature of professional organizations." A faint smile crossed her lips. "How do you know about that?"

"Several of your members have mentioned it." John stretched the truth.

"Oh, you mean the Hathaway/Logan feud." Her smile broadened.

"Feud?"

"I don't know what else to call it. Ever since Jason became editor of the journal, the Hathaway group has given him trouble. But I'll say that up until now, Jason has met them toe to toe. He's tough. . .or rather was. It's been a bit of fun to watch him parry and thrust with Medea. I sit on the board also, so I see it at all of the meetings. But I guess recent events have brought those machinations to an end." She sounded almost wistful.

"Is there anyone you can think of who might want to do him harm?" John asked.

"You mean besides Medea and her group?" Warkson chuckled. "And I don't really think that. They disliked him with a passion, but to think of harming him, I don't think so. Professionals at our level don't do things like that. Oh, they may want to in their fantasies, but no; we're not inclined to violence. There are many more ways to bring a rival down by innuendo, sarcasm, rumor-spreading. But violence, no." Warkson was quite firm in her summary of the situation. "Do you know if the police have drawn any conclusions yet?"

"Not that we know of. The coroner's report is due tomorrow, I believe," John responded.

"But for now, I think John and I should let you get back to your patients. You've been most generous of your time," Mary concluded, as John rose to leave.

"Not at all. If I can be of any help, please feel free to call on me again. It's been a pleasure to meet both of you." She turned to go back to her clinic offices, and the Braemhors exited through the front entry.

"She seems like a sweet, trustworthy, grandmotherly sort," Mary observed as they got into the Vauxhall.

"That's certainly the persona she projects, but I don't know. Something about her raised my antennae. She was just a bit too sweet, too grandmotherly to my liking. I don't know why, but. . . maybe she's just a little bit too soft-spoken for my taste." John was much more skeptical of Warkson's outward appearance than Mary.

"But before we go back to Daraichburn, I want to talk with Sinclair again." He headed the car back to Sinclair's offices.

Sinclair was about to leave when the Braemhors arrived.

"Something new, John?"

"Just one thing. Have the coroner test Jason Logan for tetrodotoxin poisoning, will you?"

"You think Logan was poisoned? It looked like a classic heart attack to me."

"It's possible. Maybe both, but if I were you I'd hedge my bets and throw a neurotoxin into the mix. Just a suggestion."

"I'll call the doc before I leave," Sinclair agreed. John's urgency had impressed him.

"Right. Mary and I are going back to Daraichburn for now. If I think of anything else, I'll call you."

* * * * * * *

"What are you thinking, John?" Mary asked as the Braemhors headed back to Daraichburn.

"This puzzle is getting more and more complicated. First we thought we had one prime suspect, Shelley Logan, the wife who is blasé about her husband's demise. Then I thought we had another candidate in Medea Hathaway, leader of the opposition in the political wrangling of the CSCA. Now another has joined the pack, Bertha, the sweet grandmother."

"Why the latter?" Mary asked.

"I don't know. Just a feeling. Also she did accompany Jason when they had dinner at that specialty fish restaurant near the hotel."

"So?' Mary was not quite following John's reasoning.

"Do you realize what the specialty of the house is?"

"No."

"Puffer fish!"

"Puffer fish!!" Mary was astonished. "But they're poisonous!"

"Unless they're very carefully prepared. Apparently the patrons go there to live on the edge, the thrill of the risk. Though I doubt there's much real risk or the restaurant would not be able to stay in business. Imagine if every evening a few patrons dropped dead of puffer poisoning. Still there's always a chance the chef made a mistake, was distracted for a moment while preparing the fish."

"John, you don't think Dr. Warkson had Logan poisoned at the restaurant?"

"I don't know yet, but remember a puffer fish was bought for him to add to his collection."

"So that's why you asked Sinclair to look for a possible neurotoxin as the cause of death."

"Yes, I think the key to this puzzle is. . . ."

". . .the fish," Mary finished his sentence. "Rita was right, wasn't she, John?"

John just smiled.

CHAPTER 6

Rita greeted them at the door of Dunmoor Cottage.

"All quiet on the home front, Aunt Rita?" Mary hugged her aunt.

"Oh, yes. Now, you promised to tell me what you learned in Edinburgh," Rita said as they sat in the sitting room with tea and the fresh scones she'd baked.

The Braemhors told Rita about their trip, interviewing the Baird Hotel staff and Dr. Warkson. They even allowed that she had made a major contribution to the investigation by pointing out the importance of the fish to the whole scenario. Rita was very pleased that she'd been so perceptive and beamed her self-satisfaction with an expansive smile that never left her face during the whole half hour they talked.

John ended the tale of their adventures with, "Tomorrow I've got to go to Melrose to return this photograph to Ann Murdock." He rose to leave.

"Should I come with you?" Rita asked. "I've decided to get hearing aids and I could tell her while we're there."

"No, I think it would be best if we wait to order your aids until after we've solved the puzzle of Dr. Logan's death." John wanted to deal with one thing at a time.

"If you think that's best." Rita acquiesced, though she was obviously disappointed.

At Ann Murdock's offices the next morning, Braemhor was fortunate. He arrived when she was between patients and was able to see him without wait.

"Here is your photograph. It was a big help," John opened.

"Glad I could help. Did you learn anymore about Jason's death?"

"Not a lot, though we did meet with Dr. Warkson."

"Why?" Ms. Murdock seemed a bit edgy.

"Well, she was the last person, so far as we know, to see Dr. Logan alive. She seems like a very kind, grandmotherly type of person. Acts like she wouldn't hurt a kitten."

"Don't be fooled." Ann Murdock's whole countenance changed. She was no longer the sweet young thing just trying to help this private investigator. She continued, "Dr. Warkson's a viper in a soft, fluffy façade. Sweet and nice to your face, but when you turn your back, in goes the rapier. I wouldn't trust her any further than you can throw a. . .a. . .fish tank."

"Interesting you should use that metaphor. What is there that's so nasty about Bertha Warkson?"

"She's part of the gang!"

"What gang?"

"Medea Hathaway's group. Bertha's the worst one because she's so deceitful, but wears this kind, sweet veneer." Murdock became more and more agitated as she spoke. "Do you know that she's the one who devised the gifts—the book and the epaulettes—the board gave Jason to imply his supposed dictatorship. Nasty. Nasty. Nasty. A fully loathsome person."

"You don't like her," Braemhor stated calmly.

"To say the least."

"Did you know she went to dinner with him the night he died?"

"Yes, everyone did."

"But do you know where they went?" John was probing.

"No."

"The specialty fish restaurant near the hotel."

"Where they serve puffer fish? My god!"

"Why 'my god'?" John asked evenly.

"Puffer fish are lethal! Oh, Mr. Braemhor, you don't suppose she fed him poison fish?"

"You seem to know a lot about puffer fish?"

"Not really. Just what I read in the write-up about that restaurant. I've never seen one, or even a picture of one. How could she have done something like that?"

"Well, I wouldn't worry too much about Dr. Warkson. I find that although the political power struggles in professional associations can be quite nasty, they seldom escalate to criminal behavior, except, maybe, financial." Braemhor tried to be more reassuring, as Ann Murdock was still quite tense.

"Well, I've taken enough of your time." Braemhor apologized. "Again, I really appreciate your sharing the CSCA photograph with me. It was a big help. Could I have one of your cards in case I need to get in touch with you again? I'm afraid I lost the one you gave me before."

"Of course, here." She handed another of her business cards to Braemhor. "And thank you again for all of your efforts on poor Jason's behalf. If I can help in any other way, you have my telephone number."

Now I think we're getting somewhere, Braemhor thought as he put the card into a small plastic bag and headed back to Dunmoor Cottage.

Shortly after he arrived back home, Braemhor was on the phone to Sinclair. "Jim? John here, John

Braemhor. Did you find a fish net in Logan's room, the kind people use for smallish tropical fish?"

"Yes, we did. It's in our evidence box until we get this case wrapped up. Why?"

"I have another suggestion."

"And?" Sinclair smiled at Braemhor's increasing involvement in the audiologist's death.

"Have the net handle brushed for prints. I'll bring you a set for comparison later today."

"Fine, John, I should have the coroner's report by then, so we can compare notes."

"Good." Braemhor hung up and turned to Mary.

"The case is becoming more complicated, but clearer," he announced, and then proceeded to tell her and Aunt Rita—she was now a partner in the sleuthing, and loving every minute of her involvement—about his conversation with Ann Murdock.

"So who do you think done it?" Rita asked impishly. "Sounds like we still have three possibilities—the wife, the rival colleague, and the vicious grandmother."

"Don't forget that the other audiologist has now entered the picture," Mary cautioned.

"It should be clear, at least in my own mind, by the time I get back from Edinburgh," John pronounced as he picked up some fruit to eat on the drive.

Mary took note of the enthusiasm that embraced her husband. She knew the case was not far from resolution.

* * * * * * *

A little over an hour later, Braemhor walked into Sinclair's office. Sinclair handed him a copy of the coroner's report. Braemhor read it quickly.

"So I was right!"

"Yes, you were. Logan's body was laced with tetrodotoxin, causing extensive muscular paralysis, including of the diaphragm. Probably paralyzed the heart as well," Sinclair concluded. "Before this, the coroner had found several small lesions on Logan's torso, but wasn't sure of their significance. Now he thinks they were the sites of entry."

"Like bites?" Braemhor asked. "So the fish bit him?"

"Looks that way. What a horrible way to die," Sinclair added. "Now we just need to know who put the fish into the bath with him."

"And took it back out again and put it into its bowl," Braemhor concluded the thought.

"But the door to Logan's room was open when his colleagues found him, so anyone could have gotten in. Possibly while he was already in his bath," Sinclair added.

"But they would have to have known about the puffer fish in the bowl, and I think I have an idea who that was," John said.

"Care to enlighten me, John? This case already has two possible prime suspects."

"Actually, there are more than two. Here. Dust this card for prints—besides mine—and I think we'll have an answer to the murder—and I do think it's a case of murder. I think the prints will match what you found on the fishnet handle." He handed Sinclair the small plastic bag containing a cream-colored business card, who then gave it to Wallace for a quick dusting and comparison.

"Coffee, John? While we wait for the results." Sinclair poured two mugs. "Now continue your scenario of the case."

"Well, you said two main suspects. I think there are two additional possibilities. First, we both jumped to the conclusion that Logan's wife was the prime suspect, since she stood to benefit financially by his death. But

Shelley Logan wasn't even in Edinburgh when Jason Logan met his end. She'd gone back to Melrose the day before. Even missed the grand photograph of all of the CSCA participants. The only way she could have been involved was to have an accomplice, or hired assassin, do the job for her. Too messy. The more people involved, the more the likelihood of a slipup. No, Shelley Logan is not our culprit.

"Next there was Medea Hathaway, Jason's political nemesis in the society. She certainly worked hard to bring him down as president of the society and editor of the journal. But I think her type of vengeance would be more intellectual and political than physical violence. Besides, as far as we know she knew nothing of puffer fish—which we now know was the poison delivery mechanism. Also, she was seen leaving the hotel the afternoon before Jason's death."

"But she could have come back in the evening and done the job," Sinclair pointed out.

"True, but I just don't see her as the type. In addition, all she had to do was wait until the end of his term as president at the end of the year and she would have gained supremacy over the society. Intellectuals are much less impatient than your ordinary murderer."

"So where does that leave us?" Sinclair asked. "And who are the other two suspects?"

"Second question first," John responded. "The third suspect has to be the woman he had dinner with the night he died—Bertha Warkson. She knew about puffer fish. They went to a restaurant that specializes in the high risk thrill of feeding their patrons puffer fish. She claims to have gone to her room about ten o'clock and that she thought that Jason had gone to his. What time did the coroner place the time of death?" Braemhor asked himself and consulted the report. "Ah, here it is, 'around eleven to twelve, midnight.'"

"So Warkson could have done it, but my guess is if you re-dust the room you won't find any prints that match hers. Besides, I think by the time Wallace returns with the results of the prints on the card, you won't need to look for more prints."

"So, you've eliminated three suspects, but you seem to think there's a fourth," Sinclair summed up.

"The card will tell us." John smiled slightly.

At which time Wallace returned with the results. "Sir, two sets of prints on the card. One we found in our database, belongs to a John Braemhor." Wallace's face broke out into a wry smile. "And the other, a smaller set, looks like from a woman. They are a perfect match for what we found on the fishnet handle, sir."

"Well done, Wallace. Have the lab boys write it up and put their conclusions into the Logan case evidence box," Sinclair ordered.

He then turned back to Braemhor. "The card has spoken, but what made you suspect Ann Murdock?"

"Two things. First I had ascertained that she was the one who'd bought the puffer fish at The Fish Tank. Mr. Trawler, the proprietor, identified her in the photograph of the society attendees. Then when I talked with her this morning, she adamantly disclaimed any knowledge of puffer fish, even said she'd never seen so much as a picture of one. Why would she lie to me? Only if she had something to hide. She knew more about puffer fish than she was willing to admit. Why? Hence Ann Murdock is the murderer."

"Very tidy, John—in your mind, and you have convinced me—but although what we have so far looks pretty strong, it won't convict by itself you realize. Where do you think we need to go from here?" Sinclair asked.

"I think you should bring her in and interrogate her very thoroughly. From what I saw this morning, she's fragile, living on an emotional edge. I think her deed has unhinged her from what little reality ties she had. I think psychologically she's about to disintegrate. Even Mr. Trawler noticed it. Said she reminded him of a jumpy guppy. They're a pretty shy and skittish fish, you know."

"Sounds like a good plan to me. I'll send two of my boys to Melrose and pick her up right away. Maybe she'll help us under questioning." He ordered two of his staff to take a green and white to Melrose and pick up Ann Murdock.

"And I'll get back to Daraichburn. Call me when the case is wrapped up, will you?"

"Most certainly, and, John, thanks. Once again, you've made my job easier."

* * * * * * *

Two days later, the phone at Dunmoor Cottage rang.

"Dunmoor Cottage Bed and Breakfast," Mary answered. "Of course, Jim, I'll get him."

"John, it's Jim Sinclair," Mary called.

"I got it on the extension," John responded. "Hello, Jim, what have you got? Good news, I hope."

"Better than that. The Logan case is wrapped up. I brought Ms. Murdock in for questioning and we'd hardly started the interview when she broke down and confessed to killing Logan with a puffer fish. Once she'd told us the whole story it was almost like a great burden had been lifted off of her. She actually appeared relieved to have confessed. Seems she'd been trying to rekindle the romance she'd once had with Logan before he married Shelley Logan. He would lead her on and on and then at the last minute drop her again. But she kept trying, getting increasingly frustrated and emotionally hurt with each new rejection. Finally, she decided that if she couldn't have him, no one would.

"About a month ago, she hit upon the idea of using a puffer fish. She was aware of his fondness for tropical fish so she bought him one at The Fish Tank, like you said. She gave it to him after his wife had gone back to Melrose. The fish was in the small bowl in which we found it. She said he seemed pleased with the gift and she thought it might re-ignite the spark between the two of them. It was not to be. She planned to have dinner with him, 'for old time's sake,' but when she got to his room to get him for dinner, she found the room empty, though the door was unlocked. She went in, looked and called for him, but no Logan. She found a spare key to the room on the dresser. Then she found a note beside the key from Bertha Warkson on a side table, also arranging for dinner that evening. She went to the fish restaurant we talked about and saw Logan and Warkson having what appeared to her to be a cozy tête-à-tête at a table in the back. Ann Murdock was infuriated.

"She returned to Logan's room, let herself in with the key she'd found, hid in the spare, unused closet, and waited. Finally, about half past ten, Logan came back, poured himself a hot bath, and relaxed. She got the fish net and took the fish from its bowl to Logan's bath, and then stood there and watched as he writhed and rapidly became progressively paralyzed and died. I think the sight of him dying and her realizing what she'd done horrified her to the point that she almost forgot to return the fish to its bowl. She did forget to lock the door, she left in such a confused hurry. End of story and end of case. With her confession we'll have no trouble convicting her," Sinclair concluded.

"But you know, John, although this is clearly a case of premeditated murder, I feel that Ann Murdock is more of a confused, bewildered, psychologically delicate being, than a cold-blooded, vicious murderer."

"It's a shame when emotionality trumps rationality and ruins so many lives. Well, I'm glad that you were able to solve the case and bring it to a definite conclusion," Braemhor spoke almost wistfully.

"Not without a lot of outside help and for that I thank you," Sinclair said.

"Don't mention it, Jim. Maybe next time you can help me with one of my cases. Stay in touch."

"Right."

Braemhor collected Mary and Rita in the sitting room and relayed the tale Sinclair had just shared with him.

"So we've been successful detectives, haven't we?" Rita gushed with self-satisfaction.

"We're a team, Aunt Rita," Mary observed, "but we have one more thing to accomplish."

"Oh?" Rita was perplexed.

"Yes, to get you your hearing aids. Maybe we should call Dr. Logan, don't you think?'

"Yes," Rita enthused, "and I'll bet she doesn't have a tank of fish in her office any more."

CHAPTER 7

It was late fall when Mary suggested to John that they travel to the Colonies—as John calls the United States—to see their son, Jim, and daughter-in-law, Jennifer, and the grandchildren.

"Rita will look after the cottage. Besides, we haven't yet seen their new house," Mary reminded John. The younger Braemhors had moved in mid-summer to a quiet village—Hiramville—across the river from New Boston so that the children would have the benefit of an excellent school system and a safe environment in which to grow and develop. They had thoroughly enjoyed their years in the city of New Boston, but the crime rate was steadily growing and invading the safer neighborhoods of the city.

"Time to find a better place to raise the family," James had said, and both he and Jennifer, being individuals of action, located a new abode for their family, close enough to the city to commute to their respective jobs, but far enough away to allow the grandchildren—Daniel and Donna—a life free of the fear of sudden violence around every corner.

The house, on a quiet, shaded avenue a short walk from the village center with its necessary shops and churches, was a twelve-room, 100-year-old Victorian surrounded by large oak and maple trees. There was even a compact granny flat on the third floor, which afforded guests the privacy of their own space, while still being a part of the overall household.

The back garden was perfect for young people's exploratory urges with plenty of room for play and secret spaces in which to create their own private fantasies. There was even enough space to allow a small family game of softball. James had taken up a liking for the American sport of baseball and on several occasions took the family to see the New Boston Blackbirds professional team.

All things considered, it could not have been a more ideal location. John and Mary looked forward to a brief respite from the mists and showers of their native Scotland.

The flight from Manchester, via Heathrow, was uneventful save for the usual hassle of moving through the flight gate security, emptying pockets of metal objects and removing their eyeglasses. At Heathrow, the security agent pulled Mary out of line for an individual wanding.

"I guess I look like a terrorist," she laughingly confided to John after they were safely belted into their seats.

"It's your steel grey hair." John smiled as he opened *The Guardian.*

James, Jennifer and the children met them outside the security area at their arrival gate in New Boston and, after hugs and kisses and astonished remarks about how tall both grandchildren were, whisked them off to the car buried in the five-story car park adjoining the terminal.

Half an hour later, James turned into his and Jennifer's driveway beside their home and the whole family went in to have a fine supper and to catch each other up on their respective lives over the past few months. Following the meal, both grandchildren entertained Mary and John with the latest pieces they were learning during their music lessons—Daniel on the cello and Donna on the violin. By then it was time for the older Braemhors to retire and correct the jet lag that was now alerting them to the need for sleep on the futon on the third floor.

For the next month, John and Mary immersed themselves in extended family life, making many short sight-seeing trips with the family to see a number of American historic sites and the eastern seashore.

Later, James was very intent on introducing his parents to an American Thanksgiving, complete with a turkey dinner, graced with cranberry sauce, dressing, smashed potatoes and peas with onions. Pumpkin pie, of course, completed the meal. Even John had to admit that "the Colonies do have some delicious traditions."

A week after the Thanksgiving overstuffing of the family, John suggested that he call the Howards in Carterville to arrange a brief visit. On two occasions the Braemhors had assisted the Howards—Stanley and Jane. The first was when they solved the ominous circumstances behind the sudden demise of Jane's great uncle, Frank Neal Winslow, in a Manchester rest home, and the second was when John and Mary had gone to Carterville and participated in solving a series of unusual deaths among the Carter University faculty which John had labeled the "crazy glue murders." Stanley Howard was the Dean of the Faculty of this prestigious liberal arts college nestled in the foothills of the Adirondacks.

Howard's response to the proposed visit was most gracious. "Of course, Jane and I will be most happy to see you both again, and I can arrange accommodations for you again at The Retreat. When would you be arriving?"

"Will day after tomorrow suit? We need to attend our granddaughter's ballet recital of *The Nutcracker* this evening," John answered.

"Excellent! I'll send a university van to the train station for you. And, John, this is a real pleasure. We look forward to seeing you and Mary."

"Day after tomorrow." John turned to Mary.

* * * * * * *

The trip north through the Hudson River Valley and west in the Mohawk River Valley was a reprise of the travel the previous spring to Carterville. The scenery along the route was again stunning, but in a different way. Now winter was setting in. Just north of Poughkeepsie, light snow flurries began and then became steadily more intense as the train snaked its way north. By Coxsackie the ground had been rendered white and visibility from the car's picture windows was restricted to but ten feet on either side of the tracks.

"Oh, John, look. Isn't it just beautiful?" Mary was entranced. Neither she nor John had had much experience with snow.

"So long as it doesn't delay our schedule." John was less concerned with the esthetics of the scenery than he was with getting to their destination on time. The train had perceptibly slowed its progress, though it steadily plowed its way west.

"Oh, John, we're on holiday. Just sit back and enjoy and be happy we brought our winter coats and boots."

"I'm not so sure our coats are up to the task. I understand that below zero temperatures—Fahrenheit, that is—are not unknown in this part of the Colonies. Just hope that Carter University has a robust heating system." Ice was forming in the spaces between cars as John spoke.

Suddenly there was a loud bang and the entire car trembled with the impact. The train slowed to a halt as the passengers—including the Braemhors—stared through the frost-covered windows in wonder. Several passengers got up and moved quickly towards the door at the end of the car. But they could see no more than those who stayed in their seats waiting.

Within a couple of minutes—though it seemed much longer—the conductor came through the car reassuring the passengers that there would be a slight delay, but that it was nothing to be concerned about.

"What happened?" John queried the uniformed trainman as he passed by John and Mary's seats.

"Nothing much. Somebody had put a railroad tie on the track. The noise and jolt was when the engine hit it and knocked it off the track. Doubt there was any damage, but the engineer is checking just to be sure. This happens every once in a while. Young people with nothing much else to do think it would be neat to derail a train. What they don't realize is that it takes more than a single railroad tie to derail a 20-ton diesel locomotive. We should be on our way shortly. Nothing to worry about." The conductor spoke in a matter-of-fact monotone borne of having had this experience a repeated number of times. He smiled as he passed along words of reassurance to all of the passengers.

Within ten minutes the engine again surged with power, and the train began moving westward, picking up speed as each mile passed. The engineer seemed intent on making up time and staying on schedule. As the train moved farther west, the less fierce became the storm, until by Herkimer it was reduced to intermittent flurries like those that began back at Poughkeepsie, though the ground had been converted from green and grey to white.

The conductor appeared and shouted out the next station stop as he walked through the car.

"This is our station," John spoke as he got up to pull their valises down from the overhead rack.

John and Mary alighted from the car via the icy steps as a young man holding up a sign which read "The Braemhors" stepped forward.

"Mr. and Mrs. Braemhor?" A broad toothy smile brightened his face.

"That's right," John acknowledged, handing their bags to the student.

"Hi, I'm Jamal. I'll be your driver for the trip into Carterville. He led the Braemhors to a reddish van marked "Carter University" parked just outside the main entrance to the enormous 19th century station and put the bags in the back luggage section.

"The snow is just beautiful," Mary remarked as they clicked their seat belts. "How deep is it?"

"Up here in the city only about four or five inches," Jamal answered, "but down at the University it's nearly a foot."

"How's the driving?" John asked the practical question.

"Not too bad. I've driven in a lot worse." Jamal smiled. "Not to worry. The roads are well-maintained by the state. And Carterville keeps the village roads open no matter what."

The Braemhors relaxed and settled back to enjoy the next hour viewing the winter wonderland. Jamal was right. The road, even along the crest of the hills, was a dark stripe amidst the whiteness, well-plowed, salted and sanded. The hills were dotted with small forest stands of Norway spruce, intermingled with maple and oak.

"Oh, look, John." Mary pointed to the right. There stood a small herd of white-tailed deer, looking frozen in the whiteness, as they watched the van maneuver up the hill. "They look so tame."

"Too tame for my liking," Jamal added. "They're more of a hazard than the ice and snow, both winter and summer. I guess you don't see much snow in Scotland?"

"Very little. Maybe a few flurries once in a while. It's a nice change for us," John said.

As they entered Carterville and drove past the village green, Mary asked, "What's going on?"

On the green, in front of the Ambrose Inn at village center, stood several small groups of individuals, one by a Christmas crèche near the bandstand, another close by the first, and yet a third nearer the curb bordering the street down which the Braemhors were being driven. All were holding signs and appeared to be shouting or singing. Since the van windows were closed against the frigid air, John and Mary could not hear what was being said and they were just barely able to read the signs held by some of the people near the street. LOVE, NOT HATE. RESPECT EACH OTHER. RELIGIOUS STRIFE IS NOT THE ANSWER. BE TOLERANT.

"I'm not sure. I think some group is protesting the crèche on public property and another is protesting the protesters. Something like that," Jamal responded as he concentrated on guiding the van down the street and to the University campus. "I don't pay much attention to village politics. Got enough to do just to stay on top of my studies."

"Wise decision, I'd say," Mary stated. "I can understand. . . ."

Soon Jamal turned into the campus and drove up the hill, past the academic buildings to The Retreat, nestled among the snow-covered evergreens overlooking the campus and the valley beyond.

"This looks familiar," Mary noted as they entered the foyer where Mrs. Parker was awaiting their arrival.

"Professor Howard left this message for you," she said as she handed Mary an envelope marked "Mr. & Mrs. Braemhor." "I have the same apartment you had on your last stay ready for you." She pointed to the stairs behind her desk. "We have several other guests also. Dinner will be at six in the dining area." She handed Mary the key to their apartment.

"It looks like we will not be here for dinner this evening, Mrs. Parker," John said as he read the message Stanley Howard had left for them. "But probably tomorrow evening."

"That will be fine; just let me know for sure by lunch tomorrow." Mrs. Parker smiled and went through the dining area to her left. John and Mary descended the stairs and found their way to the apartment.

"So Stanley and Jane will be hosting us dinner tonight?" Mary asked.

"That's right. A car will pick us up about quarter after six," John said as he and Mary unpacked the contents of their valises into the chiffonier and closet in the very tiny, austere space they were to occupy for the next few days. There was also a double bed, a small desk and two straight chairs. The bath was to the left of the entry.

Mary stood by the picture window in wonder at the gently falling snow that was adding to the already deep covering on the ground.

"Isn't it beautiful, John?" she marveled.

"Certainly not like home." He stood beside her, also marveling at the quiet whiteness. "Best we wear an extra sweater under our coats to dinner. I suspect that the Howards's home will not be as cozy as our peat-warmed cottage."

John was wrong. Jane Howard was not one to let the breath of winter invade her home. When they arrived at the Howard's house it was as warm and toasty as Dunmoor Cottage, so their cable knit woolens were not needed and were quickly shed and put in the Howard's entry closet with their coats.

"John, Mary, welcome once again to our humble abode," Jane gushed as she gave Mary a welcoming embrace.

Mary surveyed the art, fine furniture and expensive oriental floor coverings and thought, *humble?* But she returned Jane's graciousness with, "Jane, it's so nice to see the two of you again. And Carterville certainly is different from the last time we were here."

Stanley took John's and Mary's hands and responded to Mary's greeting. "We think it particularly good for you to see our campus and village in a markedly different season. I hope you brought your boots. I see you have brought warm coats and sweaters." Stanley beamed with genuine warmth at the presence of his Scottish friends.

Jane's curry-laced meal was a delicacy to behold and savor—a feast she had developed during her and Stanley's sabbatical year in Madras, India. Though she had done little meal preparation during that year—servants were plentiful and inexpensive—she had paid close attention to the local customs and particularly the cuisine, making copious notes of all of the recipes that ignited her palette.

While they were being served after dinner coffee and sweets in the small sitting room off the dining room, John asked about what they'd observed when passing through the village on their way to The Retreat.

"You seemed to have a number of groups expressing different ideas on the village green as we passed through," he observed.

"Oh, that." Stanley smiled. "Just democracy in action."

"What exactly is it all about?" Mary asked.

"Mainly a bunch of malcontents who aren't happy having a crèche on public property. They started protest standing—I call it that because they're not marching— shortly after the Village Council put the crèche up." Jane was obviously not happy about the turn of events in the village.

"They believe in a literal separation of church and state," Stanley quickly interrupted for fear that Jane would express too strongly her personal feelings on the matter. She was an active member of one of the local Protestant churches and was not sure why anyone would protest a crèche on the village green during the Christmas season. Stanley himself was on the National Advisory Board of that denomination.

"But who are the others?" Mary asked.

"Ah, this is the interesting aspect of the local politics. One group is protesting the protestors. They feel that this country is a Christian nation with a capital *C,* and that no one should object to religious symbols playing a prominent, if not dominant, role in our daily life—particularly at Christmas time. What they fail to recognize is that this community is composed of a diversity of religions. Unfortunately, this group is mostly made up of non-Carter University people, 'townees.' So the disagreement is taking on a decidedly town/gown flavor.

"You see, in part because of the presence of the university, we have a number of Protestant sects— Episcopalians, Baptists, Methodists, Presbyterians, minor evangelical groups—plus, Jews, Catholics, Muslims, Buddhists, Unitarians and other beliefs, even two or three Zoroastrians among us as well as non-believers. All feeling that they, too, have a right to equal billing. And in the middle is a group of Quakers trying to bring the two sides together in a local rapprochement—trying to make peace, not war. You see, this is where democracy can get messy."

"Interesting," John reflected.

"Indeed," Stanley agreed, then added, "the Village Council is having a public meeting tomorrow evening at the town hall. Care to attend?"

"I think it would be fascinating." Mary enthusiastically joined the discussion.

"In the meantime, I think Mary and I should go back to The Retreat and rest up for tomorrow's lesson in democracy," John suggested with a smile.

Following John and Mary's appreciative remarks to Jane, Stanley drove them back to The Retreat and suggested that they have lunch with him the next day at The Faculty Club, "if you think you can manage the snowy walk down the hill; if not, I can send a car for you."

"Oh, I think it will be a delight to walk in your winter wonderland," Mary quickly responded.

"All right, then. Say about noon. You know where the Faculty Club is? And do be careful. Snow and ice on these hills can be treacherous, particularly if you're not used to it," Stanley warned. Then he waved and drove off down the hill to the village.

"This should be fun, John," Mary said as they entered their apartment.

"And educational." John smiled.

* * * * * * *

After a leisurely lunch at the Faculty Club, renewing acquaintances from their last trip to Carterville, the Braemhors re-explored the campus. Stanley Howard had been correct, the footing on the new fallen snow was precarious and on several occasions both John and Mary almost fell. But both considered the slipping and sliding an additional learning experience to add to their already delightful memories of upstate.

Following Mrs. Parker's simple but delicious supper serving, the Howards arrived at half past six to give the Braemhors a ride to their "lesson in American democracy" at the village meeting in the town hall.

The room was overflowing. There were those who appeared to be faculty members, dressed in the obligatory tweeds and carrying unlit briars. One even had a Holmesian meerschaum. Others, by their dress, seemed to come from the less affluent, village community of shopkeepers, secretaries and store clerks. In addition there was a rural, farm group in their work jeans, barn boots and, when they took off their heavy woolen coats, wide-banded braces, keeping their jeans from falling below the rounded protuberances that marked some of their waistlines. And, of course, the students, mostly political science majors with a smattering of sociology and psychology students.

Fortunately, Stanley had sent a student assistant ahead to secure seats for the four of them in the third row from the rear where they could best observe and hear the proceedings. The first to speak was the mayor, a diminutive round woman in her mid-sixties with a cap of grey hair, bobbed to accentuate her oval face.

"Welcome, everyone. I am Margaret Burke, mayor of Carterville. We are here this evening to discuss the placement of the crèche on our village green. I think most of you know the Village Council." She pointed to the five individuals seated on the platform at the front of the room. "As you know there has been some disagreement as to the location of the crèche. I have asked two members of the council to present, briefly, the two opposing viewpoints concerning the crèche, then we will open the floor to audience discussion. First, the chairman of the council, Mr. Allen Fletcher."

Fletcher was a tall, thin man, clean-shaven and dressed in black. He fumbled with the microphone on the table in front of him, blew into it, making a loud windy sound that permeated the room, cleared his throat several times—which also made a loud noise through the sound system—and looked out over the citizens before him.

"Gentlemen and ladies," he opened with pompous intonations. "It is I who proposed to place the crèche where it is in the center of our village green. There could be no better place for it, since we of the village of Carterville are a Christian community. Remember that this nation was founded on the principles of Christianity by Christian men. This is our heritage, a heritage which binds us all together as Americans. At this season, particularly, to suggest that this glorious symbol of our lives should not be prominently represented in our village is . . . well, blasphemous." This last statement was met with a chorus of *Amens* and applause throughout the room and a few very loud groans. A shout of *bigot* was even heard from a dark corner in the back.

Stanley leaned over to John and Mary. "Fletcher has never been one for subtlety."

"Sounds to me like he's thrown down the gauntlet," John observed.

The mayor then spoke again. "Now, I've asked Councilwoman Linda Quig to give the other viewpoint."

Quig, a large-boned woman in her fifties had dark brown hair drawn back in a bun at her neck. Her equally dark eyes penetrated the audience as she rose and took the council's table microphone in hand.

"She's a member of our Political Science department," Stanley quietly informed John and Mary.

"Mr. Fletcher wants you to believe that all Americans are of one stock—Christians," Quig began, "but America is a nation of immigrants, people from different countries, with different skin colors and, yes, different beliefs. This diversity is what gives us our uniqueness among nations and our strength as a nation. I believe that to place a symbol—powerful though it may be—of one and only one religion on our village green serves as an endorsement by the state—our village government—of that religion and denigrates other religions. The citizens of this village are religiously diverse, and no one religion should be exalted above others, which is what we do as a village when we put the symbol of only one religion on village property. Better to acknowledge each and every belief and non-belief that underpins our community. Thank you."

Mayor Burke stood up. "We will now open the floor for comments and discussion. If you have something to say, go to one of the two microphones in the aisles and everyone will get a chance to be heard, in turn."

Lines formed at the two audience microphones and the harangues began. Most spoke against removing the crèche from the village green, echoing Fletcher's remarks. Then came a small—he did not stand more than 5' 3" in height—wizened man about sixty. His face was deeply lined and mildly swarthy. He had a fringe of white hair and a stubbly white goatee. He had to lower the microphone before he could use it.

"My name is Leon Goldfarb. I own the jewelry store on Broad Street. Most of you know me, I think. I was one of the group which asked the Village Council to remove the crèche from the green. I asked because America has a long and honored tradition of separation of church and state. Our founding fathers, at least one of whom was not a Christian, greatly feared that a state that allows only one church is a state doomed to fail. They had witnessed the terrible wars that destroyed church-dominated European civilizations. They wanted America to be different, to allow the free expression of all religions with preference given to no one religion."

"Go back where you belong!" came a shout from the middle of the audience.

"Yeah, Carterville is American. We don't want you or any others like you here! We're Americans!!" another voice added.

"I was afraid of this," Stanley again leaned to John and Mary and whispered.

Goldfarb was briefly shaken, but quickly regained his composure and responded, "For the information of the gentleman in the fourth row, my grandfather started our jewelry shop in the 1930s. I was born in Carterville, as was my father, and graduated from Carterville Central High, and served in the Air Force during World War II. Most of my family is buried in the village cemetery. I am an American and a citizen of this village as much as you, sir. Now, if you will let me finish. Our objection to the placement of the crèche is very simple. It should not be on public property, because there it alienates members of all of the other religious beliefs, not just those of the Jewish faith." With that, he took his seat.

John and Mary were so intent on the ongoing argument that they had not noticed Stanley get up and approach a microphone. Mary looked at John and said in a hushed voice, "Oh, dear, now Stanley's going to get into it."

"Well, he does hold a certain leadership position in the community," John observed, as he heard Stanley begin to speak.

"I am Dean Stanley Howard, as most of you know."

"Sit down!! The college runs enough of our village life without you telling us where we can put our Christmas decorations!" A gruff-looking man in the back had stood up and was shouting over the crowd.

"Yeah! We don't want any of you running our town!" another added. And suddenly the room was filled with shouts and catcalls denouncing the college, the faculty and anyone else the crowd felt was interfering with their lives.

The mayor stepped forward. "Please! Please! If we can't have a civil dialogue, I'll close the meeting and you can all go home with nothing settled."

"Suits me!!" announced a wiry man in coveralls who then stomped out the door, taking a half-dozen others with him.

Howard raised his voice into the microphone, and at the sound of the authority in his voice the room suddenly became eerily quiet.

"Thank you," Stanley continued. "What I was going to suggest was that since one of our churches is adjacent to the village green, and since the church has a large grassy plot adjoining the church building, that the Village Council consider placing the crèche there. That way it will be visible to all who are on or near the green to enjoy, yet be on private property. And thus avoid the church/state debate." A small round of applause erupted from some in attendance. But a large contingent of the audience were still not satisfied with the compromise, and the ranting and raving against moving the crèche continued for the next half hour.

As the harangues continued, John suddenly nudged Mary. "Is that Charlie MacLaine over there? Or am I seeing things?" He nodded towards the right front of the room.

"You mean seated with that very tall, dark-haired man? It certainly looks like him, but I don't know. Besides, what would he be doing here in Carterville and going to a public meeting?"

But at that moment the next audience speaker diverted John and Mary's attention. He was a medium-sized, gaunt man dressed in blue work clothes.

"Who's that?" John quietly asked Stanley.

Stanley frowned. "That's one of our local members of the KKK, Bob Wilcox. They hold occasional cross burnings on a farm a few miles south of here."

"The KKK?" Mary asked. "I thought they'd been pretty well bankrupted by lawsuits in the 80s." John nodded his agreement.

Stanley, not a little surprised that the Braemhors would be aware of the KKK, answered, "Oh, true, but the Klan has been making a comeback in the last ten years."

"I'm surprised they'd even be in upstate New York. I've always associated them more with your southern states," Mary added.

Stanley's face broadened with a sardonic smile, "Oh, we're just a diverse population."

By that time, Wilcox's remarks had become particularly hateful and threatening, amounting to a call to arms to rid the area of all these 'non-Americans.'

"I'll tell you one thing," he was shouting into the microphone now, "if the village won't do nothin' 'bout this, there are those of us that will!!! We're not afraid to protect our God-given rights; by god we'll. . ."

At that point, Mayor Burke rose in the front and quickly intervened. At the same time, there was heard a loud *click* in the sound system, as someone, no one was quite sure who, turned off the microphone Wilcox was using.

The mayor tried to put a reasonable face on the proceedings. "Well, we have certainly heard a diversity of opinions here this evening. I and the Village Council will consider all of them and render a decision with respect to the placement of the crèche at our regular meeting next Tuesday. I thank all of you for coming this evening. The meeting is closed." She rapped the desk in front of her with a wooden ruler, ending John and Mary's "lesson in American democracy."

Later, over a cup of tea, back at the Howard's comfortable home, John asked Stanley, "What do you think will be the result of the meeting?"

"I'm a pessimist." Stanley smiled. "I doubt if much at all will change. The crèche will stay where it is, the minorities who brought the complaint in the first place will grumble and write letters to our local newspaper, and the ruffians will be happy they've 'beaten' those 'intellectual types with their big ideas and language nobody understands.' Life will go on and each religious group will celebrate their particular holidays as they have always done."

"You sound rather defeated," Mary observed.

"Not defeated, just realistic." Jane looked up as she poured the tea.

"I thought your idea was a particularly good compromise." John looked at Stanley.

"Thank you, but our nation is not in a compromising mood right now. It's all or nothing, us or them, black or white. And it's a shame because democracy, real democracy, is all about working together. Compromising when things get sticky. But some people want everything their way even if it means the demise of our form of government." He thought for a moment. "And yet, there's always some humor to be found. You saw Mr. Wilcox tonight. Well, when the new health care legislation was making its way through the national Congress and the debates were quite vociferous, he was heard to object that he did not want government to interfere with his Social Security!"

"But I thought your Social Security is a government program?" Mary said.

"Precisely." Stanley smiled. "This is what we're up against."

Back at The Retreat, John queried Mary. "Well, what do you think of American democracy?"

"Like Stanley said, 'It's messy.'"

"Makes you wonder how the Colonies ever got things together to challenge the mother country successfully."

"Like we're trying to do now?" Mary reminded John of Scotland's recent efforts to secede from the UK and become an independent nation.

"But it's taken us over eight centuries. The Colonies did it in less than one. They must have something going for them." John extinguished the bed lamp.

CHAPTER 8

Next morning the Braemhors were awakened by a light tapping on their door. John, in his robe, peered through the slight crack he'd opened in the door. "Yes?"

"Sorry to bother you so early," Mrs. Parker spoke quietly, "but there's a phone call for you upstairs."

"Right. I'll be right there." He hastily donned his clothes and went to the public phone on the entry floor above.

"Braemhor here."

"John, it's Stanley. We've got trouble. The statuette for the baby Jesus is gone from the crèche. Police noticed it when they changed shifts at seven."

"What time is it now?"

"Seven fifteen."

"So not too many people know yet?"

"Chief Phillips, the mayor, me, and now you, unless some of the town folks noticed when they went to work."

"Good. I'd suggest that the mayor find a substitute doll and put it in the crèche as soon as possible." John was thinking fast to head off a major uproar when the village became aware of the theft. "The fewer people that know, the better."

"I'll call her right away and see what we can do. Shall I pick you up after breakfast, say about half an hour? I don't have a meeting until ten."

"We'll be ready for you."

After a hardy scrapple and toast breakfast in The Retreat's dining room, John and Mary walked the short path to the road just as Stanley drove up.

"The mayor found a doll in the village museum, replaced the missing one in the crèche, and has turned the crime investigation over to Chief Phillips, who, by the way, says he would like to see you and Mary again."

"Maybe we could see him while you're in your meeting," John offered.

"And then I'll pick you up at the Inn for lunch at the Faculty Club."

Stanley dropped the Braemhors at the police office in the village building.

"Good to see you again, Mr. Braemhor," Phillips said as he offered his hand in greeting, "and you, too, Mrs. Braemhor." He smiled at them both. "Come in. Come in." He led the way into his cramped office where there was barely enough room for two chairs in front of his official desk. Phillips, short, round and pudgy, had changed little since their last visit to Carterville.

"Not much of a crime for us to solve this time." He beamed as he leaned his chair back almost to the wall behind his desk, remembering how the Braemhors had worked with him before on the "crazy glue murders."

"What's your thinking on this one?"

The chief welcomed the opening to display his astute detective work. "I think it's a prank. One of the social clubs probably snitched the doll last night after that raucous meeting. I thought I saw you two there. Typical town-gown brouhaha. Yes, sir, I'd bet my badge it's down in a party basement of one of the clubs. They usually stash these things under the bar. Not very imaginative, I'd say, but it makes my job easier."

"Does this happen often?" Mary asked.

"Oh, yes, ma'am. At least once or twice every semester. They stole the university seal once—big thing, bronze, about two or three feet in diameter. Probably weighed a couple hundred pounds. Took us a couple of days to find it. They had hidden it behind the front panel of their bar. Like I say, not very imaginative."

"That must have taken a number of very strong young men," Mary suggested.

"Yes, ma'am, but that wasn't the largest snatch the students have managed. One year they made off with a Civil War Naval cannon from the local cemetery. Now that was heavy! We didn't find it for more than a week. They'd buried it in the backyard of their house. Fresh dig gave them away."

"Are there any penalties for this sort of thing?" John asked.

"Not usually, as long as they return the stolen item to its original place and no damage is done. Student pranks, that's all. Ah, here's my deputy now." Chief Phillips looked out his window. "And he's carrying the baby Jesus." Phillips smiled. "Case solved, but I do admit I was a bit concerned about this one, considering all of the ruckus at last night's meeting. Could have gotten nasty if many folks had gotten wind of it."

At that moment, the mayor entered the chief's office trailed by Allen Fletcher, who was storming and ranting about the missing doll in the crèche. He'd noticed the empty cradle early that morning as he took his morning constitutional.

Before he could turn his venom on the chief, Phillips said, "Calm yourself, Mr. Fletcher. The missing item is being returned to its original place in the crèche as we speak. There's no reason for you to raise your blood pressure."

"No reason! No reason! Someone desecrated a sacred symbol. I hope you know who the perpetrators of this heinous crime are. And I hope you'll prosecute them to the fullest extent of the law. Who were they?"

"I'm sorry, Mr. Fletcher, but I'm not at liberty to divulge that information." Phillips stood fast.

"Probably Goldfarb and his cronies. I demand that you arrest Goldfarb and the rest of his ilk and put them in the county jail," Fletcher ranted on.

"Thank you for your concerns, Mr. Fletcher. Now, if you'll please leave my office. As you can see, I have other business to attend to." Phillips nodded to John and Mary.

Fletcher left grudgingly, harrumphing as he went back down the hall to the outside exit. The mayor stayed behind.

"Margaret, this is John and Mary Braemhor visiting from Scotland. They helped me with the case of the faculty deaths in the spring."

"I'm very pleased to meet you. Harry has spoken quite highly of you both. Didn't I see you at the meeting last night?"

"Yes," Mary responded. "We found it most fascinating."

"Well, usually our meetings are more civil and calm than that, but I'm glad you enjoyed it. And don't worry about Allen Fletcher. He has a very large bark, but no real bite to speak of." She smiled and exited back to her office down the hall.

"Well, we won't take any more of your time, Harry. I know you've got more important business than entertaining Scottish visitors. I think Mary and I will take a stroll around the village while we wait for Stanley Howard to gather us for lunch. It's been very nice to get a chance to see you again, and I hope your work load is no more challenging than a few student pranks." John rose and offered Phillips his hand as he and Mary left the office and went outside into the brisk winter air. They heard the telephone ring in Phillips's office as they left the building.

"Shall we take a look at the Inn?" John asked as they crossed the street at the north end of the village green. "We didn't get to see it the last time we were here."

The Braemhors entered the Inn's lobby through two large, solid cherry doors. The space had just been refurbished in dark greens and maroons with gold leaf trim. It was stunning. Two large gas fires roared in the fireplaces at either end of the main room. John and Mary decided to sit in an overstuffed settee facing the curved, sweeping staircase to the upper floors and enjoy the ambiance while they waited for Stanley. They had not been there but a few minutes when a sinewy, athletic-looking man with grey hair and mustache descended the stairs. He looked to be about 45 or 46.

Mary grabbed John's arm. "It *is* Charlie!"

They both started to rise to greet him, but he raised his hand, palm towards them and shook his head ever so slightly from side to side. He quickly looked over the room, left and right, then moved, just as quickly to a stuffed chair located at the end of the settee on which they sat. Without a word, he picked up a local newspaper from the table in the center of the sitting group and buried his head in it.

From behind the paper, he said in a very low whisper, barely audible, "Yes, it's me. But you do not, I repeat, do not know me." John and Mary settled back into their settee and ignored this person sitting in the chair next to them.

The three sat in silence for a full two minutes. It *was* Charlie, the same Charlie MacLaine, the FBI agent with whom they'd worked in Nova Scotia, New Boston, and Vermont. He spoke again in a whisper. "Can't talk. Where are you staying?"

Mary and John carried on an animated, perhaps too animated, conversation with each other about the lovely place called The Retreat on the upper campus where they were staying.

"Gotch ya. I'll come tonight after nine." With that, Charlie threw the newspaper back on the table, got up and exited out into the Carterville winter.

* * * * * * *

Nine o'clock could not come soon enough for John and Mary, but first they had lunch with Stanley and Jane at the Faculty Club. The Faculty Club was the same three-storied, wood-shingled building the Braemhors remembered from their last trip north. The Howards had reserved a small room off the main entry hall for privacy. However, the staff asked Stanley if it would be all right to put a few faculty members in the same room, as this was a particularly busy noontime. He could hardly refuse. Professors Hollenbeck and Spento, who'd been members of a former faculty clique known as the Che, were not new to the Braemhors. When they were last at Carter University they'd met them during their investigation of the murdered faculty members.

The third member of the group who was to share the room—Professor of Political Science, Ivan Gorski— was new to them.

Consequently, Stanley, being the polite host that he was, quickly took a moment to introduce Gorski to John and Mary.

"It's good to make your acquaintance," he intoned in a deep, guttural voice. "To what do we at Carter owe your visit?"

"A holiday trip to see our old friends, the Howards," John replied.

"A holiday? Didn't I notice you in the village meeting about the crèche last night?" His questions carried an accusative tone.

"We like to see all aspects of America, even its messy politics. What about yourself?" Mary was quick to turn the tables on this man she did not take a liking to.

"Touché, madam." Gorski's smile was more of a smirk. "I, too, take an interest in American politics. And you are very perceptive; it is messy at times. But I must return to my friends at the other table." He nodded and returned to sit with Hollenbeck and Spento.

"Interesting fellow," John observed.

"He's relatively new to the faculty. Excellent teacher."

"And the campus *bon vivant*!" Jane added.

"Rumors, Jane, just rumors," Stanley cautioned.

"Well, rumors or not, he has certainly shown an inordinate interest in several faculty wives. He could easily have belonged to the Che with their reputation for fast living." Jane went on, referring to the well known group from a few years past.

"He's also very outspoken on the issues of last night's meeting." Stanley tried to deflect the direction of the conversation.

"Oh?" Mary asked.

"Oh, yes. I was surprised it was Leon Goldfarb who spoke last night rather than Gorski. I was expecting Ivan to carry the issue for the non-Christians. He's Jewish and has been the leading spokesman on issues of church and state. Known throughout the area for his outspokenness. . . . But on another subject, I understand Chief Phillips has solved the theft of the baby Jesus from the crèche."

"Oh, yes," John answered, "another social club prank. His deputy found it under a house bar and returned it this morning."

"You see, not all crimes in Carterville are at the level of violence as when you were last here." Jane smiled. "It really is a quiet, sleepy little village."

The conversation then turned to the long history of the area, as elaborated by Stanley and Jane in a most amusing and informative way. The afternoon quickly passed away until it was time for Stanley to give the Braemhors a ride to The Retreat and a quiet late afternoon in the library filled with books and religious artifacts.

"Oh, John, stop pacing. Charlie will be here. It's only a quarter to nine. Sit and read your book until he arrives," Mary chided.

John reluctantly sat and opened Samuel Butler's *Erewhon* and quickly became immersed in the early chapters' descriptions of New Zealand.

Just as Mary had predicted, a knock at their door announced Charlie MacLaine's arrival, promptly at nine.

"John, Mary, what a pleasant surprise." MacLaine held out his hands to them both. "What brings you to Carterville?"

"He sounds like Ivan Gorski," Mary observed.

"How do you know him?" Charlie was puzzled.

"Don't, really. Only just met him at lunch at the Faculty Club this afternoon. Why?" Charlie sounded as if he knew Gorski, so now it was John and Mary's turn to be puzzled. "What's Gorski to you?" John was direct.

"It's a long story, most of which I'm not free to divulge. Let's just say I've been assigned to Gorski. To find out as much as I can about him, what he does, what he believes in, who he associates with."

"An FBI assignment?" Mary asked.

"Let's just say I'm not on vacation." Charlie tried to smile away his circumspection.

"We understand he's a very outspoken advocate in the village controversy over the crèche on the village green." John tried to move the conversation along.

"That's just a façade." Charlie was very serious.

"Façade? You mean he's involved in something more serious than a passing church-state issue in a small upstate village?"

"You might say." Charlie kept his distance.

"Come on, Charlie. Loosen up a little. Maybe we can help," Mary cajoled.

"I'm not sure how." Charlie persisted in playing his cards close to the vest.

"We're close friends with Dean Howard and may be able to gather some information on the inner workings of the faculty and Gorski's place in it."

"All right. Here's what I can tell you. Gorski is a Russian Jew who came to this country about two years ago. First he had a teaching fellowship at Columbia while he looked for something more out-of-the-way, less mainstream."

"Hence, Carter University," John concluded.

"Yes, here in the upper reaches of New York State he could take on the cover of a quiet professor and drift out of the sights of anyone who might want to keep an eye on him. While it appeared to be a safe haven for him to do whatever he does, it also made our job easier. Much easier, for example, to monitor his email activity, since he uses the University's internet system—notoriously easy to hack."

"Anything there?"

"No, until about two months ago when we intercepted some very innocuous messages from a location in Maryland, near DC and the Pentagon."

"Innocuous, you say?" Mary queried.

"That was the thing. They were so innocuous we became suspicious. They were between him and his niece. The usual uncle-niece chit-chat, how much he likes his new position, what the weather is like here and how it is in the south. It was just too bland to be real. At first we wondered if the emails were in code, but so far we haven't broken it, if it is."

"Maybe they were just what they seemed—uncle-niece talk?" Mary offered.

"Except for one thing. Gorski's entire family lives in a Moscow suburb. None of them are in the U.S. . . . And, in addition, ever since he came here, the Russian intelligence service appears to be one jump ahead of our services. They seem to know what we're planning even before we know ourselves."

"So you're suggesting he's getting some sort of insider information and forwarding it through the 'niece' connection. But where would he get any international information in an out-of-the-way place like Carterville, and why can't you cut off the Gorski information at the 'niece' connection."

"We're working on that, but we don't want to cut off that avenue until we break the code—if there is one—and know the original source of *his* information.

"And that's where you come in," John conjectured.

"Yes, I'm taking his beginning course in political science as an older graduate student. So far I've gotten to know him fairly well—you saw us at the meeting together—we occasionally have an after class drink at the Carter Inn together. But it's touch and go. I don't want to try to get into his confidence too rapidly for fear he'll become suspicious. It's a slow process and one I cannot have friends involved in." Charlie's look was meaningful. "You see, if I can really get on his good side, I might even be able to feed him some false information to pass on to whoever is running him."

"How will you manage that?" Mary asked.

Charlie smiled. "That I haven't figured out yet, but I'm sure it will come to me when the time is right."

John looked up. "Who here at Carter knows you're not really a graduate student?"

"Only your dean friend and the chairman of the political science department. And now you two, of course." He paused for a moment. "I know this is going to sound odd, but for your stay here I have to ask you not to make any public acknowledgment of knowing me. I'm just another student on the campus. Totally unknown to you. Okay?"

"Easily done, Charlie. But if you can think of any way we can be of help, let us know." John concurred with MacLaine. "But where are you staying? In case we need to contact you."

Charlie smiled as he rose to leave. "Next door." He nodded in the direction of the apartment down the hall from the Braemhor's. "I'll leave a note under your door, if need be."

"What about breakfast in the morning?" Mary asked.

"Not good. I take all of my meals at the student dining hall, down the hill. I'd best be going. Got an early morning class. I'll let you know if there's anything I think you can help with." With that, Charlie exited and went down the hall to his own apartment.

"Fascinating," Mary noted.

"Indeed."

* * * * * * *

Another sumptuous American breakfast awaited the Braemhors next morning in The Retreat's dining room.

"What shall we do today?" Mary queried John.

"I thought we might see the Preston Gallery. I understand they have a fine collection of works on paper. If we can make it down the hill safely. We had more new snow overnight. Did you notice?"

Moving slowly down the hill in yet another fresh winter wonderland, the Braemhors ran into Stanley Howard, looking piqued.

"What's the matter, Stanley?" Mary inquired, responding to his distressed appearance.

"Professor Gorski missed his morning class. Most unlike him. He's always very punctual. And there's no answer at his residence in the faculty housing. I thought I'd see if I can find him."

"How did you find out?" John's curiosity was aroused.

"Your friend, MacLaine, called me. He thought it was unusual. I understand he's let you in on his little subterfuge."

"Yes, sounds like a bit of international intrigue on your campus."

"Yes, and I don't like it. We have enough intra-faculty campus intrigues on our own for my liking. I have enough trouble keeping track of my faculty without having the FBI roaming about. Well. . .the tribulations of a dean. Let's see if we can find Professor Gorski, shall we?"

The three of them walked briskly—as briskly as they could with the snow and ice underfoot—to the faculty housing on the flat, near the gallery. Stanley rapped loudly on the door to Gorski's apartment. No response. Stanley rapped even louder. Still no response.

Finally, Stanley turned to the Braemhors "I have passkeys," he said as he took a small ring of keys from his jacket pocket and inserted one into the lock.

As he started to enter, John stopped him. "Wait!" Stanley was startled and turned, frowning at John.

"Let's just touch as little as possible until we see what's inside," John cautioned. Mary immediately recognized that John's criminal investigative mode had taken hold, though she was not sure what had set it off.

"All right." Stanley was perplexed.

John slowly pushed the door open with a handkerchief around his hand. Stanley was fascinated to watch this seasoned investigator at work, though he, too, was not sure there was need for caution. After all, a professor had missed his morning class. Nothing new about that. Happens every once in a while, though not usually with Professor Gorski. Besides, Stanley had had about enough cloak and dagger with MacLaine's presence on campus. But he quietly acquiesced and followed John into the living room. Mary followed both of them.

Living room, empty. Bedroom, empty.

Stanley started into the bath. "Oh, my god!!" he shouted and backed out of the bathroom door, almost knocking over Mary, who'd followed both of them into the bedroom. She grabbed his arm and a good thing, too, for Stanley had gone faint. Fortunately, Mary was able to guide him to the edge of the bed which kept him from falling all the way to the floor.

John, who, by this time, had entered the bathroom, turned quickly to Mary, still supporting Stanley on the end of the bed. "It's not pretty," he exclaimed. Through the partially open door, Mary could see a body slumped over the bathtub and lots of blood. Though not as accustomed to such scenes as John, she was able to remain calm and ready for action.

"We need to move Stanley out of the way," John spoke crisply.

With John on one side and Mary on the other, they managed to half walk, half drag Stanley to a comfortable recliner in the living room where he could recover from the traumatic sight. Mary went into the kitchen and got him a glass of water.

John pulled out his mobile and called Chief Phillips. "Harry. We need you, an ambulance and whatever other personnel you think appropriate right away."

"What's up, John?"

"We've got a body. In the faculty housing on campus. I'll tell you more when you get here."

"A body! I'm on my way. I'll call Campus Safety. Get them to keep the curious away. Where will you be?"

"Right here in the apartment—me, Mary and Dean Howard.

It seemed an eternity before Phillips arrived with Campus Safety not far behind and the wail of an ambulance in the distance, rapidly getting louder.

While they waited, Mary comforted Stanley who sat in the chair shaking from head to foot. John went into the bathroom and ascertained that the body was indeed dead. *What a mess,* he thought.

While Campus Safety cordoned off the immediate area, Phillips came in to view the site. Even he was a little turned off by what he saw. He quickly called for state assistance and a coroner. There was little for the volunteer ambulance crew to do once the medic had ascertained that the body was, in fact, deceased, so Phillips had them check over Stanley Howard and take him to the ER for further evaluation. Fortunately, he seemed to be recovering from the shock.

John called to Mary. "Telephone Jane Howard. Tell her that Stanley will be at the emergency room at the local hospital. That he's all right. Just a bit shaken up by what he's seen. Tell her we ran across an accident and she should go to the ER and take him home."

Phillips and John went into the bathroom to inspect the body while they waited for the rest of the police personnel. It was slumped in a kneeling position by the bathtub, the head, arms and upper torso in the tub itself. Both wrists had been slit.

"Suicide?" Phillips mused.

"I think not," John said quietly. "Look at the bloody bruise on the back of his head."

"I think you're right, but we'll let the coroner pass judgment on that. What about a weapon?'

"That cast-iron dog doorstop looks to me like a good candidate." John pointed to a black and white iron doorstop shaped like a pug. "It certainly would be heavy enough."

Phillips wrapped it in a pillow case. "We'll have it dusted for prints when the lab boys get here. But tell me, John," a facetious smile crossed his face, "why is it that every time you and Mary come to Carterville, we have something like this happen?"

"It's just the dark cloud I carry with me." John returned the smile.

The coroner, a Dr. Blake, his van, and two state troopers arrived as they were talking. To Braemhor's surprise, Phillips identified the victim as Ivan Gorski to Dr. Blake.

"How did you know who the victim was?" he asked Phillips.

"It's a long story, John, but a couple of months ago I got a call from the FBI that they were interested in him and would I keep a low profile watch on him. So for the past few weeks I've been keeping tabs on him, his routines, who he pals around with, that sort of thing. Nothing out of the ordinary. Just if I note anything suspicious, to let them know. It's been pretty routine. Only thing I ever reported to them was that he was outspoken on local issues, like the crèche controversy. That's all there's been, until now. I'll have to call them as soon as I get back to the office. At any rate, that's how I got to know who he was."

John anticipated that Phillips would be hearing from the FBI as soon as Charlie got wind of this morning's events.

Blake's preliminary assessment was that Professor Gorski had been struck on the back of the head prior to his wrists being slit, but Blake did not want to be quoted until he'd finished his examination in his laboratory. By the time Dr. Blake was ready to remove the body to his van, quite a crowd of onlookers had gathered—students, University staff, and a few of the faculty who were between classes.

Charlie MacLaine was standing with the group of students, but as soon as he could he approached John, continuing in his role as a curious student, and asked, "What's going on, sir?"

John looked away from Charlie and muttered so the crowd could not hear his response, "Gorski. Dead. Blow to head. Wrists slit." He then quickly moved back to where Mary stood with Chief Phillips, who was talking with the state officers.

"Damn!!" MacLaine exclaimed, then took out his mobile and placed a call.

CHAPTER 9

John and Mary spent part of the afternoon at the Howard's home helping Stanley work through the morning trauma. He was still quite shaken by what he'd seen. Jane was almost as traumatized to see her husband in such a state of upset. But as the day wore on, and the sedative Stanley had been given in the ER wore off, he slowly overcame the shock of finding Gorski's body; Jane, in turn, calmed down as she saw her husband regaining his psychological balance. By late afternoon, equilibrium had once again descended on the Howard household, though Stanley allowed that he never again wanted to see such a scene as had passed before his eyes that morning.

In fact, by dinner time, Stanley had regained his composure to the point that he'd phoned his executive secretary at the office and dictated a memo to the University at large to be distributed as soon as he'd cleared it with Chief Phillips the next day. Fortunately, she'd already fended off the press until the next day.

John left at three o'clock to meet with Phillips to stay abreast of developing events. To his surprise, MacLaine was there, having made himself known to the chief and entered into the ongoing investigation. They had concluded that the best initial line of inquiry would be Bob Wilcox, the outspoken KKK member.

"I don't think so," John disagreed.

"Why not?" Charlie was immediately troubled by John's propensity to jump to conclusions on a scant amount of data.

"He's too obvious. Too outspoken. The KKK is a hate group, but they're not stupid. From his speech the other night, Wilcox will know that he'll be a prime suspect. My guess is that he'll have a very tight accounting of his time last night and early this morning already prepared. Are there any international possibilities that should be explored?" He looked directly at Charlie.

"Probably. I alerted home office. They can check out those possibilities. And a search of Gorski's apartment might turn up something. But, damn it, John, I was right on the verge of getting somewhere with Gorski. I had gotten his confidence as one of his students, and I think given another week or two I might have learned more about his source of information, as well as his contact in DC. And then some idiot—KKK or otherwise—has to mess everything up. It's frustrating to say the least. Oh, well, the best laid plans. . . . Now we've got to find out who screwed us up and why. Other possibilities, John, Harry?"

Both shook their heads.

"I'll get on Wilcox and we'll see where we get," Phillips said.

"And I'll see if the student population is of any help," MacLaine added.

"Let's meet tomorrow afternoon and see where we stand," Braemhor concluded.

* * * * * * *

Next morning Stanley called the Braemhors and invited them to lunch at the Faculty Club. He also informed them that one of the speakers at the village meeting, Leon Goldfarb, had been found in the back of his shop in the village, badly beaten. Nazi swastikas had been painted on the front door of his shop. John called Phillips.

"Understand you have an assault crime on your hands, too."

"John, this is turning out to be a very bad couple of days, but at least we know where Wilcox was last night."

"Oh?"

"He was at Goldfarb's shop taking out his hate on the poor gentleman."

"I can't believe he was that stupid."

"It's worse than you might imagine. He took two of his less-than-bright bully boys with him and one of them was so scared when we picked them up, he owned up to the beating before I could even apply the thumbscrew." John could hear Phillips chuckling in the background.

"Well, at least you're two for three." John added up the crime tally sheet.

"How's that?" Phillips was mildly perplexed.

"You've solved the crèche robbery and the personal assault case. Not a bad day's work, I'd say."

"I see what you mean, but that still leaves us with the big one—the murder—and one of our prime suspects has a watertight alibi, beating up an old man. Any ideas yet?"

"I wouldn't count Wilcox out quite yet, Harry. Couldn't he or his henchmen have done both?"

"Possibly, but as easily as his buddy threw in the towel on the beating. . . ."

"Maybe. Maybe. Well, give me a little time to see what I can come up with. Any word from MacLaine on a possible international connection?"

"Not yet. I'll let you know." And Phillips rang off.

John turned to Mary who'd come upstairs for breakfast. "Carterville is quite a den of crime." He told

Mary about Goldfarb and Phillips's good fortune getting a quick resolution to that one.

"However, we're no further along on the Gorski murder. Phillips thinks that Wilcox's participation in the Goldfarb beating eliminates him as a suspect in the Gorski affair, so we're down to nothing, unless Charlie can come up with some sort of international connection."

"Couldn't Wilcox have done both?" Mary quickly asked.

"Same thing I said to Phillips. He had all night and the early part of the morning to both attack Goldfarb and murder Gorski." Braemhor marveled, as he always did, at the thought patterns he and Mary shared.

"Well, the chief must be feeling very proud, solving two out of three." Mary again echoed John's thinking.

"He is, but the big one is still eluding us. Oh, by the way, Stanley wants us to meet him at the Faculty Club for lunch. Should just about give us time to see the Preston Gallery before that."

By midmorning the Braemhors had made their way down the hill to the Preston Art Gallery to view the university's fine collection of works on paper. To their pleasant surprise, the gallery also contained a traveling exhibition of oils by Vermont painters, chiefly Emile Gruppé, whose landscapes particularly caught Mary's eye. Mary was surprised that John agreed to take time from the investigation to see the art displays. As they walked through the galleries, she asked John about it.

"I decided to give my brain a rest. Right now we seem to be in a blind alley, unless Wilcox and his boys did do all of the mischief last night. Somehow I don't think so. There's got to be another player in this murder drama, and I. . . ! That's it, Mary, I think I know where to look."

"What do you mean, John?"

"Something Stanley said at lunch yesterday. Maybe Gorski's murder isn't anything as exotic as international intrigue or even a local cultural clash. Maybe it's more down to earth. Remember he said Gorski was a campus *bon vivant*?"

"Yes, so we're looking for an irate husband?" Mary asked.

"Mary, your deductive powers are excellent." John squeezed her hand as they hurried along the snow covered paths to the Faculty Club.

Stanley and Jane Howard arrived before the Braemhors at the Faculty Club. This time Stanley did not reserve a small side room, but he and Jane sat in the main dining room at a large table with several other faculty members. Stanley quickly introduced John and Mary around so that all present got to meet the visiting couple from Scotland, but their reputation had preceded them.

"So you're the couple that helped solve the Che murders when you were last here." A tall red-headed political scientist greeted them.

"We helped Chief Phillips a bit last time, yes."

"Seems to me he's going to need more help this trip," observed a diminutive woman in her mid-sixties. She was the chairperson of the French department.

"Do you have any leads yet?" a dark little man at the corner of the table muttered.

"I don't think Chief Phillips has many substantial leads as yet, but it's hardly been 24 hours since the discovery of Professor Gorski." John tried to show his questioners that the investigation was clearly Phillips's investigation, and that he and Mary were playing only minor supporting roles. Try as he, Mary, Stanley and Jane might, they could not turn the conversation away from Gorski's demise. Talk about it pervaded the campus and particularly the Faculty Club. The entire lunch was consumed with questions and assumptions about the murder and who might have perpetrated it.

Though a number at the table were only interested in the gory details of the event, Stanley, John and Mary said very little, keeping their remarks circumspect if not downright evasive, frustrating all except the dark man at the corner who finally announced, "It served him right! He was always messing about in other people's lives. I'm surprised it took so long."

"You didn't like him, Professor. . .?"

"Hauff, John Hauff. German. No, I did not. And I can't say I'm sad to see him go. He was perfectly abominable to one of my staff."

Since most of Stanley's fellow faculty members at the table had departed for afternoon class obligations, John quickly took the empty chair next to Professor Hauff and quietly asked, "What did he do?"

Hauff moved back several feet as he was obviously uncomfortable with Braemhor invading his space. "He. . .He was making advances towards my youngest faculty member's wife—Silvia Mattson. I warned him. Warned her, too. That Gorski was up to no good."

"How did they respond to your warnings?"

"Everett—that's Sylvia's husband—was quite incensed, but I think she was intrigued by the approaches of an older man. I think she quite welcomed his attention. Ach! The frivolity of youth."

"Why are you so interested?" John persisted.

"Because Gorski was upsetting one of my younger and best faculty. The strain on Everett Mattson's teaching was becoming evident. Even his students noticed." Hauff looked at his watch. "Ach! It's time for my senior seminar. I must leave you, Mr. Braemhor. Perhaps we'll see each other again." With that, Hauff exited the club.

Before he returned to the other end of the table where Mary, Jane and Stanley had been having a lighter conversation, mainly about the Preston Gallery, John quietly wrapped Hauff's knife in a serviette and put it in his jacket pocket. He asked Stanley, "What can you tell me about Professor Hauff?"

"He's near retirement as the chairman of our German department. Typical German of his era. Somewhat pedantic. Likes things to run smoothly, always. Runs a very tight ship in his department. He's not gotten along well with Gorski from the beginning, but that's a hangover from his war experiences."

"War experiences?" John asked.

"Yes, he was a child in Berlin when the Russians came in at the end of World War II. His father fought on the Russian front, was wounded and captured there, just before the end of the German campaign. He was one of many held in Russian prisons long after hostilities had ceased. Took him over three and a half years to get home. Of course, he was one of the lucky ones. He did get home and was able to carry on his life. But Hauff never forgot the treatment his father had received in the prison camps and that he and his family received during the Russian occupation."

"And what about Professor Mattson?"

"Excellent German professor, but of late he's been increasingly distracted, seems to have more on his mind than his students and his course materials."

"You know why, don't you?" Jane interjected.

Stanley raised his eyebrows, but Jane continued, "Professor Gorski was making advances on his wife.

Whole campus knew, except him of course. I think he found out and was very distressed about it."

"Where do the Mattsons live?" John asked.

"They have the apartment just down the hall from Professor Gorski in the faculty housing."

John gave a meaningful look to Mary, who, catching his meaning, said, "Oh, John, look it's almost two and I did so want to finish exploring the Preston before suppertime."

John smiled faintly. "Looks like the culture of art is calling. We'd best be going."

"Maybe supper tomorrow at our house?" Stanley invited.

"We'd like that. Jane, maybe we can talk more about the Vermont artists then," Mary said.

"Where to now, John?" was Mary's mildly perplexed question after they'd gotten outside of the Faculty Club.

"If I can contact Harry, I think we might visit the Mattsons at their apartment." He punched Phillips's number into his mobile.

"This is Chief Phillips." The gruff voice reached Braemhor.

"Harry, have you interviewed all of the people living near Gorski's apartment yet?"

"Some of them, but not all. It's only been 24 hours." Phillips voice was showing irritation.

"I know, Harry. Sorry, but I think I may have a lead. Can you meet Mary and me at Gorski's apartment. I think it might be prudent to interview a couple named Mattson who live down the hall. I can fill you in when you get here."

"I'll be there in about ten minutes."

Phillip's police cruiser pulled up quietly, but immediately attracted a crowd of students. The chief spent the next ten or fifteen minutes dispersing the gathering, assuring them that there was nothing new about Professor Gorski, that this was just a routine part of the ongoing investigation. Finally, they believed him and left.

Immediately, John told Phillips of his luncheon conversations. "It sounds to me that Mattson would clearly have a motive for murdering Gorski. Irate husbands can become pretty irrational. So I thought we might make some headway by talking with Mattson and his wife. Any word from MacLaine?"

"Haven't seen him yet today. I assume he'll get in touch if he has anything." The chief rapped heavily on the Mattson's door which oddly swung slightly open at the force of his knocking. Phillips turned, looked at the Braemhors and frowned. He called out as he entered cautiously, John and Mary right behind him. It was deathly quiet inside. No one was in either the living/dining area or the studio kitchen. He and John went into the bedroom. Phillips shook his head as he observed, "John, we've got another one." He put in a call for additional officers and, again, the coroner and the lab crew.

Mrs. Mattson was on her back on the bed, staring glassily at the ceiling. Her smock was torn, and there were obvious bruise marks on her arms and at the base of her neck.

"Irate husband?" Mary asked as she entered the room.

"Certainly a possibility," John responded as Phillips went to the living/dining area to close the front door.

When he returned, Phillips gave John another of his sardonic smiles and said, "John why don't you go back to Scotland and take that dark cloud with you?"

"As soon as you wrap up these cases."

It was almost five o'clock by the time the coroner had completed his work. Mrs. Mattson's body had been removed to the county morgue, and the apartment had been thoroughly dusted for prints and other clues to determine what had taken place. Campus Security had quickly cordoned off the area and held the curious, who were now drifting off to their own evening meals, at bay. Phillips had also put out an APB on Professor Mattson, in the hopes of finding him before he got too far away.

Stanley Howard arrived shortly after the coroner and was showing the strain the day was taking on his usual relaxed demeanor. He was looking haggard and drawn. He almost pleaded to John and Mary for support, "John, Mary, what is happening to my faculty? First Gorski. Now Mattson's wife." He was almost in tears.

"We'll try to get to the bottom of all of this as soon as possible." John tried to console Stanley, but his words were falling on deaf ears.

"It was bad enough with the Che murders, but at least they occurred over a period of years. But this. My god! Gorski this morning! Silvia this afternoon! Who's next?!"

"It's not your fault." Mary tried to comfort him.

"Oh, I know. I know. But I'm watching my faculty fall apart before my eyes." Stanley's shoulders shuddered. Fortunately, Jane arrived about that time and took Stanley back to his office where he could dictate the appropriate memos and letters. He had had the foresight to ask his executive secretary to stay on past her usual leaving time.

Shortly after Stanley and Jane left, Phillips joined John and Mary. "Good news! We got Mattson. At the local bus station. He was getting on a Trailways to the city. This should make things move along faster and smoother, I hope. I'll call you in the morning and let you know what's going on."

"Still no MacLaine?" John asked.

"Still no MacLaine," Phillips said as he turned to leave.

* * * * * * *

The call came early next morning. It was Chief Phillips wanting to speak to John.

"Good news and bad news," he announced.

"Give me the good first," John answered.

"Mattson disintegrated under questioning. Admitted strangling Mrs. Mattson in a fit of pique, but claims no responsibility for the Gorski murder, though he allowed that he was not sorry to hear what had happened to him. And, John, I have to agree with him. We've compared all of the prints we lifted from Gorski's apartment, and none of them match Mattson's. So that's the bad news. We've still got the Gorski murder on our hands and no leads. What a pain!!"

"I may be able to ease your pain," John spoke calmly.

"Oh?"

"Yes. Come up to The Retreat and have coffee with Mary and me and I'll explain."

Fifteen minutes later, the three of them were enjoying Mrs. Parker's coffee in the dining space off of The Retreat library.

"What have you got this time, John?"

"This." He handed Phillips the dinner knife from the Faculty Club still securely wrapped in a serviette. "You see, I too thought that the most likely candidate for the Gorski murder was young Mattson. I never really considered Wilcox and his crew a viable choice. Though they knew of Gorski for his local outspokenness, they are too much 'baddies'—as MacLaine calls them—of the moment. Had they thought about it, Gorski might have also been a target for their hate, but it was Goldfarb who spoke up at the meeting the other night. They concentrated on Goldfarb and forgot about Gorski's liberal views.

"Mattson was another matter. As Mary said, 'irate husband' and all that implied. So when we found Silvia Mattson's body, I thought her husband had probably killed her—I was right. But I also thought he had murdered Gorski. Now you've proven that prediction wrong. But yesterday at the Faculty Club, I hedged my bets. Another faculty member may have had just as much reason to see Gorski out of the way."

"Who?" Phillips was all ears.

"Professor Hauff, chairman of the German department."

"Why him?"

"First, Gorski was disturbing the peace and the efficient functioning of his department. Hauff is a stickler for having everything he runs go smoothly, and the more Gorski leaned on Silvia Mattson, the more distressed Everett Mattson became and the less efficient he was in his teaching duties. Reflected badly on Hauff's department.

"Second, there has been bad blood between Gorski and Hauff ever since Gorski arrived. You see, Hauff hates Russians because of the way they treated his father in their prison camps at the end of World War II and the way they treated him and his family in Berlin during the occupation.

"Consequently, I took the precaution of purloining Professor Hauff's dinner knife during lunch yesterday and held it in case the Mattson assumption did not prove correct. Since the Mattson/Gorski case has crumbled, I'm glad I did. See if the prints on the knife don't match some of those in Gorski's apartment. If so, then you've solved another case." John smiled.

"Thank you, John." Phillips beamed.

"Don't thank me until you have a match, then we can chalk it up to cooperative police work."

"More coffee?" Mary interjected midst her pride in her husband's investigative acumen.

Just before Stanley was to pick up the Braemhors for supper, MacLaine tapped on their door.

"Well, Charlie, any news on the international front?"

"None." MacLaine was disgruntled. "My guys still have nothing."

As John was explaining to MacLaine what had transpired with the Mattsons and his hope that the Hauff prints might be a help to Phillips, Phillips himself came down the stairs to the apartment level of The Retreat. His face showed that the news was good.

"You were right, John, the prints on the cast iron dog and elsewhere in Gorski's apartment were Hauff's and when confronted with the evidence, he agreed not to contest the charge of Gorski's murder. Once more I'm in your debt and I didn't mean that comment about you going back to Scotland."

"I know that, Harry. We just work well together." John was pleased, too, that his assumptions proved accurate.

MacLaine, too, was pleased to see the case resolved and his old friend, John Braemhor, receiving due recognition. He put his hand on John's shoulder, turned to Phillips and said, "He's a good man to have on your side when the going gets tough."

"I guess it's time for me to go back to my Utah haunts," MacLaine continued. "John, Mary, it's always a pleasure to see and work with you. Maybe someday we can just have a vacation together." Charlie left to go pack for his trip home where he would await his next FBI assignment.

As Phillips was leaving, Stanley arrived to pick up his supper guests. The evening was spent eating Jane's sumptuous meal and tying all of the details of the last few exciting days together.

Just before the Braemhors went back to The Retreat, Mary asked, "By the way is Professor Edwards on campus?"

"Ah, our resident hypnosis researcher? No, he's on leave this semester, and he'll be taking our Edinburgh study group in psychology this spring. Why do you ask?" Stanley queried.

"We bought two of his books in Fort Ewen in the Highlands earlier in the year and thought it would be interesting to meet him."

"Oh, he's an interesting fellow. Maybe he'll be here on your next trip." Stanley offered an oblique invitation to visit Carter University again.

"Or maybe we can seek him out in Edinburgh," John suggested.

CHAPTER 10

The trip back to New Boston was uneventful and after another ten days with James, Jennifer and the grandchildren, the Braemhors returned to Daraichburn and the comforts of Dunmoor Cottage.

Aunt Rita greeted them at the door and informed them that all was quiet at the cottage while they were away.

"The fairies didn't once make a sound or do their dance," Rita informed them with her customary twinkle. "And I would have heard them with my new hearing aids," she announced firmly.

"That's good, Aunt Rita," Mary said as she hugged her aunt. "I'm glad that it was quiet for you."

"I fixed a shepherd's pie for your homecoming. It should be just about ready." Rita led them into the kitchen where she had a table set for a scrumptious Scottish meal.

"I took a little coach ride Sunday," Rita suddenly announced while they were eating.

"Where did you go?" Mary asked between mouthfuls.

"To Beggar's Knob. They have an artists' colony there and since John has taken up painting, I thought I'd see what other artists are doing. I bought you a picture," Rita proudly stated, as she unwrapped the package by her chair.

"Oh, Aunt Rita, you shouldn't have done. . . . Why Aunt Rita, it's beautiful! And you got it just down the road?" The painting was of a woodland scene along a dirt road with trees and low foliage, a typical Scottish stone roadside wall and a small pristine lake just beyond the berm.

"It really is!" John concurred, quite taken by the artistry displayed in the image. "That was very thoughtful of you, Rita. I think it will go very well above our fireplace in the sitting room. Don't you think, Mary?"

"I do indeed! Let's see how it will look." Mary took the painting into the sitting room and placed it on the mantle. All the while Rita was grinning from ear to ear with pride at the reception of her gift. She couldn't have been happier.

"I think it goes there very well." Mary assessed the painting's placement. "From the artists' colony at Beggar's Knob?"

"Yes, and they have a lot of other artists' shops and galleries there." Rita glowed.

"Maybe we should go tomorrow and see what else they have."

"Oh, I'd like that. Maybe I can find something for the castle." Rita was referring to Dunmoor Castle, Mary's ancestral home near Blanefield.

"A good thought, Aunt Rita," Mary agreed. "Let's plan on a day trip tomorrow. All right, John?"

"I think that's a fine idea."

In their room later, after having unpacked from their trip, John offered an observation.

"I think I've seen that place in the painting."

"Oh, where?" Mary asked as she turned down the coverlet on their bed.

"If I'm not mistaken, it's just down a small side road off of the B712 towards Bigger. I saw it one time when I was searching for landscapes to paint. Thought it was just about a perfect view to render onto a canvas. Sorry I didn't do it, when I first saw it. Well, it's nice to know that I have an eye similar to the professional artists."

"You know, John, you have more artistic talent than you let yourself believe."

"Flattery will get you everywhere." John smiled as he turned out the light.

* * * * * * *

The ride to Beggar's Knob was short, only about 13 kilometers, and all three were in high spirits—Rita because of the obvious delight John and Mary found in the painting she'd bought them, John and Mary because it was so comfortable to be back in their own haunts again after an exciting, but tiring holiday in the snow covered Colonies. Even nature seemed to bless the excursion with the usual cold, misty precipitation they loved so much about winter in their native Scotland.

Beggar's Knob was a small village at the crossroad of two minor highways. The roofs of the cottages were thatched, with the walls washed in bright colors—reds, yellows, greens, blues. The shops were clustered along the main streets of the intersection. Almost all were galleries of individual painters, though one was a co-op containing the works of several artists.

"Where did you buy the painting, Rita?" John asked.

"At the Tawell Gallery, next to the co-op." Rita pointed.

"We should start there, then," Mary said. John parked the Vauxhall.

The Tawell Gallery was one of the larger shops on the street, painted a lush green with gold trim about the entry. Inside, all four walls were covered with paintings of various sizes and subject matter. There were landscapes, seascapes, still lifes, and a few portraits.

"Can I be of assistance?" The thin man behind the desk against the back wall spoke with an equally thin voice. He wore a sharply pointed white goatee and carefully crafted white mustache. Cascading down over his broad, pale forehead was a well-managed, wavy head of bushy white hair. His hair and facial growth belied his age, for all else about him spoke of a man in his early thirties.

"Ah, Ms. Erskine, so good to see you again." The proprietor recognized Rita from her last visit and came forward, his hand extended to her in greeting. "Back for more paintings. . .I hope?" A broad smile lit his face.

Rita was delighted to be recognized. "Maybe. Maybe." She beamed. "These are my niece and nephew. Mary, John, this is Mr. Tawell. He painted that lovely picture I gave you."

"You have a great deal of talent, Mr. Tawell." Mary greeted the artist.

"Thank you. That's most kind. I try to render scenes as I see them, not necessarily as they are."

"That must take an unusual degree of skill." John joined the conversation.

"Skill or good fortune, I don't know which." Tawell was flattered.

"Do you ever revisit the landscapes you've painted?" John asked.

"Oh, dear, no. Unlike Monet and his grain stacks, I don't revisit the scenes of my crimes." He chuckled. "Once I have the view on my canvas I bring it home here to the gallery and never go back."

"Are your landscapes of local areas? I thought I recognized the scene Rita bought." John strolled in front of the wall of landscapes.

"Quite a few. Quite a few. Most, I'd say. Within a few kilometers of the gallery, more or less. Mostly off on side roads and paths where few travelers go."

At that moment, a couple—clearly Americans by their dress and accents—entered the gallery. "Oh, look, Bill, here's a picture of the pottery we just saw." She pointed to a bright white and yellow painting of a young woman bending over a large unfired clay bowl."

"Yes, but I don't remember the young woman."

"Maybe it was her day off," she offered. "But that sure is the pottery we just saw."

Meanwhile, John gathered Mary and Rita and headed them toward the door. He turned and waved to Mr. Tawell. "Perhaps we'll come back later."

"Please do. Enjoy the rest of your travel." He turned to the Americans to offer them any assistance they might require.

Outside, John turned to Mary and Rita. "Odd, don't you think? Mr. Tawell looked very young, except for his facial hair and the great shock of white hair on his head. Did you look at his skin? It was the skin of a 20- or-30-year-old."

"And pale," Rita added. "Reminded me of a ghost."

"Well, we can't all be so robust and mature as John." Mary smiled.

"I'm serious, Mary." Rita did not share Mary's levity. "He scares me—though he seems very nice—did the first time I was here, when I bought the picture. Just something about him."

"I agree with Rita," John added. "I know that name—Tawell—from somewhere in the past. Can't quite put my finger on it. . . . Oh, well. What about some lunch?" John broke the trend of the conversation.

"There's a tearoom across the street," Mary observed. "Maybe we could get a bite there."

"Excellent! Then we can explore more of the galleries after lunch," John suggested.

The afternoon was spent perusing other galleries in Beggar's Knob. There were five or six in the space of a few blocks from the main intersection. Most seemed to specialize in a particular subject, one offered mostly seascapes; another dwelt on still life, mostly fruit and flowers; one had a whole wall devoted to people engaged in various trades and crafts—barber, cheese maker, tatter, potter, slate cutter, porcelain decorator, hairdresser, farmer, even a painter at work on a portrait of a small child. A smaller gallery—the Greene Gallery—down the street on the same side from the Tawell Gallery seemed to specialize in landscapes.

"Oh. Look," Rita exclaimed as they entered the shop, "here's the same scene Mr. Tawell painted."

"You're right, Rita," John agreed, "but not nearly as well-done." He made the last statement under his breath as he stood near Rita and Mary. He did not want to offend the artist, who was standing by the opposite wall arranging paintings.

"Help you?"

"Are your landscapes local?" Mary asked.

"Oh, yes, most of us in the colony paint locally, or mainly. And the scenery around Beggar's Knob lends itself so well to artistry." The proprietor was an older man. Somewhat bent with age. His skin had the look of an outdoorsman, dark and lined with sun damage. His hands, John noted, were gnarled and twisted with arthritis.

"This scene seems particularly popular." Mary pointed to the picture Rita had noted when they first entered the gallery.

"Oh, yes, most of us have painted the same scenes at one time or another."

"We saw one at the Tawell Gallery," John said.

"Oh, yes, James Tawell's place. He's a newcomer. Came in only last year and opened up his gallery. Very talented, but very possessive."

"Possessive?"

"I shouldn't say this, but Jim seems to feel that the scenes he paints belong to him. He actually gets a little offended when he sees something similar to what he's painted. That one, for instance. He really took umbrage that I'd painted it before he did—I did mine a couple of years ago. Even offered to buy it from me. Reduce the competition, I guess. Odd fellow, that, but nice enough if you don't paint the same scenes he has." Mr. Greene chuckled. "I guess we artists are all a little odd."

"Is there a lot of competition?" Mary asked.

"Not really. In the main, we're a sociable lot. Oh, there are some petty jealousies, but you have them in any group. Some of our younger members are always a little jealous of newcomers, of course. Geoffrey Lawrence, for example, took a particular dislike to James Tawell when he arrived. Don't know why, but he always seemed to be competing with Jim. There has always seemed to be bad blood between the two of them. Geoff has his gallery across the street there." He pointed.

"Of course, I guess Tawell feels a little left out, seeing as he's the newest in the area. Give him another ten years and he'll be accepted as one of the old guard." Greene chuckled again. "Can I interest you in anything?"

"Not today, thanks," Mary answered. "We're just browsing. But we live nearby, so it's an easy trip back to your shop."

"All right, then. If you'll excuse me, I'll continue my straightening up." Greene went back to adjusting the paintings on the opposite wall.

"Let's see if we can find this ubiquitous landscape that I saw before," John stated. "See if it's as pretty as Tawell painted it. We can still be back at the cottage before supper."

From the B712 he turned north on the same dirt side road that had led him last spring to the scene depicted in the painting Rita had just bought. The twisting road slowed their speed by more than half, but no matter, as the three travelers were in no hurry. Suddenly, after a ninety degree turn followed by another ninety degree in the opposite direction, John pulled onto the verge and announced, "Here it is." He set the brake and turned off the engine.

"Here is what?" Rita exclaimed.

"The scene in the painting you gave us," he responded.

"I don't see it," Rita said.

"Neither do I," Mary concurred.

"You're right, but I'm sure this is where it was." John looked in puzzlement. Before him was the stonewall that had been rendered in the picture, the trees and the low bushes. But the beauty was not the same. "It looks so dead," he observed.

"Of course, John, it's winter," Mary suggested.

"It's not that," John protested. "Granted the trees are leafless and there's not much in the way of foliage and grass, but it's more than that. Everything looks *dead*."

He was right. Even in winter, there remains life in the Scottish rural scenery. The view that the three now stood before was not just shorn of the verdant splendor of spring and summer. It was barren in the extreme. The browns were closer to a decayed grey with specks of black dispersed throughout. The stones of the wall were lichen covered as never before. The lake itself had taken on the appearance of a bog with broken and stubby tree trunks rising ghost-like from the putrid looking slime. And the conifers were brown, not the muted dark green of an ordinary winter. Enveloping the scene was the look and feel of deterioration, and John had correctly characterized it, *death*. It was as if John, Mary, and Rita had left their normal spatial dimension and stepped into a different, unreal, two-dimensional achromatic space. It seemed also as if the temperature had decreased by ten degrees.

"Strange," John observed, "it was so beautiful and alive when I was here before."

"And in the painting I bought you," Rita observed.

"Even stranger, John. Look up the road ahead and the road we just travelled," Mary pointed out. Sure enough, the area covered by the painting was distinctly different from the rest of the scene. Behind and ahead was the normal winter scenery. The conifers were in full splendor and the deciduous trees, though stripped of leaves, retained the muted coloration of sleeping giants, not shriveled and dead remnants. The morbid scene before them was very circumscribed as if carved out by a giant hand. And only to the extent of the scene depicted in the painting. All else around was as it should be.

"What do you make of it, John?" Mary asked.

"I don't know what to make of it. It looks as if that particular area has been poisoned or burned over. Like someone or something was determined to destroy the beauty that was once there."

"Maybe the fairies did it," Rita offered just enough levity to bring laughter back to the otherwise somber scene.

"I doubt it, Rita," John responded.

"Why not?" Rita did not want her idea so summarily dismissed.

Through his chuckles, John answered, "Because they didn't leave themselves any space to dance."

"We passed a small pub on the 712. Maybe the proprietor can help us understand better what happened here," John suggested as the three got back into the Vauxhall. "It's too cold to stay here."

Once back in the car, with the heater warming their frost-burned faces and hands, John turned the car around and went back to the B712 where they soon found the Yellow Finch Wayside Pub.

John parked in front of the pub. "Would you like some tea while we see what information we can gather?"

"Good idea," Mary agreed. They went into the pub and ordered some tea and afternoon scones.

The Yellow Finch was tiny, a diminutive oak bar before which stood three small tables with wire-backed Coca Cola chairs. "Quaint," Rita noted.

When the waitress brought their orders, John opened the conversation with, "We just drove down the dirt road off the 712. What happened by the lake?"

"Oh, you noticed, too. Everybody asks. Ve don't have da foggiest." She was a round, pleasant person with her blond hair pulled back in a German style bun to match her accent. "Vone day, tree veeks ago or so, it vas a beautiful voodland scene mit big green evergreens unt low bracken on 'tother side of da vall. Now it's vhat you just seen. Scary like. Looks like everyting just died."

"It happened suddenly?" Mary joined the conversation.

"Quick like. Veek or so. I live just beyond the curve by da lake. I'm not sure I vant to vork here anymore. Might go home."

"To Germany?" Mary queried.

"Ja, unt not too soon. At least dere ve know vhat does tese tings."

"Oh?" Mary said.

"Ja, in da old country it vas da Beast of da Vood, it vas." She set their tea and scones down and hurried back to the kitchen behind the bar.

"Seems to scare the locals," John observed just as a large well-fed dark-haired man in a chef's apron stepped from behind the bar and approached the table.

"You've seen our local mystery?" He smiled. "What brought you to that out-of-the-way place?" He was wiping his hands on a somewhat soiled dishcloth.

Mary answered. "We bought a painting at Beggar's Knob of that scenic view and drove around looking for it. It was quite a shock when we found it. Do you have any idea what happened?"

"Not at all. Like Uta—that's my waitress—said, it was very sudden. Couple of weeks. Scared her pretty bad, I'm 'fraid. I called the Forestry Commission, but they were no help. Sent a couple of their foresters to look at it, but they were as puzzled as we were." He paused for a moment and then, having ascertained that Rita and the Braemhors were nothing more than Scots on holiday, abruptly said, "Well, gotta get back to me bakin'. Enjoy your tea."

* * * * * * *

The trip from the Yellow Finch to Dunmoor Cottage was initially made in silence, Rita enjoying the beautiful scenery, Mary and John pondering the sight of desolation they'd just left.

"How can that be?" John opened the conversation. "The lake view from the road was more like a moonscape than the Scottish lowlands. It looked as if it had been burned to destruction . . . and yet there was no scorching on the ground or the tree trunks. I don't think it was the 'Beast of the Wood.'"

"Could someone have sprayed it with a herbicide?" Mary asked, "and if so, why?"

But, as always, Dunmoore Cottage welcomed the Braemhors and Rita home with its cozy warmth, further enhanced when John lighted a peat fire in the sitting room.

After a hardy supper, the three settled into the sitting room, Rita reading the day's newspaper and John and Mary catching up on the post that had accumulated while they were away. Since John and Mary were still fatigued from the overseas travel and the day in Beggar's Knob had been tiring, they and Rita all retired early.

In their room, Mary continued to deal with the collected post while John started reading through the newspapers that had arrived while they were away. Suddenly, he took particular notice of a small news story on the back page of a two-week old paper.

"Look at this, Mary," he exclaimed and pointed to the article.

"What is it, John?"

"Says that the Forestry Commission is investigating a number of rural sites where it appears the foliage has unaccountably died back. They have no idea what has happened. Nor do the local farmers. The particular areas appeared healthy, and then within a week or two, the ground cover and trees turned brown as if struck by some sort of blight, although they were not aware of any in the area. Their teams of investigators have as yet to offer a plausible explanation. All of the blighted areas are within five kilometers of Beggar's Knob!

"This sounds exactly like what we saw yesterday. I want to go back to Beggar's Knob."

"We've got guests coming in tomorrow evening, John."

"Rita could watch the cottage for us."

"That will be fine except that if she learns we're on another investigative excursion, she'll be crestfallen." Mary did not like leaving Rita out.

"This may not be another adventure. Maybe there's a logical explanation for what we've seen today and what is described in this news item"

"But you doubt it." Mary smiled in the darkness of their room.

"Yes," John admitted, "but I think, in deference to Rita, we'll just have to delay the trip back to Beggar's Knob for a day or two."

"That's all right. It will give us time to straighten up from our visit to the grandchildren, and you can see if there's anything more in the old newspapers about Beggar's Knob."

John, seeing the wisdom of keeping Rita involved, agreed to the delay, and Mary was very appreciative of her husband's flexibility. They always worked so well together and she knew that usually there was no distracting him when he was on the scent of another mystery.

"Thank you, John. I do hate to disappoint her."

"I know, and it's not like this is a matter of life and death—yet."

* * * * * * *

While Mary with Rita's help got the cottage ready for guests, John perused the papers, and having found nothing more about dead landscapes, decided to pay a call to the Forestry Commission office nearby in Melrose.

"I'll be back for lunch," he told Mary.

When Braemhor made his interest in the landscape destruction known, he was ushered into the office of Charles Greenhagen, district forester at the commission station. Greenhagen was a large man with a genial nature who immediately took a liking to this interested citizen. His ample abdomen challenged the buttons on his green forester shirt to do their job. John introduced himself and explained that his interest in the newspaper article about Beggar's Knob was aroused by the fact that he and Mary had seen one of the damaged areas off of the 712. He wondered if their investigations had led to a logical explanation for the destruction.

"Not as yet," Forester Greenhagen admitted.

"What do you think happened?"

Greenhagen smiled. "We're not sure ourselves. The locals want to blame it on something called the Beast of the Wood."

He's talked to Uta, John thought.

"But we think it's more prosaic than that. Possibly some sort of herbicide was used on the areas. The destruction is pretty complete."

"Will it grow back?"

"Oh, eventually, but it might take several seasons. What puzzles us is why anyone would do such a thing. Pure and simple vandalism."

"Maybe not too simple."

"What do you mean?"

Braemhor explained his background as a retired investigator and that he gets involved occasionally when a particular event or happening captures his attention. "If you wouldn't mind too much, I'd like to look around a bit and see what I can find. Unofficially, of course."

"Help yourself all you want, Mr. Braemhor—unofficially and cost free." Greenhagen smiled even more broadly. "We're happy to get any assistance we can from the local citizenry. But I can't openly condone whatever snooping you might do. Here's my card in case you find anything."

"Fair enough." John was irritated by Greenhagen's turn of phrase—"snooping"—but contained himself in deference to gathering more information. "Before I go, where are the other areas you're investigating? I'd like to see as many as I can."

Greenhagen stapled a printed list to his card before he gave it to Braemhor. "Let me know if you find anything." He smiled again.

* * * * * * *

When John got back to the cottage, he immediately took out a map of the local area and began comparing it with the list Greenhagen had given him. Sure enough, all of the areas of landscape destruction were within five kilometers of Beggar's Knob. He marked each locale on the map and mentally prepared the route to take when they went back to the area.

Two days later, after the last of their B&B guests had left, the Braemhors and Rita headed west to seek out the areas on Greenhagen's list.

Looking for the obscure, out-of-the-way places was not easy. Finally, they found the first on a narrow, two rut byway just north of the village. Near a layby was a little used path leading into a thickly wooded area, except that none of the trees and undergrowth showed any signs of life. The conifers were brown and shorn of their needles and the undergrowth was a brownish grey.

"Looks just like what we saw the other day," Mary observed while John took a picture of the scene.

I wonder if all these scenes look like this, John thought.

For the next hour and a half, the threesome slowly motored around the area and found all five similar, dead-looking landscapes. Each was narrow and not very deep, much as one might see in a painting of the view. All had an ashen brown appearance in which no live foliage was to be seen. John took pictures of all the areas. Down a path from one such scene a man in heavy tweeds, with a hemlock walking staff was exercising two dogs.

"What happened here?" John asked, pointing to the dead space.

"Don't know. One day it was a pretty little patch, a week later it was just as you see it now. Wasn't always that way. Now me dogs shy away every time we come by. They used to like to play in the grassy area, but no more. Strange."

"Did you notice anything odd about the area? Any activity nearby?"

"No. Only that painter fellow. He used to paint pictures of this area. Now, he don't come back anymore."

"How long was he here?" Maybe what the man had seen was important.

"'Bout a week. He painted every day. Everything was fine. Then he finished his painting and went away, and within a week everything turned grey."

"Before he went away or after?" John thought the timing might be important.

"Like I said, all the time he was painting it looked fine. He went away and by the next week it changed to what you see. What do you want to know for? You from the government?"

"No, no, just interested travelers," John reassured the man.

"Well, there are another couple of places just like this up the road." He pointed in the direction from which the Braemhors had just come.

"Yes, we saw them. That's what aroused our curiosity," Mary told the man. "Enjoy the rest of your walk."

"Thank you, ma'am." And he strolled on until he reached the desolate area where the two dogs suddenly shied to the other side of the path. They whined pitifully until their master led them past the section of the forest that fascinated John so much.

"What do you think, John?" Mary asked when they had gotten back into the car.

"I'm not sure, but I think we've got enough time to get lunch and then visit Mr. Tawell again."

"It's the other fairies," Rita suddenly announced.

"What other fairies, Rita?" Both John and Mary were incredulous.

"The evil ones."

"What evil ones are you talking about?"

"Don't you know? There are good fairies and evil fairies." Rita was deadly serious.

"And I suppose the good fairies lure people into their circles and make them disappear?"

"That's right. And the evil ones destroy everything about them."

"And making people disappear isn't evil?" John baited her.

"Not in the same way as destroying all of the beauty around."

"She has a point, John." Mary took Rita's side.

"If you say so." John was not to be drawn into a pedantic debate about relative evils at this point in his exploration of dead landscapes. "Maybe we can deal with the fairies when we get back to Daraichburn," he grumbled as he again parked the Vauxhall in front of the tearoom across the street from Tawell Gallery.

After lunch and just before entering Tawell Gallery, John instructed Mary to distract Tawell with questions about his other works while he compared Tawell's paintings of landscape scenes with the photographs he had taken.

"Ah, good to see you again." Tawell seemed genuinely pleased to see Rita and the Braemhors a second time. "Enjoy exploring the local area?"

"Very much so. I was wondering, how long it takes you to paint a landscape usually?" Mary asked.

"Depends on the weather. I usually allot three to seven days for each rendering. But that includes my sitting and enjoying the scene before I start. It helps me feel a part of the scene before I carry it away on my canvas. It's like painting a portrait. I like to get to know my subject very well before I start, their inner feelings, what the real person is like, not just their superficial appearance. Landscapes, like portraits, must capture the soul of the subject, otherwise it's but copy work, a sort of paint by the numbers, if you see what I mean."

"Oh, I do," Mary assured him, "but it must make it personally difficult to part with your paintings, if they are so much a part of you."

"It does. It does. But one must earn a living. There are expenses to be paid, rent on my gallery space, paints, brushes, canvases. So I must part with some of my children, but I try to select patrons who are worthy of their care." He turned and smiled at Rita, who shyly smiled a smile of embarrassment. "You see I try to make sure that each of my paintings is unique, not to be found anywhere but on my canvas."

"Is this a member of the local gentry?" Mary inquired, pointing to a particularly large life-sized portrait of a middle-aged baronet in full tartan regalia.

"Yes, it is. Sir William Brunart. His estates are near here. I hope to finish it within a week or two."

John joined Tawell and Mary. "Very nice," he said, viewing the portrait.

"Oh, I have been very fortunate to capture his likeness. I think the real soul of the man is there on the canvas. As I was telling your wife, I try to capture the essence of my subjects from these fleeting moments we call life, before the great beyond swallows them up never to be seen again." Tawell had gotten almost misty in his delivery and appeared to be more reminiscing to himself than being part of the conversation with Mary and John.

"Well, Mr. Tawell, it's been most interesting talking with you and hearing the perspective of a painter whose art is his livelihood. I dabble a bit in painting myself. But for me it's strictly a hobby."

"Good for you, Mr. . . . ? "

"Braemhor," John finished Tawell's sentence.

"Braemhor, ah, yes. If you're at all interested, I offer classes for hobbyists at all levels. Here is my card."

"Thank you. I'll keep that in mind. Rita, Mary, time we were on the road."

But at that moment, another partially finished painting caught John's eye—a crofter's cottage. The stonewalls and the surrounding setting were apparently complete, but the thatched roof had yet to have its finishing touches.

"Is this near here also?" he asked.

"Oh, yes, just off the verge on the main road south. Pretty little relic of the past, don't you think?"

"Yes, when do you expect to finish it?"

"By day after tomorrow at the latest. Depending on weather, of course."

At that point, John indicated that he'd concluded his perusal of Tawell's landscapes and was ready to go. At John's signal Mary interceded. "Time to go, John. We just have time to get home for supper."

"Yes, Mr. Tawell, thank you again for the hospitality of your gallery. Mary's right. We need to go. Perhaps again sometime."

"Hope to see you again," Tawell said as the three left the gallery.

"What did you find, John?" Mary asked once they were on the road.

"Every one of the pictures I took of those areas of desolation is replicated in one of his paintings. Except that, his pictures are the image of life, vibrant with color."

"Maybe he painted them in the spring or summer."

"No, it was more than that. I can't quite put my finger on it, but more animated, pulsating with life."

"Like he captured the soul of the scene?" Mary offered.

"Yes, you might say."

"That's what he would say. In fact, that's what he did say about his painting. That he tries to capture the soul or basic essence of his subject, no matter whether it's a landscape or a person."

"Sounds very artsy."

"Or philosophical."

"Or crazy." Rita entered the conversation.

"What's that, Rita? Crazy, like insane?" Mary asked.

"Well, yes, but insane is too strong a word. Maybe I mean affected, like someone playing a role. Not a real person." Rita had become very serious and more analytic than either John or Mary had ever heard her to be.

"Like he's trying to be the sort of person the public thinks an *artist*, in quotes, should be?" John asked.

"Something like that," Rita agreed.

"And yet, John," Mary came back into the discussion, "there's something about him I don't like. I feel vaguely uncomfortable around him, and yet he's a fascinating person."

"Maybe more than fascinating. Care to see an old crofter's cottage before it disappears?"

"What do you mean, John?" Rita was perplexed. "Buildings don't disappear. Even the fairies can't do that."

"Maybe not. Maybe not."

The ancient crofter's cottage was set back from the road to Daraichburn a kilometer or so east of Beggar's Knob. It was marked as a heritage site to be developed. John pulled off on the verge and set the brake.

"Oh, John, it is beautiful . . . in an old sort of way," Mary observed.

They walked around the structure. The front door was padlocked. By peering in the windows they could see that it was a two-room building; on one end of the entry was a fireplace made of the same stone as the walls of the cottage. There were a few wooden chairs, a table and a bedstead in the other room, left, they guessed, from a time long, long gone by. Unable to gain entry, John took pictures of the cottage from several angles before the three made their way back to Daraichburn.

CHAPTER 11

That night, back in Dunmoor Cottage, John, Mary, and Rita pondered the day and Tawell and his dazzling paintings of what were now barren scenes.

"Let's suppose he's going out and killing the scenes he paints. To what end?" John opened the conversation.

"Profit motive. You said yourself, profit is one of the main driving forces behind a lot of crime. If his paintings are unique, he can demand a better price."

"But he didn't overcharge me," Rita countered.

"Maybe he took a liking to you, Rita." John smiled. "But when I checked the pictures of the other devastated views that we photographed they weren't overpriced, I didn't think."

"I guess we can put the profit motive on hold, then," Mary summarized. "Maybe Mr. Tawell just has a peculiar view of his own artistic importance."

"Or unimportance."

"You mean he's trying to boost his low self-esteem, as the psychologists call it?"

"Stranger things have motivated people, and he certainly did not strike me as being well self-contained. Our Mr. Tawell appears to be a whole collection of oddities."

"Oh, John, maybe he's just eccentric."

"Let's hope so. Let's hope so. Game for another trip to Beggar's Knob?"

"Let me check our reservation book." Mary got the book from the front hall. "Not for another day or two,

John. We have two couples coming tomorrow. Maybe day after."

"Would you mind terribly if I went alone? I want to keep an eye on that crofter's cottage, and I thought I might explore the pottery those Americans were talking about a couple of days ago."

"That would be fine. Aunt Rita can help me around the cottage while you're away."

"Then I'll leave first thing in the morning."

But next morning, Rita had other ideas. "I'll come with you, John, I've never seen pottery making and you know how I love a mystery."

"But. . .but. . . ." John sputtered at this unexpected turn of events.

"That's a splendid idea," Mary quickly interceded.

John knew there was no use resisting. And he did not think at this stage of his investigation there was any potential danger. *Besides,* he thought, *Rita will be company.* "Fine, Rita, bring a warm wrap; it's cold this morning, and it looks like the mist is turning into rain."

"Where to first?' Rita asked, once they were on the road.

"I thought we'd stop by the crofter's cottage we visited yesterday. It's on the way."

A few kilometers west of Daraichburn, the crofter's cottage came into view, and in front of the cottage was Mr. Tawell in the midst of folding up a portable easel. John pulled the car over.

"Ah, Mr. Braemhor, Ms. Erskine, so nice to see you again. Back to Beggar's Knob this morning?"

"Yes, but we saw you and thought we'd stop and see how your painting is coming along," John told him.

"It would be coming along very well, thank you, except for the weather. I'd hoped to finish by noon, but

I think I'll have to wait until tomorrow. Going back to the gallery to open up. Stop by if you have some time."

Before John could quiet her, Rita burst out, "Oh, we'd like to very much, wouldn't we, John?"

"If we have time, Rita. If we have time." He took her arm and guided her back to the Vauxhall.

"Next time, Rita, let me decide where we're stopping," he admonished her as gently as he could.

"All right, but where are we going next?" Rita smiled her impish smile.

"Let's start at the pottery the Americans were talking about. Their comments caught my ear the other day.

"Tawell had a painting that was probably done there—a young woman decorating pottery. I'd like to stop there on our way back into town." John turned west and in a short time a sizable local pottery shop appeared on the right. He parked in front.

The front door opened to a long counter behind which were about twenty tables at which worked a variety of crafts persons, some working on potter's wheels, some decorating pottery to be fired in a line of ovens near the back wall. A gentleman at the counter greeted John and Rita.

"Welcome to Beggar's Knob Pottery. Can I help you with something in particular?" He was a short, thin, balding man of about 45 years and wore a blue denim apron which was flecked with spots of moist clay. His hands, too, showed evidence of having recently been working at a wheel.

"Not really. We saw some paintings in the village of potters at work and thought we'd stop and see the subjects of the artwork," John answered.

"Oh, that would be that artist fellow's work. He often comes out here to paint some of my staff while they're working. Nice fellow. Excellent artist. When he works he usually positions himself on the casting floor near the potter he's painting. Did one recently, our best decorator. She sat over there." He pointed to an empty table in the center of the room.

"But there's no one there," Rita observed.

"Sadly, yes."

"What happened?" John asked.

"I'm not at liberty to say, sir. Perhaps you'd like to talk to Mr. Clemons, our manager." The warm glow and friendliness suddenly faded, and the man behind the counter became cold and decidedly distant.

"That would be nice, if we could." John maintained a warm, nonthreatening attitude.

"Excuse me a moment." He turned and went to the bank of enclosed offices along the right wall of the work area. He soon returned with a short, round, red-faced man in his 60's. He did not appear pleased about being disturbed at whatever he'd been doing.

"Mr. Clemons, this is Mr. . . . ?"

"Braemhor, John Braemhor. This is my assistant." He pointed to Rita who beamed at being made an official part of the investigation. "Mr. Clemons?"

"Yes, what do you want?" It was not a friendly question.

"Just want to ask you about the empty table in your work space." John held up the official ID Peter Kilmart had provided him during his work on the murder by Hadrian's Wall a few years back.

"Again? You another copper? We had the place crawling with your kind when it happened. Don't you talk to one another?" Mr. Clemons was clearly irritated.

"Sorry, it's just that sometimes it helps if we have different people review cases that are still pending." John was careful not to offend Mr. Clemons any further.

"All right. Come on back to my office where can talk in private." Clemons had calmed down somewhat.

The three sat down in Clemons's cramped office.

"I'm sorry to bother you again, but please tell us what happened—from the beginning."

"We're not quite sure. An artist from Beggar's Knob inquired if he could paint some of our personnel. Said he wanted to do a series of paintings of local people at work. A number of our people agreed. I think they were flattered. And we certainly had no objection. Figured it was good advertisement for the pottery.

"He started working with Nancy, Nancy Hartwell, our very best decorator. He was here about four days, all day, painting and making small talk with her and the nearby staff. Even shared their tea breaks. Everything seemed fine, though Nancy did complain of not feeling quite well, like she'd took sick. But then the day after he finished his picture—and it was a very nice picture, I must say—Nancy didn't show up for work. We called her home and her Ma told us she'd died in the night! Can you imagine? Died! One day she was decorating our pottery; the next day she was gone! It was a shock, I can tell you."

"What did she die of?" John asked.

"Don't know, but I think your fellow coppers said the doc blamed it on her heart. Just gave out. Imagine. She was only 23!"

"And the Hartwells live here in the village." John looked into a small, leather bound writing pad as if he were consulting some of his notes.

"Oh, yes, just down the road a bit on the edge of the village." Clemons had relaxed by this time and was more giving of information.

"Yes, that's what I seem to have here," John concurred as he stared at the blank sheet on his notepad.

"One other thing before we go. Know anything about Ms. Hartwell's social life?"

"Not much. Not much. She used to spend most of her free time at the Dragon's Claw, pub down the road. But I already told the other coppers that." Clemons's irritation flared again.

John quickly turned to another blank page in his note pad. "Oh, yes, so you did." John looked up. "Sorry, I had it on another page in my notes. Well, Mr. Clemons, I think I've bothered you enough. Like I said, it just helps if different investigators review the data in these cases. We'll be on our way. And I do appreciate your willingness to talk with us again."

John and Rita rose and threaded their way through the casting floor to the front door.

"Why were you looking at blank sheets in your note pad when you were talking with Mr. Clemons?" Rita asked when they'd reached the car.

"We couldn't let him know that we're not a part of the police investigation, now could we?"

"Oh, just another of your investigative techniques? How clever." Rita smiled to be a part of this investigative deception, if only as an "assistant."

"Let's go see if we can get lunch at the Dragon's Claw." John drove the short distance from the pottery to the pub.

When the middle-aged waitress brought their pot pies, John asked, "Did you know Nancy Hartwell?"

"Oh, yes, sir. Nice young woman. Such a shame. She was so young."

"She came in here often?"

"Near every evening after she got off from her work at the Pottery."

"By herself?"

"Oh, no. She was much too pretty for that."

"Had lots of suitors, did she?"

"Up 'til a month ago. Then she and that artist fellow from the Knob were a regular item. Why they were even in here the night before she died. Can you imagine? I served her her last meal. I shudder to think about it."

"You're right. That was a very sad thing." John began his pie.

"Just about killed her Mum, I can tell you," the waitress said as she went back to the kitchen.

"So Mr. Tawell was taking Nancy out for pub meals," Rita stated.

"I'm not sure, Rita. I'm not sure. But eat up. We'll go gallery shopping before we go back to Daraichburn. You promised Mr. Tawell we'd stop in this afternoon."

The first gallery John and Rita visited was owned by a painter named Geoffrey Lawrence, Salt Hill Gallery. Like the others on the main street it was small but filled with numerous paintings. He had painted some of the same traditional landscapes that Tawell had. But more than any of the other galleries, he concentrated on Kandinsky-like abstractions.

"Oh my, John, look at the bright colors in these." Rita pointed to a wall covered with Lawrence's modern art.

"May I help you?" The young man standing by the wall of paintings that Rita was admiring asked. He looked to be in his 30's. His auburn hair and contrasting pastel green eyes gave him an unsettled, wild look, in Rita's estimation.

"Just admiring your work," John responded. "Do all of you here in Beggar's Knob paint the same landscapes?" He pointed to the other wall.

"Oh, yes, it's very lovely around Beggar's Knob. A plethora of scenic views for painting. Part of the reason there's such a large art colony here."

"Congenial group?" John asked.

"Pretty much, until Tawell arrived," the young man groused.

"Oh?"

"Yes, Jim Tawell seems to think if he paints a scene, he owns it. Very jealous and very unforgiving if any of the rest of us paint it or a similar view. But I got him."

"How did you do that?" John was intrigued.

"See those abstracts where the lady is standing? Most of them are of the same landscapes, but Tawell doesn't recognize them. Shows how much of an artist he really is." Sarcasm figuratively dripped with his every word.

"You don't like him?" Rita innocently asked.

The green eyes flashed. "You noticed. It's not a secret. We haven't gotten along since he came up from London a year or so ago."

"How do you develop an abstract from a realistic scene?" Rita asked.

"It's really very simple." Lawrence's countenance changed dramatically as he found someone genuinely interested in his artistic techniques. "Here, I'll show you."

He brought out a sketch pad and a pencil-shaped piece of charcoal "First, you start with the realistic scene. Take this one, for example." He happened to choose the very landscape Rita had bought from Tawell. "Then you block it out spatially." Drawing as he explained. "Then you use the prominent areas and..." He went on, making a series of sequential sketches, that by the time he finished, pictured each change he described. It was a splendid and quick lesson in modern art.

Rita was awed by Lawrence's instruction. "That's fascinating, and you made it so clear. You're an excellent teacher.

"Thank you. You can see it's really very simple, if you know what you're doing. Tawell doesn't." He returned to the same old negative narrative.

"Well, thank you, Mr. Lawrence, but we really must be going. Have to get home in time for supper," John intervened.

"Yes, and if you want any good—really good— abstract paintings, now you know where to come. And here, Ms. . . . ."

"Erskine," Rita added.

"Erskine. Take these sketches with you. Maybe they will inspire you to come back and purchase a final product."

John and Rita crossed the street to the Tawell Gallery.

"Did you notice his hands?" John asked Rita.

"You mean his ring? Yes, I did," Rita admitted, "on his right hand, a large signet ring."

"Yes, quite large."

"You'd think it might get in the way when he paints."

"Maybe he's left-handed," John mumbled. He was deep in thought. Not only did he have the feeling that he knew Tawell's name, but both Geoffrey Lawrence's name and the name of his gallery—Salt Hill Gallery— aroused vague reminiscences from the past. *What is it that's so familiar about these names at Beggar's Knob?* But try as he might he could not quite solve the mystery of his cloudy memory.

The stop at Tawell's gallery was brief, just long enough to fulfill Rita's earlier promise to stop and say "hello."

"We saw the Pottery," Rita brightly said, "saw the table where the young woman used to decorate."

"Ah, yes, Nancy. Such a shame. She was so full of life until I painted her. I can't imagine what must have happened."

"It's like you painted the life right out of her," Rita continued. John cringed in the background.

"Well, I do transfer my subjects to canvas, but not quite that dramatically." Tawell was embarrassed by the direction of the conversation and noticeably uncomfortable. "She died not long after I finished, you know. Not quite the reputation an artist tries to cultivate." Tawell was shaken.

"And we saw some of the scenes you painted," Rita persisted.

"And they're quite beautiful." John quickly jumped in, grabbed Rita by the elbow and started to guide her towards the door.

"Quite beautiful!" Rita protested.

"Yes, beautiful. Lush, beautiful landscapes, Rita." John pressed her arm. "By the way," John turned to Tawell, "do you think you'll be able to finish the crofter's cottage tomorrow?"

Tawell's tension subsided as the conversation veered away from Rita's misbegotten questions.

"Yes, I think I might. Stop by in a few days and you can see the final product." He managed a weak smile.

"We'd like that," John said. Then as he and Rita walked towards the door, he turned back to Tawell.

"I wonder if you'd mind awfully if I took a photograph of you with Ms. Erskine? I know she'd very much prize having a picture of herself with the artist whose landscape she bought, but I'm sure she'd be embarrassed to ask."

"Not at all. Not at all. Ms. Erskine," he called, "come stand with me in front of my landscapes so Mr. Braemhor can take our picture."

Rita was delighted. "Oh, that will be so nice." She scurried to stand by Tawell. He put his arm around her shoulders and smiled while John recorded the event on his digital.

Then John quickly ushered Rita out of the door and towards the car.

"Rita, you must not interfere like that!"

"Like what, John?" Rita innocently asked.

"Your comments on his landscapes. If Tawell is up to mischief you could easily have scared him off." John was quite irritated.

"I'm sorry, John. I didn't think."

"You certainly didn't!" John was not happy.

As they got back into the Vauxhall, Geoffrey Lawrence stood at the window of his gallery watching them depart.

"One more stop before we go back to Daraichburn. I want to talk to the waitress at the Dragon's Claw again briefly."

Braemhor parked the car in front of the Dragon's Claw and turned to Rita. "You wait here. I won't be but a moment."

True to his word, they were on the road home within ten minutes.

* * * * * * *

Mary met the two at the door of Dunmoor Cottage. "Supper is just about ready." She hugged Rita and gave John a peck on the cheek.

"I need to make some telephone calls first," John said and went into his and Mary's bedroom to use the extension. The first call he placed was to Forester Greenhagen, who was just about to leave his office.

"Braemhor here. I have some information for you."

"What did you find out?" Greenhagen was slightly irritated at being caught moments before he wanted to leave his office.

"I think the Heritage Site Crofter's Cottage may be in danger tomorrow night."

"What makes you think so?" Clearly, Greenhagen was skeptical.

John explained to him as briefly as he could that a certain artist from Beggar's Knob had painted all of the landscapes which recently had been mysteriously decimated, and that he was preparing to finish a painting of the cottage tomorrow. "I know that this is very thin circumstantial evidence, but each time this artist completes a landscape, that landscape is destroyed. You've seen them. You gave me a list of the recently vandalized areas. Well, I correlated each with the paintings in the Tawell Gallery, and they match perfectly."

"Interesting theory, Mr. Braemhor, but nothing you've told me says Mr. Tawell is going about the countryside destroying the flora. You'll have to come up with something more substantial than that. We're very busy here at the commission. What do you expect me to do? Have one of my foresters stay up all night watching a crofter's cottage."

"That's exactly what I had in mind."

"Well. . ." Greenhagen's voice trailed off as he thought over what Braemhor was suggesting. He thought John's whole theory was cockamamie, yet he recognized that if he dismissed it out of hand, he might regret it.

Finally his voice continued, "I do have a young forester who's been working on the problem of the landscapes. I'll talk with him, and if he's willing to sit up all night near the cottage, I'll put him on it.

"Thank you. That would be very helpful. If I'm right we—John included Greenhagen in his investigative theory—may be able to clear up the demise of our landscapes. If I'm right."

"If you're right." With this final remark, delivered with sarcasm, Greenhagen hung up.

Next Braemhor called DCI Sinclair in Edinburgh.

"Hello, John," Sinclair's voice boomed through the connection, "Thought I'd hear from you soon."

"Why's that?" John was taken aback.

"Got a couple of my boys working on the death of the young pottery decorator near Beggar's Knob. Not far from you, so I thought you'd get involved before too long. I was right." Sinclair smiled through the telephone.

"You're a good detective, Jim. What have you got so far, then I'll tell you what I'm thinking."

"As you probably know, a young pottery decorator at the Beggar's Knob Pottery—Nancy Hartwell—was found dead the other morning. Only 23. The local doc attributed it to a heart attack. I can't resolve that with her age. Oh, it's possible I guess, but the probability doesn't calculate. I've asked the coroner to do a thorough review of the body."

"Tell him to look for cyanide poisoning," John advised.

"What? Why cyanide?" Sinclair was startled.

John then gave Sinclair a summary of why he'd concluded that Nancy Hartwell had been poisoned with cyanide, how he thought the poison had been delivered, and who delivered it.

"Wait a minute, John. You know as well as anyone that I appreciate an interesting investigative theory, but this time you're on pretty thin ice. I can't arrest a suspect on the grounds that he's reliving a piece of history from the 1840's."

John smiled. "Let me know what the coroner says."

"I should have the report day after tomorrow."

"Good, by then, if the Forestry Commission does their job, they may already have your prime suspect in custody."

"Why the Forestry Commission?" Sinclair was beginning to get confused.

Braemhor then explained that he'd alerted the commission to an impending crime the next night at the crofter's cottage near Beggar's Knob by an artist wanting to enhance the value of his paintings. "You see, Jim, I believe these two cases dovetail very nicely. Or at least I hope so."

"I hope so, too, John, because, if so, you'll have saved me a lot of work. I'll let you know as soon as I hear from the coroner."

* * * * * * *

At supper, Rita held center stage as she delighted in telling Mary all she could remember of her adventures in sleuthing with John in and around Beggar's Knob. Mary was glad she'd sent Rita on the trip. John was the only one who had genuine reservations about taking Rita on another investigative expedition.

"Oh, really, John, what was the harm? And Rita thoroughly enjoyed herself."

"Number one, she could have easily scared Tawell off. Number two, she nearly told him of our visits to the landscape sites. I didn't want him to know that we were aware of the destruction at those sites. Unfortunately her mouth runs ahead of her brain and her thinking. This is a very complicated case and I found her presence a distraction. Fortunately, on the drive home she was quiet, and I got to do some uninterrupted thinking. I finally realized why the name Tawell was so familiar."

"And?"

"John Tawell was a very famous murderer in the 1840s. Famous because the case was the first to be solved through modern—for that day—telecommunications technology. He had a long history of criminal activity, forgeries and the like. At one point he was transported to Australia rather than suffer the death penalty.

"After his return to London, his wife and two children died of tuberculosis. He then took up with the nurse he'd employed to care for his wife through her last illness, a woman named Sarah Lawrence. He married again but also maintained his liaison with the nurse. He installed her and the two children born to that relationship in Salt Hill."

"The name of Geoffrey Lawrence's gallery," Mary interrupted.

"That's right. But he had difficulty keeping knowledge of his paramour from his second wife, and so he murdered Sarah with prussic acid, cyanide. The police missed the train he boarded for London, but through the telegraph they were able to wire ahead to Paddington and he was apprehended in London. Subsequently, he was executed for the murder of Sarah Lawrence, who by that time had changed her name to Hart."

"So you think our artist, Jim Tawell, is descended from John Tawell and inherited some of his criminal tendencies."

"Certainly a possibility. Tawell is not a very common name. Could he, I thought, have been the one destroying the landscapes he painted. Compared to murder, the destruction of woodlands is not a major crime, but it is criminal. Just ask Greenhagen of the Forestry Commission. But why? I asked myself. And you supplied the answer."

"Profit motive. Makes his paintings more unique and therefore more valuable."

"Precisely," John concurred.

"But, John, where does Geoffrey Lawrence fit in?" Mary was fascinated by her husband's thought processes.

"That's the real puzzle, so bear with me on my next fantasy flight. Note that his last name is the same as the woman John Tawell murdered in the 1840s. And. . .he's named his gallery Salt Hill."

"The place where John Tawell murdered Sarah Lawrence." Mary was now on top of the story.

"So could Geoffrey Lawrence be a descendent of the murdered woman and. . . ."

"Destroyed the landscapes to implicate James Tawell and rain vengeance from the past down upon him." Mary took up the thread of the story.

"Exactly. But now the case gets complicated."

Mary rolled her eyes at that statement, thinking it was already complicated enough.

John continued, "Now we have the death of a young decorator in the local pottery. A woman Tawell had painted. Did Tawell kill her as he did—if he did—the landscapes?"

"Or did Lawrence? Continuing the path of trying to make his nemesis, James Tawell, look like a major criminal," Mary continued the thought. "Either way these are pretty drastic actions, you must admit."

"Right. Now Rita and I found that an artist was the last person to see Nancy Hartman alive. Rita thought it was Jim Tawell. I wasn't so sure, so I arranged to take a photograph of Rita with Tawell in his studio and then showed the picture to the waitress at the Dragon's Claw. She did not recognize him! So Tawell was not there when Nancy Hartwell made her last visit to the pub."

"So where does that leave us, John.?"

"Waiting for events to unfold themselves. If the crofter's cottage is damaged tomorrow night and if Greenhagen's personnel apprehend whoever attempts it, and if Sinclair's coroner finds what I think he might find, then we'll know which of our little sub-theories is more likely correct."

"It's a lot of ifs, John."

"Enough to sleep on, I think." John smiled.

* * * * * * *

And now the long wait began, the part of any investigation Braemhor found so tedious and anxiety provoking. *If, and that is a big if, Greenhagen condescends to send a forester to stake out the crofter's cottage. If the coroner finds cyanide poisoning. If the tools Braemhor expects to find in Tawell or Lawrence's gallery.* As Mary said "a lot of ifs."

Every time the telephone rang John jumped, hoping it was either Greenhagen or Sinclair, even though he knew that the information he sought would not be available until the next day. The day dragged on, as did the evening. The night was no better because sleep was elusive as he turned over and over in his mind the few pieces of data he had to work with.

By morning, John was pacing like a caged panther. Mary had seen it all too often and so she quietly went about her cottage chores and tried to ignore the anticipation that drove her husband.

Finally, about nine, one of the telephone calls Braemhor was anticipating arrived.

"Mr. Braemhor, Charles Greenhagen here. I want to thank you for your help. I admit, day before yesterday I was very skeptical that watching the crofter's cottage would yield anything of value. But we in the Commission have you to thank for insisting that we put the cottage under surveillance. We now have a man in custody who we caught deliberately trying to burn down that magnificent structure from our past."

"Geoffrey Lawrence," John interjected.

"Er, yes, how did you know?" Greenhagen was surprised.

"Let's just say it's another one of my theories based on circumstantial evidence." Braemhor smiled.

"Well, theory or not, I have to admit that you were right."

"I'm very pleased, but one thing more I have to ask. Please keep Lawrence in custody for now. I hope that by later today he'll be wanted by the Edinburgh police for a far more serious crime. I'll have DCI Sinclair contact you as soon as I can."

John hung up and turned to Mary. "Greenhagen has caught the man responsible for the destruction of the landscapes. I think when the Commission searches his gallery they'll find an inordinate quantity of liquid herbicide."

"And maybe even more," Mary concluded her husband's sentence.

"Right," John said, all the while appreciating Mary's involvement in his investigations.

Sinclair's call came ten minutes later.

"John, you were right, as usual. Nancy Hartman died of cyanide poisoning. And another thing, she was pregnant!"

"Now you have both a motive and a means. I just spoke with the Forestry Commissioner, Charles Greenhagen. He's apprehended Geoffrey Lawrence for attempting to burn down a heritage site, a crofter's cottage near Beggar's Knob. I asked him to hold Lawrence for a day or two until you call him."

"Why me?"

"Because, if I'm not mistaken, Mr. Lawrence has not only been involved in the crimes of landscape destruction in this area, but is also the individual you will want in connection with the death of Ms. Hartman."

"Another one of your theories?" Sinclair was a little skeptical.

"You might say. But I think if you search Lawrence's gallery, the Salt Hill Gallery in Beggar's Knob, you'll find a large quantity of apples and the equipment for reducing the apple seeds to a fine powder."

"You're ahead of me, John."

"Just search the gallery and let me know what you find. I'll explain later. For now, call Greenhagen at our local Forestry Commission office. The two of you can coordinate your search of the gallery. I assure you, it's not a wild goose chase."

"Only because I know you, John. I'll call you later."

John hung up and turned to Mary and Rita. "I think we've about wrapped up the cases of the disappearing landscapes and the decorator's death at Beggar's Knob, in one stroke. I should get final confirmation by evening."

By midafternoon, Sinclair was back on the telephone with, "John, I don't know how you do it but your 'theories' are correct. Greenhagen and I went to the Salt Hill Gallery and, sure enough, the herbicide he used on the local flora—and, as you predicted, the apples—and a large pestle and mortar containing a fine powdery residue were there. Testing showed it to be a high concentrate of prussic acid, cyanide. We took Lawrence into custody from Greenhagen and now are having him arraigned for the murder of Nancy Hartman. He made our work easier by breaking down under questioning and admitting both the murder and the vandalism of the local landscape. As I told you, Greenhagen had caught him red-handed trying to set fire to the crofter's cottage. Two cases closed in one action. Thanks to you. But I do have three questions."

"Yes?" Braemhor was pleased that his theorizing had paid off.

"First, how do you think Lawrence delivered the cyanide to Hartman?"

"With his signet ring, of course. He was still wearing it, wasn't he?" John responded.

"Yes."

"Well, check it for apple pit powder residue. That will be your cyanide. The ring is a variety of pillbox ring, also known as a poison ring, used in the 16th century to deposit poison in an enemy's food or drink. The killer surreptitiously passed his hand over his enemy's plate or cup while opening the ring and allowing its contents to fall into the food or beverage."

"Clever," Sinclair admitted, "and the apples?"

"While most people today are unaware of it, apple pits contain cyanide. Simple and easy source of poison, if you have that turn of mind," John continued.

"Finally, why did you think Lawrence would have used apple pits?"

John explained the connections from the past that linked both Tawell and Lawrence, and he detailed the Tawell case of the 1840's to Sinclair. "And this is critical, the original Tawell's lawyer, Sir Fitzroy Kelly, tried to exonerate his client by claiming the murdered woman had died because she'd eaten too many apple seeds during a festive season. Even earned Sir Fitzroy the sobriquet of 'apple-pip Kelly.'" Braemhor chuckled at this last revelation.

"So you think Lawrence was reliving a case from over a century ago?"

"Yes, first he wanted to discredit Tawell because Tawell's ancestor had murdered his ancestor, Sarah Lawrence. Then when he found himself trapped by the pregnancy of the young Nancy Hartwell, he reverted to the role that Tawell's ancestor had played in the past and murdered her with prussic acid."

Sinclair sat back unable to speak. Finally, his words came through the phone, "Well, John, I'm certainly impressed with the conclusions you reach based on the thinnest of evidence. Even reaching back over the centuries to build a case. But I do thank you for all of the help you give me in the present with your razor-thin theories."

"Glad to help. And remember not to eat the apple pips."

CHAPTER 12

Over breakfast the next morning, Rita let the Braemhors know that she thought she should get back to Blanefield and her own abode. "I've been away more than a month, you know. Time to tidy up my own place and see the rest of the family. Besides, I think I've had enough sleuthing for now." A coquettish smile brightened her face.

"When will you go?" John asked as he cracked the shell on his soft boiled.

"I thought I'd take the morning train tomorrow. That way I can be home by midafternoon."

"Rita, I want to take you back to Beggar's Knob. Maybe we could go this afternoon. I'd like to buy you a painting as thanks for all your help these past few days," John said. Mary was as startled as Rita who gushed at the idea.

"That would be so nice," Rita acknowledged. "I'd love to have one of Mr. Lawrence's abstracts, but I suppose that isn't possible now." She sounded disappointed.

"Probably not, Rita," John admitted, "I imagine the police have impounded all his work now that he's in gaol, but I'm sure Mr. Tawell will have something to your liking. We'll have to shop around."

That afternoon John and Mary took Rita back to Beggar's Knob and the Tawell Gallery.

"I'd just love to have one of Mr. Lawrence's abstracts," Rita confessed to Tawell.

"I think you may be in luck." Tawell beamed. "The police allowed some of us with galleries here in Beggar's Knob to buy up his stock now that the case is solved. I purchased a few. See if there's anything you like."

Rita was delighted to find Lawrence's abstract rendering of the area near the Yellow Finch pub that Tawell had portrayed in the painting she gave to John and Mary. "This will do just fine!" she announced as she handed it to Tawell for packaging. John paid for the painting, and the three drove back to Daraichburn.

Next morning, John and Mary took Rita to the station in Melrose and bid her a warm goodbye.

On the way back to Daraichburn, John posed a question. "Care for another brief holiday?"

Mary was puzzled. "Where to this time?"

"The morning paper said that Professor William Edwards is giving a series of lectures on hypnosis in Edinburgh starting day after tomorrow."

"The one from Carter University? The one whose books we bought in Fort Ewen?"

"The very same," John confirmed.

"That would be very interesting. I don't think we have any bookings for another week or so. I'll check when we get home." Mary liked spontaneous excursions.

* * * * * * *

The trip north on the A703 was brief, and the Braemhors arrived before supper at the small hotel near the university. After supper they walked around the university grounds and oriented themselves to the large lecture hall where Dr. Edwards's evening lecture was to be held.

They decided to go to the hall early to secure good seats, and it was a good thing they did. The hall began to fill almost an hour before the talk was scheduled. By the time of the lecture, the room was filled to overflowing with many students standing along the wall and sitting in the main aisles. John and Mary, fortunately, found seats in the third row in front of the lectern.

Dr. Edwards arrived a few minutes ahead of lecture time and shuffled and arranged his note papers on the lectern to the audience's left. He was of medium height and slender in weight. His brown hair cascaded over his left eye, giving him a more boyish look than one would expect for an American professor. His dress was casual—tweed pants, an open-collared, button-down shirt and a grey cardigan with leather elbow patches. He looked up at precisely half past seven and began.

That evening's lecture, he explained, was about the long and tumultuous history of hypnosis, beginning with the ancient Egyptian, Grecian and Roman sleep temples centuries before the birth of Christ, passing through the Hindu and Chinese cultures, and, of course, the most well-known practitioner, Franz Anton Mesmer of the 18th century. Naturally, Edwards covered two well-known Scottish hypnotists—James Esdaile and James Braid. The latter, Edwards told his audience, was credited with coining the term *hypnosis*. He concluded his lecture by introducing the audience to the work of the modern practitioner, Martin Evarts, and researchers Humphreys and Edmonds. It was an unusually thorough introduction to his topic in the short space of one hour.

At the conclusion of the talk, John and Mary went forward to meet the lecturer and to compliment him on his two books which they'd purchased recently in Ft. Ewen.

"Ah, yes, the Braemhors. Your reputation precedes you."

"Oh?" Mary responded.

"Yes, I was on campus when you helped Dean Howard and the local police clear up that nasty business of the deaths of some of our Carter University faculty. Learned about you then. I heard it was a very clever bit of detective work."

John smiled. "Just trying to help out a friend."

"Well, modesty or not, I was impressed by what I heard."

"And we're impressed with all we've learned from you about hypnosis," Mary said. "I see you're giving three lectures. What aspects of hypnosis will you be discussing in the next two?"

"Tomorrow afternoon I'll cover the various phenomena of hypnosis. You know, like amnesia, age regression, time distortion, analgesia, and the creation of multiple personalities. Then tomorrow night, how each of these can be used clinically, and I'll also review some of the more common hypnotic induction techniques."

"Not going to teach the audience how to induce hypnosis?"

"Oh, no." Edwards smiled. "Hypnosis is for the professionally trained, not amateurs. Couldn't do it even I wanted to—which I don't—since here in the UK you have much more restrictive statutes with respect to hypnosis. Will you be coming tomorrow?"

"Decidedly."

"Good. Would you two care for some libations before going back to your hotel? There's a nice pub just off campus on Lothian. I often go there after I've discharged my duties with my study group from Carter.

I could meet you there in about 15 minutes. Need to straighten up my notes here before I leave. It's called the Meadowlark."

"Excellent. We'll meet you there," Mary agreed.

The Meadowlark was a short walk from the campus. The Braemhors settled into a booth as far from the front door as they could find. The pub was large as pubs go—*to accommodate the students*, John thought—with an oaken bar stretching across the back wall and halfway down one side wall. Heavy tables and chairs filled the central space with booths lining one entire wall as well as the walls on both sides of the front door.

John had just ordered his and Mary's tea when Edwards entered, quickly looked around, spotted them and strode toward where they sat.

"I see you found the Meadowlark all right. Let me place my order and I'll be right back." He went to the window next to the bar.

The conversation among the three of them centered, naturally, on Edwards's lecture that evening and the interesting history of hypnosis.

"It's been around in one form or another for a long, long time," Edwards summed up.

"It certainly has, but you mentioned something that you'll talk about in tomorrow afternoon's lecture, I'd like to ask about." Mary said.

"What was that?"

"I think you said 'time distortion.' What exactly is that?"

"Something all of us experience on a daily basis. Time distortion happens to all of us. Think about a time when you were doing something that you find very fascinating and interesting. It seems like you have only been at it for a very short time but actually much more time has passed than you think."

"Like when you're painting, John," Mary said.

"Right. I start painting and I get so caught up in the process that before I know it Mary's calling me for supper. I may have been painting for three hours but it seems like I just started."

"That's one form of naturally occurring time distortion. But now think of the opposite, a time when you're doing something very boring, or something you want to finish so that you can move on to something else you're really looking forward to."

"And time seems to drag on and on and on," Mary concluded.

"Right. Those are the two forms of natural time distortion in which subjective time—time as you experience it—does not seem to match world or clock time."

"So through hypnosis you can make a subject think that a lot of time has passed when it really hasn't?" John asked.

"Or that very little time has passed, when, in fact, a long period of actual time has passed." Edwards expanded on his explanation.

"For instance?" John wanted something more concrete.

"Well, for example, a colleague of mine was working with a concert pianist who was afraid she did not have sufficient time to practice for an upcoming concert. He hypnotized her and suggested that she could fully review her concert pieces note by note— they were Beethoven's Pathétique and Appassionata Sonatas—in the space of five minutes of actual time."

"And it was successful?"

"Oh yes. She reported that the concert went exceptionally well. In fact, he gave her a post-hypnotic suggestion that she could hypnotize herself and 'practice' any time she had a free five minutes."

"Sounds almost mystical," Mary observed.

"Mystical or not, that's the sort of way in which hypnotic time distortion has been used." Edwards smiled.

"What about hypnotic age regression?" Mary next asked.

"Ah, now there's a phenomenon that has attracted more than its share of charlatans. It's a process in which it's suggested to the person being hypnotized that they return to a previous time in their life, for example, to recall a lost memory. But some of the less professional practitioners have carried this idea to extremes, such as claiming that they've taken a person back to a previous life. There have been several notable cases chronicled in books and popular magazines."

John was astounded at the extremes people would go just to gain some notoriety and probably money.

Edwards continued, "Even some professionals have been caught up in the hype. One published an article claiming to have age regressed a patient back to the point of his conception in the womb, complete with detailed imagery!

"But it's been shown that lost memories can sometimes be recovered, if not fully, at least in part. Can be a very valuable tool in the course of psychotherapy."

"Are these recollections accurate?" John was skeptical.

"Good point. Sometimes yes, and sometimes no, but for some patients in psychotherapy the accuracy of a memory may not be so important. What may be just as important, or more so, is that the patient views the memory as accurate and so is influenced by it. Hypnotic age regression can be a very useful tool in the hands of a well trained professional."

"It sounds to me that this and hypnotic time distortion might well be of value in investigative work," John concluded.

"Very much so, I'd suspect," Edwards agreed. "Also hypnotic amnesia, in which it's suggested to the patient that he cannot remember certain things, unless he's given a prearranged signal. And remember, minor and major surgeries have been carried out solely with hypnotic analgesia. Some professionals have used it for surgery as major as caesarian sections and amputations!"

"With no other analgesic or anesthetic?" Mary was a bit incredulous.

"Yes. You see, in the right, well-trained hands, hypnosis and its various phenomena can be very valuable clinically. . . . Well," Edwards looked at his watch, "you've heard most of my next lectures and the hour is such that I need to get some rest before a very long day tomorrow. I'll be going back to my university room."

"This has been most informative and most interesting, Dr. Edwards," Mary said.

"Call me Bill, please."

"Bill, we look forward to tomorrow and learning more about your fascinating subject." John rose with Edwards and shook his hand.

"John, Mary." He took Mary's hand after John's. "It has been pleasure. I shall look for you in the audience tomorrow." With that, he exited the Meadowlark."

"Well, John?"

"Dr. Edwards—Bill—deals in one of the more interesting topics of human behavior, and I certainly think some of the ways in which hypnosis has been used would be valuable in investigative work. I'll have to think more about it."

The Braemhors returned to their hotel.

Next day, John and Mary spent all morning sightseeing in the university area of Edinburgh and, after lunch, went to hear Professor Edwards's lecture at two. Edwards was right; their conversation at the Meadowlark the evening before had covered most of his afternoon and evening lectures, though as he listened, John thought that the phenomenon of hypnotic amnesia might also be of value in investigative work. "It might be that induced amnesia could be a double-edged sword, of use to both an investigator and a criminal," John said as they sat down at the Meadowlark for a pub meal before the evening lecture.

"How so, John?" Mary was intrigued.

"Supposing the police wished to insert an undercover agent into a criminal gang. Give the agent, through hypnosis, amnesia for his or her true identity as a police undercover agent. Then if confronted by the criminal gang, he or she would have no recollection of being a police officer, much less an undercover agent. That way you could protect the agent from discovery. By the same token, the criminal element could induce amnesia in one of their own. Then, if caught, he or she would have no recollection of engaging in unlawful activity and so would not be able to provide the police with any information about the criminal group."

"It still sounds like hocus-pocus to me, but I'd think it would equally apply to espionage." Mary offered.

"Hocus-pocus or not, it would be interesting to explore. Maybe I should contact Nigil Street when we get back."

"You mean of MI6?"

"Precisely."

"I think you're stretching a bit, John. Maybe we should talk to Bill Edwards first." Mary wanted to calm the boiling waters in her husband's mind.

"You always make sense, Mary, and keep me from jumping too quickly into the unknown." John smiled.

That night after Edwards's last lecture, the professor and the Braemhors returned to the Meadowlark for a brief respite of drinks and closing conversation. John asked Edwards about the possible use of hypnotic amnesia in investigative or criminal activity.

"Or espionage?" Mary broadened John's query.

"Oh, very definitely. A colleague of mine wrote an entire book on the uses of hypnotic amnesia in espionage. Even claimed that he'd participated in such applications during World War II. We never knew whether or not to believe his stories about applying hypnotic amnesia to espionage, but he claimed it was a fact, insisting it was too secret for anyone in government to admit."

"But that sort of argument closes off the possibility of verifying his story," Mary pointed out.

"Exactly. That's why many of my colleagues put his stories off to fantasy if not downright fabrication. But he stood by his narrative, and I have to admit that, theoretically, the possibility exists for using hypnotic amnesia as he described it. I suspect that one would have to dig very deep into the inner sanctum of clandestine governmental activity, like with our CIA or your MI6, to find out, however."

From there the conversation drifted to other topics including the beauty of Professor Edwards's academic home, Carter University in New York.

"You might be interested to know that a prominent academic magazine recently named Carter University the most beautiful college campus in all of the United States," Edwards informed them.

"That's quite an honor, I'd imagine," Mary said.

"We're all very proud of the designation, that's true," Edward's agreed.

Finally, the Braemhors returned to their hotel after making promises to stay in touch with their new friend.

"Shall we go back to Dunmoor Cottage tomorrow?" Mary asked when they'd gotten back to the hotel.

"Fine. Except I thought it might be nice if we could have lunch with Jim Sinclair before we go back. I could call him in the morning and see if that's possible."

"I think that would be nice, if he's free to meet us somewhere," Mary concurred.

* * * * * * *

John and Mary spent the morning visiting several old bookstores in the university district. At the last one, John found a very used copy of the book by Edwards's colleague that he'd mentioned. It was titled simply, *Hypnotism in War and Peace.*

"Should be an interesting bedtime read," John observed as he riffled the pages.

The Braemhors timed their bookstore search so that they could meet Sinclair in a pub near his office for lunch.

"Glad you can take a little time off from what I imagine is a busy schedule." John greeted him.

"Always try to make time for good friends," Sinclair's voice boomed throughout the main room of the pub as he approached the booth where John and Mary awaited their friend. His voice belied his small frame. People usually expected a quiet almost shy voice from a man of his stature.

After a brief discussion of the lectures he and Mary had just attended, John discussed his notions about the ways in which some hypnotic phenomena might be used. Sinclair took more than a passing interest in John's ideas.

"Sounds like the sort of innovation I could use," Sinclair said.

"Busy time?" Mary asked.

"I've certainly got enough on my plate to fill several meals." Sinclair laughed.

"What are you working on at present?" John was pleased that Sinclair thought hypnosis might be of help in investigations.

"My main focus right now is a series of house burglaries across the area. Three of them in your area to be specific, one in Lanark and the others in Peebles. The one in Lanark is particularly vexing, since it involves a large landed estate—the Brunarts. The other two sites are in very rich, but not landed, homes. In all cases, the thief, or thieves, knew right where to go. Nothing else disturbed. No household belongings strewn about like they were searching for valuables. Like I said, they seemed to know right where the valuables were."

"Brunart? Wasn't that the name of the baronet in the large portrait Mr. Tawell did?" Mary intervened.

"Yes, it was," John answered, then turned to Sinclair. "We've just seen a new portrait of the present baronet in an art gallery in Beggar's Knob—Sir William, I think."

"That's the one. Owns extensive acreage in Lanarkshire. One of the oldest families in your area. Goes back to the time of King Robert the Bruce. A piece of the family's most precious heirlooms has gone missing from the castle. Given to the present Sir William's ancestor, Robert Brunart, in recognition of his participation in the Battle of Bannockburn—a gem-encrusted dagger. It was in the family quarters, not locked up. There was no sign of a break-in, no doors forced, no windows smashed."

"Insider's work?" Mary asked. "Servants?"

"You might think that, but Sir William and Lady Brunart vouch for all of them. They've been with them for years. All of the staff is well spoken for by the family. The location of the dagger was known only to Sir William and Lady Brunart. Inside job? Certainly not family members. All of the valuables on the estate are willed to family members. No need to steal."

"Unless debts are pressing," John offered.

"First thing we checked." Sinclair smiled. "But no, no family member has any pressing, unmanageable debts."

"Anything else missing?" John asked.

"Nothing, although there was another priceless Bruce-era relic in the castle at the time—a gold and silver Bruce crest badge. It wasn't locked away either. We guess the thief probably did not know it existed. We've sent out a general description and photos of the dagger to antique dealers and jewelers. So far, nothing."

"I'd imagine that a dagger would be hard to move, but if the individual jewels were extracted, they might be easier to unload," John observed.

"Right. And it would be an additional tragedy to see such a priceless relic destroyed for the jewels." Sinclair displayed a sense of historical concern the Braemhors had not seen before.

"But still, a gem-encrusted dagger would be hard to remove from the estate without being noticed. How did they get in and out with it without being detected? Unless they were part of a work crew. Any repairs done

on the castle during the period the dagger disappeared?"
John was speculating aloud.

"No repairs. No workmen about. Only the servants
and Sir William and his wife."

"What about tours? Many of the landed estates find
offering tours of the castle and grounds a way of
making ends meet in this economic climate." Mary
continued. "Could someone have come in with a tour
and gone out with the dagger?" Mary asked.

"That's a possibility we're considering, but we've
not had time to follow it up."

"Of course, getting to a relic while being part of a
tour group would not be easy," Mary continued.

"Well nigh impossible, I'd think." John jumped in.

"Unless by a pregnant woman," Mary persisted.
"You know with a large coat and oversized dress."

"So all we need to find is a large pregnant woman
with an overly large coat who likes to go on castle
tours, with a penchant for 14th century sharp-edged
weapons." John chuckled.

"All right, you two, you've had your fun." Sinclair
smiled again. "But I'll follow up on the tour idea."

"We can do it right here," Mary said as she produced
an IPhone from her purse. "Christmas gift from our son
and daughter-in-law. Very handy." Mary touched the
screen icon marked "Google" and typed in "Scottish
castle tours."

"Ah. Here it is. 'Brunart Estate Tours. Weekly tours.
Saturdays. Contact, etc., etc.'"

"Well done, Mary. I appreciate your quick detective
work." Sinclair smiled. "You've saved my DS some
computer work, and I'll have her check with Sir
William and see if there's a temporal connection
between Brunart castle tours and the disappearance of
the dagger."

"Meanwhile, we need to get back to Daraichburn so you'll have the time to develop a list of all of the pregnant women in Lanarkshire." Mary smiled as the Braemhors took their leave to return home.

"Keep us apprised of how the case goes, will you?" John asked. "It sounds like an Edgar Allen Poe mystery."

The three friends left the pub, Sinclair going to his office and John and Mary to Dunmoor Cottage.

CHAPTER 13

At home after supper, John said to Mary, "Your idea of a castle tour as a cover for the robbery at Brunart Castle was excellent, except for one thing."

"Oh?"

"How did the thief know where to locate the dagger? The castle is large, I assume, and someone on the tour couldn't wander about for any extended time without being missed. He or she couldn't search about. Had to know right where to go in order to find it quickly, hide it on their person and rejoin the tour. All in a matter of a very few minutes or even seconds," John explained.

"She had to be nimble," Mary added.

"Who did?"

"The pregnant woman in the large coat." Mary smiled.

John took up the lighter side of the conversation. "So now we're looking for a large, *nimble*, pregnant woman in an overly large coat who likes to go on castle tours, with a penchant for 14th century sharp-edged weapons. We'll just have to wait for Sinclair's list of pregnant women in Lanarkshire. But that still leaves us with the question of how did she know where the dagger was, if only Sir William and his wife knew its whereabouts."

"One of them told her," Mary continued the back and forth.

"Why?" John quickly rejoined.

"Maybe the one who told her didn't know they told her."

"Or told her and didn't remember they'd told her."

"Like amnesia?"

"Something of the sort."

John always thoroughly enjoyed these fast-paced exchanges that he and Mary often had when working on a case. They sharpened their insights and often led to conclusions that would otherwise not be reached. The brain works in mysterious ways, two brains even more so.

Without her I probably wouldn't solve most of our cases. We're a team, John thought, as they talked. *We need more data.*

"I think we need more data, John." Mary shadowed his thoughts.

"And maybe some sleep to let out brains work out the puzzle." John agreed.

* * * * * * *

Next morning, over soft boileds and burnt toast, Mary asked, "Solve the puzzle?"

"Not yet, but I think it might be enlightening for us to take a tour of Brunart Castle, say this Saturday?" John suggested.

"Data gathering?"

"You might say. I'll call and make reservations for us."

After arranging for Saturday's tour, John sat in front of a newly-made peat fire in the sitting room and started reading *Hypnotism in War and Peace*, the book by Edwards's colleague at Carter University. By noon, he was astounded by what he'd discovered. He'd gotten so engrossed in his reading that lunchtime arrived before he realized it. *Natural time distortion, I think Edwards called it,* he reflected as he went into the breakfast room for lunch.

"Do you know, Mary, this professor presents a very convincing case for using various hypnotic phenomena in espionage, particularly amnesia," he announced as he sat down.

"I'll have to read the book, too."

"Fine, I should be finished by midafternoon."

Indeed, he'd just finished at three when the telephone rang. Mary answered it, then turned to John. "John, it's for you. A Sir William Brunart."

"As in castle?"

"I suspect so." She handed the receiver to her husband.

"Braemhor here," John opened.

"Mr. Braemhor. This is William Brunart. I've just been talking with Inspector Sinclair in Edinburgh. As you know, we've had a precious family heirloom stolen from our estate. So far the police have not been able to help much. They've been able to keep the theft from the news media, which is a help, but we need results. I asked Inspector Sinclair if he could recommend a private investigator, and he recommended you. I'd like to engage your services, if you're available."

"I'm slightly familiar with the case, and I'd certainly be willing to see what we might accomplish together, but first I'll need to have a great deal more detail. In fact, my wife and I have arranged to take the tour of Brunart Castle this Saturday. Perhaps we might meet after the tour and discuss your loss and what might be done about it. Would that be satisfactory?" John was hesitant to make a formal commitment immediately.

"Let me check my calendar. Yes, that would be fine. The tour ends at noon. Perhaps you and your wife could stay afterwards. We can discuss the matter over lunch."

"Fine," John agreed.

"Then we'll meet on Saturday. Just let the tour guide know who you are, and he'll see to your coming to the private quarters after the tour." With that, Sir William hung up.

"He wants us to take lunch with him after the tour on Saturday," John informed Mary.

* * * * * * *

After a pleasant morning viewing Brunart Castle, the Braemhors were taken by the tour guide to the dining area in the Brunart's private quarters located in one of the turrets of the old structure. The original arrow slits had been enlarged to admit copious amounts of sunshine into the room, which was done in a pale green and gold motif. The damask table cloth had a green border with gold swirl designs on the central surface. The seats of the chairs were done in gold brocade with pale green images of the castle. The flatware was not silver, but gold. Elegance stood out.

Around the walls were gold-framed portraits of various family members, mostly ancestral paintings, but a few of more modern vintage. One of the latter, on the back wall to catch the light from the windows, was of a present-day couple.

"Sir William and Lady Brunart, I'll wager," John whispered to Mary as they entered the room.

"Quite right, Mr. Braemhor." The voice came from a large, barrel-chested man in his sixties with grey hair combed straight back from his forehead without a part. He was six and a half feet tall, if an inch. His complexion spoke of a man of the outdoors, ruddy and wind worn. His narrow, penetrating eyes caught John's eye, and a broad smile developed across his face.

At his side stood a diminutive woman of equal age, with an equally ruddy countenance. She, too, had spent a good deal of time outdoors riding to the hounds and playing other outdoor sports as lent themselves to the female side of the family. Whereas Sir William projected the image of a relaxed, not easily flustered lord of the manor, she seemed more high-strung. Even at an initial glance, she appeared a tight wire ready to respond with high anxiety energy to any and everything. A more contrasting couple one could not image.

"Sorry to startle you, Mr. Braemhor," Sir William apologized, "but this room has exceptional acoustics. You can whisper in any spot, and it will be heard clearly in any other place in the room. Here, I'll show you." He quickly crossed the room and stood by the outer wall. "Welcome to Brunart Castle," he said in an unvoiced whisper. Every syllable was clearly projected throughout the room as if he'd spoken into a megaphone.

"It's exceptional," John agreed as he approached Sir William to greet him.

"Quite so. And as you and your wife can now see, the portrait is of us. I'm William and this is my wife, Breathag."

"And I'm John, and this is my wife, Mary."

"Your castle is extraordinary," Mary commented.

"We like it, but it's far too big. Too much to care for—even with a permanent staff—and too much upkeep for modern times. Just keeping the portraits maintained is a worry," Lady Brunart explained.

Following a few more ice-breaking remarks by all four, Sir William suggested they be seated for dinner. He waved a signal to the elderly woman standing in a doorway at the back of the room, obviously waiting to serve the meal.

Very shortly after the meal began, Sir William's manner became more serious than his initially jovial, genial welcoming of John and Mary to the castle.

"Now to the matter at hand. What information do you need in order to undertake assisting us?"

"Tell me all that you can about the theft. Where was the dagger kept—it's a gem-encrusted dagger, is it not? Who knew where it was kept? When was it missed? How many and who have access to the family quarters? I assume it was not kept in any public area of the castle?"

"The missing heirloom is a dagger given to my ancient ancestor by King Robert Bruce for services rendered at Bannackburn. We simply kept it in a drawer of a chest in Breathag's sitting room."

"It was not locked away?" John was a little taken aback.

"No, we saw no reason to keep it under lock and key. It was a family heirloom, yes, and extremely valuable, as an antique. But there are far more things in the castle that an ordinary thief would be interested in taking. The flatware, for example." He held up his fork and waved it slightly.

"Of course, go on," John suggested.

"My wife and I were the only ones who knew its whereabouts. Oh, yes, our personal servants might have known—though I doubt it—but they've been with the family for generations. I really think they're above suspicion, and we have not had any workmen in the private quarters for two or three years."

"It's about time though," Lady Brunart added meaningfully.

Sir William smiled at her and went on. "We first noticed its absence a couple of weeks ago, on a Sunday. We were preparing to go to church when Breathag came into my room and told me that she could not find the dagger."

"Ordinarily, I don't keep track of it. It's always there in the drawer beneath some personal clothing of mine. But that morning I was looking for something and happened to see that the dagger was not in its place. I told William right away," Lady Brunart finished the story.

"Was anything disturbed in your room?" John asked.

"No, why?"

"Like someone had been searching through your clothes, perhaps?"

"No, everything was as neat as it should be. Nothing out of place. Except the dagger."

"Breathag is a stickler for having all of her personal items neatly in place."

"I can't stand for anything to be out of place or just spread about." Lady Brunart was beginning to sound a bit anxious as she spoke.

"Of course." John tried to tamp down her growing agitation.

"Had there been a tour the Saturday before?" Mary interjected.

"Yes, we have them every Saturday morning," Sir William responded. "You don't suppose someone from a tour got into the family quarters, do you? I really do not see how that would be possible."

"And even if it were possible, the thief would have to know exactly where the dagger was kept," John concluded. "Was the dagger insured?"

"Oh, yes, for quite a large sum."

"And who is the beneficiary or beneficiaries?" John queried.

"The estate, of course. It really belongs to the family, no one individual. So we drew up the policy in the name of the estate."

John hesitated a moment and then, "Sir William, I'm sorry to ask this, but I need to know to take in every possibility. Was the estate in any financial difficulties? I note that you do offer tours and that usually indicates an estate that may be having some difficulty making it through the present economy."

Sir William broke out laughing. "I see what you're driving at, and I'm not offended by your thoroughness. In fact, it tells me I've chosen wisely in seeking to engage a private investigator. But the answer to your question is *no*. The estate is solid, but I like to always prepare for the worst. The tours bring in a little additional revenue for a rainy day, as they say in America."

All four sat silently until Sir William spoke again. "Well, Mr. Braemhor, what do you think? Can you help us?"

"I don't know at this point if I can, but I'm willing to try."

"Excellent. Then consider yourself. . . and your wife," he looked at Mary, "engaged. You may set your own terms, and when can you start?"

"Our terms will be quite reasonable, and I believe we've already started," John spoke, as the corners of his mouth turned up into a faint smile.

"What next then?" Sir William was anxious to move Braemhor's investigation along.

"First, I think it might be a help for us to interview each member of the family and each of the house staff individually. We could start immediately. How many are there?"

"Well, there's my wife's maid, my man, the cook and Mrs. Bauer, who served the meal. But I'm afraid neither I nor Breathag are available this afternoon. There are no other family members here."

"That's fine. Perhaps we might interview the staff this afternoon. Would you and your wife be available, say, Monday afternoon?"

"That will work out. Shall we say about two? In the meantime, I'll arrange for the staff to meet with you within the hour. You can see them here in this room, if you like."

"I think a smaller room would be better and one not so acoustically alive as this. In here, I'm afraid our interviews would be overheard throughout the house." John smiled.

"Of course. Of course. I'll set things in motion and my man—Harold is his name—will show you to a smaller, less *alive* room for your work. And Mr. and Mrs. Braemhor, I'm pleased that we've come to an understanding. I'll look forward to results."

Shortly after Sir William and Lady Breathag left, Harold entered and led the Braemhors to a small room where they could speak individually with the staff.

Interviewing the staff took up the greater part of the remaining afternoon. All were very cooperative, but very protective of the family. Harold, Sir William's man, allowed that the staff, including himself, were unaware of the presence of the dagger in the castle. None had seen it and certainly did not know where it was kept. He reiterated Sir William's observation that someone wanting to steal valuables from the Brunarts could just as easily, and probably more profitably, have made off with some of the gold flatware. How long had he been in the service of Sir William? Just under 22 years.

Mrs. Bauer confirmed Harold's statement that none of the staff knew of the family heirlooms, much less a dagger from the 14th century. She'd been serving the table for 17 years and had acted as an assistant cook for 14. "If you think we walked off with an heirloom, you're wrong. It would be much easier for us to pocket a piece of flatware any time we needed money, don't you think?"

The French cook, Ms. DuBois, had only been with the family for ten years, replacing the previous chef when he died. "It took me a year or two to convert from French to Scottish cuisine, but I manage to sneak in a few French delicacies from time to time." A twinkle in her eye gave her a coquettish demeanor.

"Like the soufflé this afternoon?" Mary asked.

"And the *crème caramel*."

"Both were delicious, but tell us when you first became aware of the missing heirloom," John intervened.

"When the police began questioning us. We could not imagine what had happened. We thought there had been a terrible accident when suddenly there were police officers roaming throughout the castle. But then Sir William called us all into the library and told us what had happened, and asked us not to breathe a word of it outside of the estate. We were all just thunderstruck that such a thing had happened. The Brunarts are like our own family. So too bad."

Lady Brunart's personal maid, Constance Crane, was the last to be interviewed. A slender woman in her mid-fifties, who'd been in service for eight years. She appeared to be the picture of calm and serenity, so much so that Mary commented on it.

"Oh, I have to maintain my calm and togetherness if I'm to serve Lady Brunart."

"Why so?" John asked.

"Because Lady Brunart is a bundle of nerves. . .all the time. She flies off at the slightest thing. If one thing is out of place in her sitting room or bedroom, it's as if the world has come to an end. And if she gets too upset she might even start to throw things. Oh, sir, one of the two of us has to stay reasonable and calm or the whole house would be in a constant uproar. I'm the one to stay calm. That way Lady Brunart can have her daily upsets, and no one is the worse for it."

"It sounds like a very demanding job," Mary commented.

"Oh, it is, ma'am. . .sometimes. But then she can be so sweet and caring at other times that all the chaos is not so bad. I just feel so sorry for her. She seems to be tormented at times."

"Does she receive any regular medical care?" John asked.

"Oh, yes. She has weekly appointments—and just recently she began seeing a new doctor in addition."

"Why?"

"I don't rightly know. Her regular doctor has her on a lot of different pills, mostly to calm her down, I think."

"Like tranquilizers?" John was curious about Lady Brunart's medical history.

"Like I said, I don't rightly know, but sometimes they seemed to calm her down and at others they didn't seem to matter much."

"Do you know what the new doctor's treatment is? How does it differ from what she was receiving before?"

"Oh, I don't think he gives her any pills. Lady Brunart told me that he teaches her how to relax and not be so tense."

"How does he do that?"

"I don't know, but when she comes home from her appointments on Friday—that's when she sees the new one—she does seem to be calmer and a nicer person."

"You don't like her?" Mary jumped in.

"Oh, no, ma'am; I like her fine. It's just that she can be a trial sometimes. That's all I meant."

Suddenly John shifted the focus of the interview. "Harold tells us that none of the staff knew of the existence of the heirloom dagger much less its location in the family quarters. But you knew, didn't you?!?"

It was as if he'd struck her physically. Even Mary was stunned at the rapidity with which the tenor of his questioning had changed. Ms. Crane was dumbstruck and for a few moments could not respond to his accusation. "No, sir. I didn't know anything about the dagger until Sir William talked with all of the staff. Honest, sir, I didn't know nothing about it. I didn't steal it, honest, sir."

Mary had become alarmed by this point. John gave Mary a quick meaningful look and nodded to her.

"Of course, you didn't steal the dagger," Mary spoke in sympathetic tones, trying to comfort the distraught woman. "Pull yourself together. Pull yourself together. It's all right now."

"Please. Please. Sir. Ma'am. I don't want to lose my position here. I like the family, and I especially like Lady Brunart. Please." Her voice broke away into a whisper.

"Don't worry. You won't lose your position because of our interview today. Of that I can assure you. But we have to ask these hard questions if we're going to get to the bottom of the disappearance of the dagger. Now dry your eyes." John handed her a tissue. "Everything will be all right."

John and Mary gave Ms. Crane some time to dry her tears and recompose herself before letting her go back to Lady Brunart's quarters. Then they left the castle and drove back to Daraichburn.

"You were pretty hard on her, John," Mary chided.

"I know, but she's the only one of the servants who might have known the whereabouts of the dagger, since she has unfettered access to Lady Brunart's rooms. I wanted to be sure of her before we left, that's all."

"And are you?"

"Yes, I think so. But I'll double-check with Sir William though when we see him next week."

The next day was the usual scene of John pacing and fretting, thinking and stewing.

"John, please sit down." John complied. "What are you doing?"

"Trying to get some things clear. Putting pieces together."

"What pieces?"

"It's something Ms. Crane said about Lady Brunart."

"What?"

"Do you remember that she said that Lady Brunart was seeing a new doctor?"

"Yes?""And that the new doctor was teaching her how to relax."

"And?"

"Well, I've finished reading Professor Edwards's book, *Hypnosis and Relaxation*—the one we bought in Ft. Ewen—and in it, he makes the case that relaxation is the basis of hypnosis."

"So you think the new doctor is using hypnosis with her?"

"It's certainly possible. And if you combine what Edwards has to say with what his colleague said in *Hypnotism in War and Peace*, you could have a scenario."

"You mean its uses in espionage?"

"Yes. Using hypnosis as a means of either inserting certain information into a person, or. . . ."

"Extracting it from a person," Mary finished.

"Precisely!"

"So you think this new doctor, whoever he is, could be extracting family secrets. . . ."

"From Lady Brunart. And. . .and leaving her with amnesia so that she has no memory of revealing them." John was up and pacing again with the exhilaration of this last thought.

"Like the whereabouts of the dagger?"

John nodded.

"That still would not account for how the dagger was stolen," Mary contested.

"But remember that the dagger was taken without disturbing anything in the castle. The thief knew exactly where it was. He or she did not have to search for it," John countered.

"But John, even if all of your suppositions are correct, how are you going to prove it?"

"By age regressing Lady Brunart back to her therapy sessions with the new doctor. It's elementary." John smiled.

"All right, Sherlock, but getting her to agree to follow your suggestions will not be easy." Mary again admired her husband's facility for putting together fragments of information and then developing a procedure for solving a puzzle.

"You're right, and involving Lady Brunart in that way might tip our hand and put her in danger. We'll have to think of another way."

The evening ended with both of the Braemhors in a heightened state of anticipation, waiting for their meeting with the Brunarts the next day.

The Braemhors arrived at the castle a little before two and were ushered into the library.

"Ah, the Braemhors." Sir William entered and strode towards them, hand outstretched in greeting. Lady Brunart was just behind him. "Shall we sit in here?"

"I think I'd prefer to interview you separately, if you don't mind." John was very formal.

"Of course. Breathag or me first?"

"We can start with you, sir."

"Fine." Sir William nodded to Lady Brunart. "Come back in about. . ."

"Half an hour should do," John finished.

Lady Brunart left the room. Sir William sat at the central table and waved the Braemhors to chairs on the opposite side.

John started by asking Sir William to repeat what he'd said before regarding the time of the theft—"Two weeks ago yesterday"—who discovered the loss—"Lady Brunart"—and the like.

"Were there any other similar items of value in the castle?" John queried.

"Yes, there was also a gold and silver Bruce crest badge bestowed on my ancestor at the same time as the dagger by Robert Bruce. Strangely, that was untouched, though it was in a different drawer."

"So it might seem that the thief was unaware of this second priceless heirloom."

"It would seem so," Sir William agreed. "It seems to me that if any of the staff were aware of the dagger, they surely would also be aware of the crest, though, as I said Saturday, I'll personally vouch for all of the staff. They are most loyal and well paid."

"Which leads me to another question," John went on.

"Yes?"

"Are you satisfied that Ms. Crane is trustworthy? She's the one member of the staff who might have inadvertently seen the dagger in Lady Brunart's rooms."

"Oh, most definitely."

"So, as far as you know she did not know where the dagger was kept."

"That's right. No, Mr. Braemhor, I think you can eliminate Constance as a suspect."

"Then I have no more questions at this time. Perhaps we could see Lady Brunart now?"

"I'll send her in." Sir William rose and left the library.

Before Lady Brunart arrived, Mary asked a quick question. "So you're satisfied with Ms. Crane's innocence?"

"I think so. Sir William doesn't have concerns about her honesty. . . .Ah, Lady Brunart. Please have a seat here." He pointed to the chair Sir William had just vacated.

Braemhor began by having her reiterate the story of her discovery that the dagger was missing. "Two weeks ago yesterday, is that right?"

"Yes, we were just preparing to go to church when I made the discovery. It was very unnerving."

"I imagine so," Mary agreed. "What did you do then?"

"Why, I searched all of my drawers. I was frantic. I emptied all of the drawers. All over the floor. But. . .but it wasn't there!" Lady Brunart was beginning to act and speak hysterically. "It wasn't there! I was beside myself!"

"And you did?" John asked.

"I went immediately to William's rooms and told him. And told him we had to do something! Right away! But he just smiled in his usual calm way and told me I shouldn't get so upset. Shouldn't get upset! Easy for him! I was the one who had it in my rooms! What would you have done, Mr. Braemhor?"

"It sounds to me that you did just the right thing, Lady Brunart."

"There wasn't much else you could do, was there?" Mary added, trying to calm Lady Brunart.

"No, no. But it was very upsetting!"

"And that was two weeks ago?"

"Yes! And we're still no closer to getting the dagger back! The police haven't found it! I wonder if they know what they're doing!" Lady Brunart was fairly shrieking now. "You've got to find it, Mr. Braemhor! You've got to find it!"

"That's what we're trying to do, Lady Brunart. Now if you'll try to calm yourself, I only have a few more questions. It won't take much longer."

"Thank god for that!" The hysteria continued.

"Now we think the dagger was stolen two weeks ago. Anything else happen in the household about that time?"

"No, why?"

"Sometimes when things like this happen it's helpful to know what other changes might have taken place in the family routine around the same time. No new staff? No new people about the castle?"

"No. The only thing I can think of is that I started seeing another doctor about a month ago, but I can't see how that has anything to do with the dagger being missing."

"Why did you start seeing another doctor?"

"Well, as you can see I'm a very high strung person." She smiled faintly. "My regular doctor has had me taking tranquilizers for a year or so, but I didn't think they were helping me that much. So I asked if there might be some other treatment that might help. William thought it a good idea. My doctor, Mr. Holt, said that sometimes relaxation therapy could help, but he didn't know of any doctor he'd recommend in our area who did that. Then I saw an ad in the newspaper about the wonders of relaxation therapy for very nervous people who had trouble sleeping—a Mister Peel, Dabney Peel. So I called him and he agreed to see me for evaluation."

"And when did you start seeing him?"

"It will be a month ago this coming Friday. I see him on Friday afternoons, and I've been so much calmer than before."

"What does he do, exactly?" John was fishing.

"Well, I sit in a reclining chair and he, in a most soft and soothing voice, speaks to me about relaxing my whole body. Then, after I'm relaxed, he suggests ways I can stay calmer and not be so high-strung."

"Do you remember everything that goes on while you are in this relaxed state?"

"Mostly, but not always. It's a way to help me forget what makes me so tense, he said. And I do feel better after I see him. But I still take my pills, you understand."

"So he's helped you to forget things. What about remembering things"

"I don't understand."

"Does the relaxation help you remember things that, say, you've forgotten?"

"Oh, yes! Once I had mislaid a letter opener. I couldn't find it anywhere. But Mr. Peel suggested that I could remember, and I did. Went home and found it right away! I was so pleased."

"That's very interesting. So you say Mr. Peel helps you to relax and sometimes to remember things you may have forgotten—and to forget things that make you tense ?"

"And he's such a nice person, not standoffish like my regular doctor. Now don't tell William, but he even gives me a little hug when we finish each session. Makes me really feel like he cares, not so clinical as Mr. Holt—my regular doctor."

"I'm glad you've found someone you feel is helping you," Mary said.

"Just one more question, Lady Brunart," John moved on.

"Yes?"

"Your lady's maid, Constance Crane. Is she trustworthy?"

"Oh, most certainly. I trust Constance as I would my own daughter. I'm sure she had nothing to do with this, Mr. Braemhor."

"Well, then, I have no further questions, Lady Brunart. Do you, Mary?"

Mary shook her head.

About that time, Sir William returned and John and Mary took their leave. "We may want to talk with the two of you more later, if that will be all right?"

"That will be fine. Whatever is needed to get to the bottom of this theft. Call us anytime," Sir William answered.

"One more thing. Do you have a list of the individuals who've taken the castle tours in the past month?"

"Not all of them, but most. Anyone who made a reservation—as you two did—will be in the business records, but walk-ins will not. Harold can give you a copy before you leave."

"That might be very useful."

"Wait here then; Harold will get a copy for you. But how will that help?"

"Don't know if it will, but I. . . we like to be very thorough." John smiled.

"Of course. Of course. Have a seat while Harold makes a copy for you." Sir William was impressed with the Braemhors' thoroughness and pleased that he'd engaged them.

On the road back to Daraichburn, Mary was the first to speak. "Penny?"

"I think we need to talk with Bill Edwards again, get more detailed information on hypnosis."

"You think that's what Mr. Peel is using?"

"It's becoming more of a possibility in my mind."

When they got back to Dunmoor Cottage, John put in a call to Edwards who'd just finished his last lecture of the day. He quickly outlined the case he was working on in very general terms, omitting the names involved, and asked: "Would it be possible for someone to hypnotize the lady in question and extract information from her—family secret information—and then cause her to have no memory of divulging the information?"

"Oh, very possible. That would be simple hypnotic amnesia. It's possible she would not remember a thing about the session. Who is this possible criminal hypnotist we're talking about, if I may ask?"

"The lady is seeing a Dabney Peel for 'relaxation therapy,' he calls it."

"Ah ha. Our well-known Mr. Peel!" Edwards exclaimed. "He's Edinburgh's resident charlatan. Even I, an American, know of him. We use him in the States as an example of hypnosis misused. Calls it 'relaxation therapy,' does he? That's just a way to get around the UK's restrictions on non-professionals using hypnosis. But a rose by any other name. . . Read my book." He chuckled.

"I did and I came to the same conclusion," John said. "You've been a big help, Bill."

"Let me know how it all turns out."

"I will after we wrap it all up." John hung up.

"Mr. Peel is a very real possibility for the role of villain in our little drama," John told Mary. "Bill confirmed that it would be possible to extract information from Lady Brunart and for her to have no memory of it. Let me put in a call to Jim Sinclair."

"Sinclair here." The voice crackled over the wire.

"This is John Braemhor."

"Solved my case already?" Sinclair laughed.

"Almost." John spoke seriously, "but I need a bit more information before you can make an arrest."

"I was joking, John." Sinclair too became serious.

"Well, I'm not, James. You mentioned there were other robberies besides the one at Brunart Castle."

"Yes, but in those cases there was a break in, door forced, but again nothing in the houses was disturbed. No sign of a chaotic search for valuable items. Just valuables missing."

"Like at Brunart Castle," John noted.

"Still think the tour's involved? I thought Mary's idea was a good one."

"More of a possibility. But we're not necessarily looking for a pregnant woman." John chuckled but he quickly resumed his serious demeanor. "Can you find out if anyone in the houses where the other thefts took place was seeing a Mr. Dabney Peel for therapy? But it has to be done very obliquely, so that, if Peel is being seen, it doesn't get back to him."

"Ah, Edinborough's resident non-hypnotist," Sinclair exclaimed.

"You've heard of him?" John was surprised.

"Know of him well. He's been skirting around the fringes of the Medical Care Act for years. Tried to make a case against him a year or so ago for his using hypnosis without proper credentials, but he calls it 'relaxation therapy.' Oh, yes. Mr. Peel is on our radar. I think we can do it. I have a very diplomatic sergeant who I think can get your information without raising any flags."

"Excellent! Then, depending on what that information tells us, I may have another request."

"Dare I ask what?" Sinclair was fascinated by the rapidity with which Braemhor seemed to be moving on the case.

"Let's get the information first. Then we'll see where we go from there." John avoided the question. "And, James, can we gather this information as soon as possible?"

Sinclair smiled. "I'll send my sergeant out tomorrow, first thing. Should have something for you before the day's out, hopefully by noon."

"James, I do appreciate all of your help," John said.

Who's helping whom, I wonder, Sinclair thought as he hung up the receiver.

John turned to Mary. "James said he can find out if Mr. Peel has been involved with any family members living in the houses where the other two robberies took place. Might even have it by noon tomorrow."

* * * * * * *

Again the worst part of any investigation—the waiting for vital information to become available. John had a restless night. Could not shut his brain down from working on the case. *What if Peel isn't involved in the other two? Then where are we? Maybe I'm looking at this all wrong. Maybe Ms. Crane is the thief. Maybe the Brunarts are involved, for insurance. . . . I hadn't thought of that angle. What's wrong with me? I must be losing my edge with age. Well, I've got to relax and get some sleep,* he thought as he tossed and turned, knowing that the more you think about going to sleep the harder it is to get to sleep.

John awoke at five, an hour earlier than usual, after a restless night. He began turning the case over in his mind. To no avail. *It just won't come straight until I have the information from Sinclair.* He kept thinking about it even as he was doing his morning exercises. After breakfast, the pacing began.

"Oh, John, please sit down. You know James will call as soon as he has anything." Mary knew that calming him down was a futile task.

"I know. I know." John gave her a sheepish smile. "Maybe I'll try to read a little." He took up the morning paper.

At eleven the phone rang and John fairly burst from his chair. *At last,* he thought as he said, "Braemhor here."

"John, it's Jim, Jim Sinclair. The answer to your question is 'yes,' Peel is seeing the wives in both families."

John relaxed. "Good. Good. Now we're getting somewhere."

"Where, John? Don't you think it's time you let me in on it?"

"Of course, James. Sorry, but you know me. I get very involved in these cases and forget there are others who need to know what I'm doing."

Braemhor then quickly outlined his thoughts on the Brunart robbery and how Peel might be involved.

"That's all well and good, John, but I'm the one who will have to take this case to court. How am I going to prove all of your suppositions? If Peel is involved, I'd like to get him this time and not have him slip through my fingers once again."

"Understood. But I have to talk again with Sir William before the next move. If he agrees, can you get a story released to the media about the Brunart Castle robbery?"

"Of course, but Sir William was very clear, he wanted no publicity," Sinclair reminded John.

"I know. I know. But I think he'll agree once I tell him what I have in mind. I'll see him today and get back to you as soon as I can. All right?"

"Let me know, John," Sinclair said as he hung up.

"Back to the castle?" Mary had been listening to John's end of the conversation.

"If Sir William can see us. I'll call him right now," John answered.

After a brief phone conversation with Sir William, John told Mary, "He can see us at two."

Back at the castle, Sir William received the Braemhors once again in the library. John quickly asked his permission to run a story in tomorrow's news media about the dagger's disappearance that would include a statement—and this was important—that the thief or thieves had missed an even more valuable gold and silver crest from the 14th century.

"That just sounds like you're inviting trouble," Sir William huffed.

"Exactly. You see, we'll be trying to lure the thief to return to Brunart Castle for a second valuable heirloom," John explained. "Where is the crest kept?"

"In my wife's sitting room. Same as the dagger, except in a different drawer." Sir William was beginning to see the logic of John's request.

"And just you and she know where it's kept?" John wanted to ascertain that the circumstances regarding the two heirlooms were the same.

"That's right."

"Fine. Now there's one other thing. And this is very important, too. I think it would be best if your wife knows nothing of our plan.

"That will be no problem, but what you're saying disturbs me. Do you think Breathag has taken the dagger? And why would she do that?" Sir William was taking on the appearance of a lord talking to an underling, and an underling he doesn't much care for.

"No. No, Sir William. Nothing of the sort. But she could be unwittingly involved in its disappearance. And if she is, she'll be the perfect conduit for entrapping the thief, but only if she's absolutely unaware of her role in the plan. That's all I'm saying." John was deferential.

"Well, that's a relief! I must admit I do not quite understand all of the intricacies of your plan. But I assume you know what you're doing."

"I do. Trust me. And one other thing."

"Yes?" Sir William was becoming a bit overwhelmed with Braemhor's demands.

"For Saturday's tour, I'd like to replace Ms. Crane with a plainclothes female police sergeant. Perhaps you could arrange for Ms. Crane to be in another part of the castle for the day."

"How about we give her the day off?" Sir William seemed now to be playing a willing part in Braemhor's plan.

"That might be even better," John admitted. "I think that about covers what we had to go over with you. Mary and I will take the tour on Saturday, just to be here to see how things play out. Inspector Sinclair will have his sergeant arrive early in the morning to be sequestered in Lady Brunart's rooms. It would be very helpful if you could arrange for yourself and Lady Brunart to be away from the castle Saturday. I'll bring you a substitute crest Friday afternoon while Lady

Brunart is at her therapy appointment. You can then replace the real crest with the substitute, and Lady Brunart will not know that the real heirloom has been moved. I'd advise you then to place the real crest in a different safe place. Am I making myself clear?" John had taken over the dominant role.

"Perfectly." Sir William was again satisfied that he had made a good choice in hiring the Braemhors to recover the stolen dagger.

As the Braemhors left, John reminded him that it was absolutely imperative that Lady Brunart know nothing of the plans for Saturday.

As they drove back to Daraichburn Mary asked, "How can you be sure James will provide you with a sergeant?"

"Oh, I think he will. He wants to close this case as much as we do."

John was right. Following a call from Braemhor, Sinclair arranged for the news release in Thursday's papers as well as for several of his officers in plain clothes to be in the castle on Saturday, and even offered him a valuable-looking base metal crest to hide where the real crest was kept. All in all, a quick and efficient phone call.

* * * * * * *

Thursday's newspapers all carried a low-key story of the dagger theft at Brunart Castle, including information that the thieves had missed an equally valuable crest badge of similar vintage.

Friday morning Braemhor went to Edinburgh to obtain the substitute crest and make final arrangements for Saturday's tour. That afternoon he took the crest substitute to Sir William while Lady Brunart was at her therapy appointment.

"I think everything's in place. Just one more item to check. Where is the list Harold made for us of the people taking the castle tour the last two Saturdays?" John asked Mary when he returned.

"Right here where you left it, John." Mary handed it to him and shook her head as she saw, once again, the growing agitation in her husband.

"Good." He quickly glanced down the list. "Ah ha, here she is."

"Who is, John?"

"The woman who came to both of the last two tours—Catherine Knowles. Now at least we know what name we're looking for tomorrow."

Suddenly, Mary had a horrible thought. *What if the thief did not read the story in the papers!* But she decided to keep that thought to herself. *John is agitated enough.*

Saturday dawned bright and clear, unlike the usual Scottish misty, raw winter morning.

"Maybe a good omen," John observed over breakfast.

"Let's hope," Mary agreed.

They timed their drive to Brunart Castle so that they would arrive just before the tour at ten. To their surprise, the tour participants included Jim Sinclair.

"I've never seen the castle," he explained as John and Mary walked up to him. He then continued in a very low tone, "All set. The sergeant's in Lady Brunart's rooms, and two other officers are at the stables with a car." He brightened as Harold and the tour guide appeared. "Let's enjoy the tour, shall we?"

Harold slipped a copy of today's list of participants to John along with the brochure describing the castle which was given to each of the visitors. John pointed out one name to Mary—Catherine Knowles. "So far, so good," he whispered.

One of the female participants drifted to the rear of the group as the tour moved through the public areas of the castle. She was a large woman with grey-streaked black hair. She wore a large grey wool coat and carried an equally large handbag hanging from her left shoulder. Right after John spotted her, he signaled Mary and they moved in front of two or three visitors just ahead of the woman. Sinclair was another two or three individuals ahead of the Braemhors, alert to any movement they made.

As the group passed an oversized oak door on the second floor, marked "Family Quarters, No Admittance," the woman under observation hesitated, quickly glanced around, then tried the door. Finding it open, she quickly slipped inside the family quarters. John and Mary fell back in front of the door. Sinclair joined them.

"Let's give her a few minutes to find the crest and be confronted by your sergeant," John suggested as he looked at Sinclair. Sinclair quickly called for his other officers to bring the car to the castle main entrance.

Within three minutes the door opened and out came the woman—Catherine Knowles, John assumed— handcuffed by Sergeant Williams. Sinclair took over. "Where's the crest?" he asked Williams.

"She put it in her handbag, sir," Williams answered as she indicated that she now had Knowles's bag over her shoulder.

"John, Mary, I'll stop by Dunmoor Cottage later today for some tea and we can wrap things up. All right?" Sinclair smiled broadly as he and Sergeant Williams led their captive through the public areas and to the waiting police car. "And, John," he called back, "thanks again."

Mary was just setting out tea by the peat fire in the sitting room when Sinclair parked in front of the cottage. The three of them settled into the settees for a roundup of the recent events. Sinclair started.

"John, Mary, you made this one easy. Ms. Knowles—that was her name—fingered her partner, Dabney Peel, before we even got her back to Edinburgh. Said she wasn't going 'to take the fall this time.' I'm not sure exactly what she meant by that, but she made our task easier. We raided the good doctor's clinic shortly before one o'clock and took him into custody. And—you and the Brunarts will be very pleased with this—we recovered the dagger. Peel apparently had not yet had time to get rid of it or break it down for the jewels, though I don't know why. There are dozens of fences out there who would love to get their hands on an item like that."

"Maybe he was going to keep it as a token of his criminal prowess," Mary joked.

"Maybe. But it's not the sort of thing the normal citizen can show off to his friends and relatives." Sinclair smiled.

"I'm sure the Brunarts will be pleased," John stated

"Oh, they are. I contacted them as soon as we took possession of the dagger. Of course, it will have to stay with us until the trial is completed, but at least they know it's safe once again."

"And another thing. This clears up the other burglaries as well. Seems Peel was obtaining information from family members under his care as to the whereabouts of valuables in their homes. Of course, Peel and Knowles had to actually break into the houses in those cases. No tours to ease their entry. But, as you know, the scenario was the same. Once inside they could go directly to the valuables. No messy searching around.

"Now, John, how did you and Mary come to suspect Peel in all of these robberies?" Sinclair asked after he had finished his side of the story.

"Elementary, my dear Sinclair." John smiled as both Mary and Sinclair winced.

John then outlined how he and Mary became acquainted with Professor Edwards and had attended his lectures on hypnosis in Edinburgh. After that, both had read up on various hypnotic phenomena and their possible uses.

"As you know, one thing that fascinated me about this case was the fact that the thief apparently knew right where the dagger was, no searching of Lady Brunart's rooms. Its location had to be given up by someone, but Sir William and Lady Brunart seemed to be the only two individuals who knew where it was kept, and it was unlikely that either of them would knowingly or willingly give up that information.

"Then they told us that Lady Brunart began seeing a new doctor—Dabney Peel—shortly before the dagger's disappearance. Both you and Professor Edwards confirmed that Mr. Peel uses hypnosis—though he calls it 'relaxation therapy'—in his practice. Now from what we learned from Professor Edwards and our reading on the subject, hypnosis can be a powerful tool for getting information from a hypnotized person and then leaving that person amnesic for having divulged the information.

"I wondered, could Peel have gotten the location of the dagger from Lady Brunart during treatment and then left her unaware that she'd told him? That would account for the thief not having to search the family quarters in the castle to find the heirloom. Then you confirmed that the same was true in the other robberies and that Mr. Peel was seeing a member of the family in each of those households also. This last information cemented all my suppositions together in my mind, and everything lined up.

"Like elementary, John?" Sinclair smirked.

"You might say," John rejoined.

"Well, John, again I'm in your debt. And so is Sir William." Sinclair rose to leave. "Oh, by the way, Sir William did have one message for you, besides his thanks."

"Yes?"

"He said for you to send him your bill." Sinclair shared a smile with Mary and John as he left.

"Satisfied?" Mary asked.

"I think so, but how will we spend the rest of the winter?" John asked.

"I'm sure something will turn up," Mary predicted as she went into the kitchen.

THE END

ABOUT THE AUTHOR

 Owen Magruder is the *nom de plume* of a retired college professor. He has authored three professional books and a small volume of remembrances of the American Civil War. In addition, he and his wife have co-authored a brief biography of a little known abolitionist from upstate New York for the National Abolition Hall of Fame. From 1989 to 2005, the couple ran a small publishing house that specialized in original letters and journals from the American Civil War.

Magruder's ancestral home is a castle just north of Glasgow given to the family by King Robert [Bruce] III of Scotland, hence the Scottish link to his mystery novels. One of his ancestors was Alice Edmonstone Keppel, mistress of King Edward VII of the United Kingdom.

Death at Beggar's Knob is his fourth book of the John and Mary Braemhor mysteries. Owen Magruder resides in upstate New York.